The Gulls Fly Inland

More Handheld Classics

Betty Bendell, *My Life And I. Confessions of an Unliberated Housewife, 1966–1980*
Henry Bartholomew (ed.), *The Living Stone. Stories of Uncanny Sculpture, 1858–1943*
Algernon Blackwood, *The Unknown. Weird Writings, 1900–1937*
Ernest Bramah, *What Might Have Been. The Story of a Social War* (1907)
D K Broster, *From the Abyss. Weird Fiction, 1907–1940*
John Buchan, *The Runagates Club* (1928)
John Buchan, *The Gap in the Curtain* (1932)
Melissa Edmundson (ed.), *Women's Weird. Strange Stories by Women, 1890–1940*
Melissa Edmundson (ed.), *Women's Weird 2. More Strange Stories by Women, 1891–1937*
Zelda Fitzgerald, *Save Me The Waltz* (1932)
Marjorie Grant, *Latchkey Ladies* (1921)
A P Herbert, *The Voluble Topsy, 1928–1947*
Inez Holden, *Blitz Writing. Night Shift & It Was Different At The Time* (1941 & 1943)
Inez Holden, *There's No Story There. Wartime Writing, 1944–1945*
Margaret Kennedy, *Where Stands A Wingèd Sentry* (1941)
Rose Macaulay, *Non-Combatants and Others. Writings Against War, 1916–1945*
Rose Macaulay, *Personal Pleasures. Essays on Enjoying Life* (1935)
Rose Macaulay, *Potterism. A Tragi-Farcical Tract* (1920)
Rose Macaulay, *What Not. A Prophetic Comedy* (1918)
James Machin (ed.) *British Weird. Selected Short Fiction, 1893–1937*
Faith Compton Mackenzie, *Tatting and Mandolinata* (1931 & 1957)
Vonda N McIntyre, *The Exile Waiting* (1975)
Elinor Mordaunt, *The Villa and The Vortex. Supernatural Stories, 1916–1924*
E Nesbit, *The House of Silence. Ghost Stories 1887–1920*
Jane Oliver and Ann Stafford, *Business as Usual* (1933)
John Llewelyn Rhys, *England Is My Village, and The World Owes Me A Living* (1939 & 1941)
John Llewelyn Rhys, *The Flying Shadow* (1936)
Malcolm Saville, *Jane's Country Year* (1946)
Helen de Guerry Simpson, *The Outcast and The Rite. Stories of Landscape and Fear, 1925–1938*
J Slauerhoff, *Adrift in the Middle Kingdom*, translated by David McKay (1934)
Ann Stafford, *Army Without Banners* (1942)
Rosemary Sutcliff, *Blue Remembered Hills* (1983)
Amara Thornton and Katy Soar (eds), *Strange Relics. Stories of Archaeology and the Supernatural, 1895–1954*
Elizabeth von Arnim, *The Caravaners* (1909)
Sylvia Townsend Warner, *Kingdoms of Elfin* (1977)
Sylvia Townsend Warner, *Of Cats and Elfins. Short Tales and Fantasies* (1927–1976)
Sylvia Townsend Warner, *T H White. A Biography* (1967)

The Gulls Fly Inland

By Sylvia Thompson

With an introduction by Faye Hammill

Handheld Classic 40

This edition published in 2024 by Handheld Press
16 Peachfield Road, Malvern WR14 4AP, United Kingdom.
www.handheldpress.co.uk

ISBN 978-1-912766-86-4

1 2 3 4 5 6 7 8 9 0

Series design by Nadja Robinson and typeset in Adobe Caslon Pro
and Open Sans.

Printed and bound in Great Britain by Short Run Press, Exeter.

Contents

Acknowledgements

Sincere thanks are due to Susanna Dammann, who generously provided written recollections of her grandmother and an outline of her life and work. I am very much indebted to Keith Parsons, whose extensive knowledge of Thompson's life and writing has substantially informed this Introduction. Keith's meticulous biographical research, together with his collecting of periodical materials by or about Thompson, and his careful reading of the novels themselves, have helped me enormously, and our email exchanges have been most stimulating. The information relating to Thompson's educational records was kindly provided to Keith by archivists at Cheltenham Ladies' College and at Somerville College Archives and Special Collections.

Faye Hammill

Faye Hammill is Professor of English Literature and Canadian Studies at the University of Glasgow. She is author or co-author of six books, most recently *Modernism's Print Cultures* (2016), with Mark Hussey; *Magazines, Travel, and Middlebrow Culture* (2015), with Michelle Smith; and *Sophistication: A Literary and Cultural History* (2010). She has recently edited Martha Ostenso's novel *The Young May Moon* for Borealis Press (2021), and her current project, 'Ocean Modern', is about literature and ocean liners.

Introduction

BY FAYE HAMMILL

In Paris in the spring of 1933, the young celebrity author Sylvia Thompson met the distinguished artist Jacques-Émile Blanche (1861–1942). He immediately wanted to paint her. Writing in American *Vogue* in 1960, she recalled her sittings with Blanche, whose previous subjects had included Marcel Proust, Virginia Woolf and Vaclav Nijinsky. After he had been working for a few hours, Thompson was allowed to see 'how the portrait had begun (a hat, a face, and pearls ghostly on a dark ground)'. Blanche completed two portraits of Thompson and offered to give her one but, uncertain whether she was expected to pay for it, she made an excuse: '"*Hélas*," I said, "but I have no *walls*!"' Thompson wonders what became of the portraits, speculating that the economical Blanche would have used the canvases again, perhaps for one of the landscapes he painted near his home in Normandy shortly before his death in 1942. 'Do my swagged pearls lie, silted with time, in that buried world of the 'thirties, beneath, perhaps, the very cliffs that were to be the drop-scene for the tragic, heroic Dieppe raid?' she writes (Thompson 1960, 37).

Like the canvas which Thompson imagines, *The Gulls Fly Inland* (1941) evokes the already–buried world of the thirties and overlays it with the contemporary moment of the Second World War. This compelling, elegiac novel takes the form of a journal written during the early months of the war by a young Frenchwoman. Her name, Blanche Lancret, perhaps echoes that of the painter Thompson knew. In stormy weather, gulls fly inland to wait for the return of calm. So Blanche takes refuge at a house in rural England and waits for news of her American lover, Vernon, who is driving an ambulance in France. She passes the time by recording the story of their romance, which began when she was still at school. She also writes of her father who lives in Italy, and of her aunt in Paris who is married to an Austrian; these sections of the journal evoke a leisured, cosmopolitan world that had suddenly become unreachable.

Sylvia Thompson herself belonged to this world: she and her husband, the American-born artist Peter Luling, travelled continually. They had a series of homes in England but spent much of their time in Spain, Italy, France, Switzerland and the US. Thompson's words to Jacques-Émile Blanche – 'I have no *walls*' – were, therefore, almost literally true, and they can be applied in another sense to her writing with its cosmopolitan sensibility. Many of the fictional characters she created (including Blanche Lancret) are highly mobile, multilingual creatures, rarely confined within a single country, still less within a single set of physical or intellectual walls.

'She made a real stir': Sylvia Thompson's life and career

Sylvia Elizabeth Afiola Thompson was born in Bearsden, near Glasgow, on 4 September 1902, and spent her early life in Scotland. Her mother, Ethel Hannah Levis, came from a wealthy German Jewish family with interests in the rubber and tea industries (Ryan 31). Her father, Norman Arthur Thompson, was likewise from a prosperous, cultured background and became a pioneering aviation inventor, although his aeronautical business failed after the First World War. In 1910 Ethel Thompson separated from her husband and relocated with her son and daughter to Kensington and later to Oxford. Life as a child of divorced parents was not easy in this period. However, Ethel and her children maintained a relatively comfortable lifestyle in Kensington; the 1911 census shows that they had three resident servants.

At sixteen Sylvia Thompson went to Cheltenham Ladies' College. Margaret Kennedy, whose second novel *The Constant Nymph* (1924) would make her famous as a writer, attended the same school, although she was six years older than Thompson and therefore her school days had a different ambience. Kennedy's biographer Violet Powell comments that photographs of Kennedy and her contemporaries show 'little change from the starched shirts and ankle-length skirts of Victorian times', whereas Thompson 'had a precocious appreciation of clothes and cosmetics' and 'shocked her dormitory mates by her dashing silk pyjamas, and the aroma of bath salts which hung about her cubicle' (Powell 37). There is a story that she got into serious trouble for pawning a pair of stockings (Thompson 'Success'). These images of Thompson at Cheltenham have similarities to the portrait of Annabelle Strudwick, Blanche's school-friend in *The Gulls Fly Inland*, who sprays herself with Coty's Lilas Blanc in the dormitory: 'She always scented herself before getting into bed, "to get into practice for a husband", she said' (23).

At Cheltenham, Thompson began writing fiction. In a 1931 article for *Britannia and Eve* magazine she recalls: 'I wrote my first book when I was sixteen and very much disliking my life at boarding school'. Finishing it quite quickly, she then forgot it for a while, until she met a 'large, kind young man' at a dance who had heard she had written a novel and asked to see it. This unnamed man, himself an author and working in publishing, sent the manuscript to the Oxford publisher Basil Blackwell who, much to Thompson's astonishment, accepted the book (Thomson 'Success', 51). *The Rough Crossing*, a novel of school life, appeared in 1921. The American edition was brought out by an equally influential firm, Houghton, Mifflin of Boston.

Meanwhile, in 1920, Thompson had gone up to Somerville College, Oxford – as her mother had done before her – and was a student alongside Kennedy, Vera Brittain, Winifred Holtby and Naomi Mitchison. Writing in *Time and Tide* in 1928 under a pseudonym, Holtby described this generation of women students, remembering that Thompson 'made a real stir by her clothes, her blue shoes (then a novelty), her audacious wit, and her habit of coming in to breakfast when everyone else was leaving' (GREC [Holtby] 1272). Brittain recalled Thompson in similar terms, writing that, 'her dark beauty and flair for publicity made her the central figure of a picturesque if somewhat hectic Oxford generation, which was already beginning to revolt against the reflective seriousness of the post-war undergraduate' (Brittain 122). Both Holtby and Brittain note that Thompson's reputation as an author was already in the making when she came to Somerville. Her university career, though, was not wholly successful: college records show that she missed two terms of residence and, after changing from modern history to an economics diploma programme, eventually went down without a degree. The Oxford gossips speculated that she would either come to a bad end or achieve great success.

At Oxford, Sylvia Thompson met her future husband, Theodore Dunham Luling, always known as 'Peter'. He came from a wealthy and cultured New York banking family (Ryan 29–30). After Oxford he studied at the Slade School of Art, and during his career as an artist he specialised in water-colour painting, woodcuts and linocuts. He also worked in interior design. Thompson and Luling were married in 1926. Thompson's career as a writer took off in the same year, when her third novel, *The Hounds of Spring*, appeared. Opening just before the outbreak of the First World War, the novel tells of the experiences of one family over the course of several years. Its exploration of conflict, peace and international relations unfolds alongside a complex love story and an analysis of the gendered dynamics of the more privileged ranks of English society. When this book was published, according to Holtby, 'suddenly everyone knew that Sylvia Thompson had done very well indeed. She had written a real best-seller – immensely and immediately successful on both sides of the Atlantic. It spoke of Youth, it depicted post-war Europe, it had a strong sense of situation and vivid narrative power' (GREC [Holtby] 1272). From this point, Thompson was increasingly in demand: she was frequently mentioned in the North American and British press and became well known on the US lecture circuit.

Thompson was soon combining her literary career with the responsibilities of motherhood. She and Peter Luling had three daughters: Rosemary (born 1927), now the eminent Catholic theologian Rosemary Haughton; Elizabeth (1929–60), who became an actor, and Virginia (1939–2013), whose career was in anthropology and human rights. Eventually the Lulings would have twelve grandchildren. One of them, Susanna Dammann, remembers Sylvia Thompson in this way:

> She was beautiful and wayward and one of those people who attracted immediate attention when she walked into a room. She could be quite startlingly rude if she thought it would be amusing, but also had enormous charm and charisma. Unsurprisingly, she was a wonderful story-teller who held her grandchildren spell-bound with long tales of imaginary animals and their magical adventures. (Dammann 2023)

The family had an itinerant lifestyle and a fluctuating income which depended a good deal on the level of success of each of Thompson's books. In total she published sixteen novels, one co-authored play, and a large number of stories, serials and essays which appeared in at least forty different magazines and newspapers. Her books from *The Hounds of Spring* through to *The Gulls Fly Inland* were brought out in London by William Heinemann, a major literary publisher of new works and reprints of the classics. Her last two novels appeared in the UK under Michael Joseph's imprint, and *The Hounds of Spring* was republished as an early Penguin paperback in 1936. American editions of Thompson's novels appeared under several imprints but her main US publisher, from 1926 onwards, was the prestigious Boston firm Little, Brown. A number of her novels were also brought out in Canada by McClelland and Stewart, or as Tauchnitz paperbacks for sale in mainland Europe.

On 30 December 1931, Thompson left Southampton for New York on the RMS *Olympic*. She was going to undertake her first lecture tour in the US, where she would speak on subjects including 'What is Happening in England Today?', 'The English Theatre of Today' and 'European Novelist's Workshop' (see the anonymous newspaper reports 'Miss Thompson'; 'The Drama League'; and 'Sylvia Thompson'). Thompson also did radio and newspaper interviews on this tour. Among her fellow passengers was the writer Alec Waugh, who was likewise departing on a lecture tour. He recalled in *A Year to Remember: A Reminiscence of 1931* (1975) that since the ship was so empty, he had chosen to travel second-class instead of first, as had Sylvia Thompson: 'I had met her once or twice, but this was the first time I had had a chance of a real talk with her. 'This trip was the start of a friendship that I was to value greatly'. Waugh comments on the calibre of her novels and on the excellence of the short stories that she sold to high-paying magazines, but observes that she 'ceased writing early'. Indeed, her last book, *The Candle's Glory* (1953) appeared fifteen years before her death on 27 April 1968, although in her later years she continued to contribute to periodicals. Lamenting that he failed to get in touch with her after the war, Waugh says he felt both guilt and regret on reading of her death, adding: 'She was a rich rare person' (Waugh 78).

The Gulls Fly Inland: 'the phase of suspense'

'While I lie here the lovely places of Europe come to me like ghosts' says Blanche Lancret's Austrian uncle, Otto Behrens, towards the end of *The Gulls Fly Inland* (160). Otto lies ill in Nice in early May 1940, just a few days before the start of the Battle of France. His words seem to reveal the novel's fictional method. Blanche, waiting out the anxious months from October 1939 until the following August, finds that her thoughts, like Otto's, are dominated by ghosts of the lovely places of Europe. Writing about them offers not only a consolation but also a way of memorialising these sites, which are now under threat of destruction. Blanche describes her past stays at her aunt's house on the French Riviera and at her father's villa near Venice. In particular, she writes of Paris, where she was mostly brought up:

> Earlier in this journal I have said that I had three Parises in my life: the inherited Paris of my mother; the dulled Paris of my adolescence; and the Paris which, for Vernon and me, was a mirror in which the invisible enchantment of our love became visible, our delight taking on the form of the river, our wonder assuming the properties of Notre-Dame, our sweet or foolish moods reflected in a striped awning, a bunch of mediocre violets, a shabby green bus careering headlong towards Montparnasse.
>
> But now I experienced, not three days, between May the sixth and May the ninth, but a fourth Paris. A Paris at whose gates there was already a dark angel. (166)

The date of this entry gives it a special resonance: it is 18 June, four days after the Germans entered Paris. Several temporalities are overlaid as Blanche, in the dark weeks of late June, remembers these three days in May, when her ardent expectation of Vernon's arrival mingled with a 'presentiment' about Paris (166) which she was unable to understand at the time. Simultaneously, she recalls the ways that her vision of the city has shifted over the years as she saw it under the influence of different people or experiences.

This journal entry, like so many others in the novel, reveals Thompson's abiding preoccupation with the relationship between place and emotion. City streets become repositories of feeling in her narratives, while the atmosphere of a house often infuses itself into personal relations. She describes interiors with great skill, evoking her characters partly through their rooms and furniture. In Italy, Blanche and her father sit down 'in the cool among the fugitive blue and rosy and gold pallors of his frescoes' (84). Vernon likes 'big pale spaces and few pieces of furniture' (123) but Leonora, the American woman who comes between him and Blanche, prefers 'massive Spanish furniture, hangings and portières of brocades in purples, reds, and golds, imitation stone walls on which were hung ironwork candelabra, pieces of old armour, [and] Persian rugs' (123–4). Leonora also displays piles of the newest books in French and English. Her rooms and her miscellaneous artefacts reveal, not precisely her personality, but rather the intense effort she makes to acquire the outward signs of a European high culture to which she has, in fact, no connection.

Escaping from these elaborate interiors, Vernon and Blanche spend time in a New England farmhouse, sleeping in a room with 'three windows, and a white wallpaper with small yellow stars on it'; here, they find an 'absolute peace of sun and pines and snow' (122). The phases of Blanche and Vernon's relationship are defined in relation to the places in which they are together. The novel inscribes a transatlantic erotic geography as their romance evolves from their meeting in England through her visit to Boston, and then their time together in Italy, the northeastern US, and Paris.

Indeed, one crucial scene actually takes place on a transatlantic liner. This episode is foreseen by a fortune-teller, who informs Blanche that she will soon be invited by a female friend to take a long trip across water. The improbably-named Madame Smith also speaks of a man whom Blanche will meet on the boat, saying that this encounter will prove a turning point in her life. The prediction suggests the conventional formula of the shipboard romance, familiar from so many novels of the period. Ocean liners were frequently represented in interwar and mid-century literature and film, often as the setting for love or crime (see Hammill 2020). Atlantic crossings feature often in Thompson's novels: see *The Battle of the Horizons* (1928), *Helena* (1933), *A Silver Rattle* (1935), *Recapture the Moon* (1937) and *The Candle's Glory* (1953).

Yet Blanche is in fact soon asked by Annabelle (Vernon's sister) to accompany her on a visit to her parents in America. On the outward journey, Blanche does not meet anyone, but as she embarks for the return trip on the SS *Normandie*, Vernon appears in her cabin and says simply 'Please come, darling' (120). These words remind us of Blanche's description of the moment when they first kissed, in Italy a decade earlier: 'he says "Please come": as if he were afraid, himself, to come to me. And I went' (52). These are two pivotal moments in their relationship, revealing Blanche's courage (which is greater than Vernon's) but also her willingness to follow where her lover beckons. Thompson once described the occult as 'the oddest mixture of the bogus and extraordinarily veracious' (Thompson 'Round'); the fortune-teller in the novel conforms to this description. Her predictions are slightly jumbled but largely accurate, and they have a certain power in the narrative, helping to construct Blanche and Vernon's love as something determined by Fate and therefore not subject to ordinary moral conventions.

Their relationship also has a symbolic value. Blanche herself articulates this when describing her feelings as she goes aboard the *Normandie*:

> I arrived early at the dock, and when I had embarked I stood on the deck for a time, surveying the sparkling vivacity of the air, the quays and the shipping on the river, and permitting myself sensations which went through me like verses of poetry: some about the America that I was leaving, with its qualities of hope and freshness of heart; others about the Europe, familiar and mysterious, to which I was returning. And as it happens in poetry, metaphor and truth became intertwined; and in thinking of America I thought also of Vernon. (119)

The Gulls Fly Inland, then, is a novel of transatlantic relations just as much as it is a story about the Fall of France. Both themes invite reflections on national character and cultural difference. Of her aunt Julie – surely the most memorable character in the novel – Blanche observes that her Frenchness consists in 'her good sense, in her ingrained avarice (caused by toil for small gain), in her warmth of heart and her matter-of-fact sensuality' (158). She explains: 'resentful of politics, contemptuous and fearful of war, what Tante Julie was ready to defend sulkily, stubbornly, and to death, was quite simply *the habit of being French*' (158). Yet Julie is never hostile to people from other cultures: she welcomes Blanche's American and English friends, and falls in love herself with Otto Behrens, whose surname indicates that he is Jewish. Blanche watches them setting off into the Parisian evening: 'They went out taking with them an atmosphere of ripe expert enjoyment', she writes, adding: 'The atmosphere of Boston seemed very far away' (46).

It is precisely in terms of differences of 'atmosphere' that Blanche characterises the various cultures of Europe and America. Many of her observations centre on questions of good sense and humour versus seriousness. She remarks that two Americans experiencing romantic difficulties would tend to 'idealize their problem; to interpret it morally, rather than (as two French people would have) in terms of "good sense" *versus* "love"' (125). She considers that Americans can be 'strong and simple from lack of humour' (125) and quotes her father's view that England is a nation with a sense of humour, while the Italians have 'gaiety but no humour … and the Germans not even gaiety' (131). A sense of humour stands, in the novel, for an ability to see things from another's point of view, a refusal to take oneself too seriously, and an awareness of relative values. The implication is that such qualities are needed in order to ensure good relationships and avoid conflict, on the international stage as well as in personal life.

Although humour and gaiety are among the primary values celebrated by *The Gulls Fly Inland*, the wartime context darkens the mood. In this respect it contrasts with another novel of transatlantic relations which Thompson published just two years earlier: *The Adventure of Christopher Columin* (1939), a story with an enchanting fairy-tale quality. Christopher, an American marketing executive, suddenly leaves his dull job and tiresome wife, departing on the RMS *Queen Mary* for England. Once again, an ocean crossing marks the start of a new phase of life. Christopher experiences the transformative power of the marine environment: the feeling of 'the whole Atlantic morning shining and tearing and singing and throbbing about his ears' (Thompson 1939, 49) makes him recognise his own freedom and autonomy. Christopher's mind-expanding journey contrasts strikingly with the joyless sightseeing of his former wife Alice, whose response to European travel is one of mild disgust: 'Alice stopped twice to consult the Blue Guide and hold her handkerchief to her nose' (ibid 111). She dutifully inspects many tourist sites, but her only real pleasure is in planning the descriptions she will give of them to her friends back home.

Christopher, for his part, locates some distant relations living in a Cornish rectory and is accepted into their family, enabling him to discover English culture from the inside. In these scenes, transatlantic comparisons are presented in a wholly comic mode, focusing on differences of language, manners, dress and food: '"Skon?" asked Christopher, puzzled, and they were all delighted to discover that Christopher called scones "hot biscuits", and biscuits "crackers"!' (ibid 68). Next he takes a trip to Provence, visiting another newly-discovered relative, Sophie. French life and manners, too, are explored from a perspective of intimacy and inclusion, and Sophie gives him 'a kind of hospitality which he had never known, letting him stay among the tranquil and gay and lovely qualities of her character' (ibid 187). Hospitality is a prominent motif in Thompson's novels and was evidently important to her – Susanna Dammann observes that the seventeenth-century Surrey farmhouse which Thompson and Peter Luling bought in 1953 'offered generous, glamorous hospitality to all, including her grandchildren' (Dammann 2023).

In *The Adventure of Christopher Columin*, hospitality is embodied in characters from various walks of life: not only in the elegant Sophie with her spacious villa but equally in the Cornish vicar who supports a large family on a very modest income. Their hospitable gestures take on a meaning beyond the personal, representing also a form of internationalism: a welcome extended to visitors from abroad.

The theme of hospitality takes on more poignancy in *The Gulls Fly Inland*, not only in relation to war but also in the context of the financial crash of 1929. Blanche says of Mr Strudwick, father of Annabelle and Vernon, that he 'had a sensitivity of imagination to see how financial disaster must destroy, not only all the accumulated exquisite ornament, but the very pillars of fine living, how it had carried away hospitality and generosity' (115). Yet while Mr Strudwick is defeated and becomes mentally unbalanced, his daughter manages to sustain her graciousness of living even after the crash. Annabelle's 'serenity became more gay when they became poor; as if, in losing her inherited wealth, her whole nature had been relieved of an inherited high "seriousness"' (87). Annabelle, always open to the influence of foreign cultures, is also attuned to their multiplicity: 'here is yet another Frenchness' (167), she declares. It is Annabelle, too, who exclaims: 'Don't let's forget all the *goodness* in Germany, Blanche. Don't let's pretend that Germany isn't full of women, like you and me, just aching all the time with anxiety, and [...] so afraid – for their children' (172). Her attitude finds a parallel in the behaviour of Blanche and Vernon, whose hospitable response to the German refugee child Sohni has far-reaching and painful effects on their own relationship. Blanche sees Sohni 'not only as his infinitely touching self, but as a forerunner' of all the other children who will suffer as a result of wartime atrocities (128). Indeed, war is understood in *The Gulls Fly Inland* entirely through its effects on domestic lives and on civilian populations, including those of aggressor countries.

War does not dominate the narrative but it determines its shape. Blanche's detailed recollections of the 1920s and 1930s are interrupted, at the start or end of many of the diary entries, by a brief bulletin from the present moment: 'No letter from Vernon. But the American mails are delayed now. His last letter took three weeks' (20). Each evocation of the lovely scenes of the past is given a certain pathos by the awareness that the houses and streets, the cultures and lifestyles described might be wholly destroyed by the conflict. The novel begins with the statement 'Inaction is difficult to bear. Since I am forced into inaction, here, I shall write' (1). Writing in effect becomes a form of action, and in this respect the book has similarities with Margaret Kennedy's *Where Stands A Wingèd Sentry*, which likewise appeared in 1941. While Thompson wrote a novel in diary form, Kennedy chose to publish her actual diary of the months from May to September of 1940. In both books, a woman retreats to rural England for safety and spends her time caring for those around her and writing journal entries that evoke a sense of living through history. They record the daily uncertainty of 'the phase of suspense', in Thompson's words (130), or 'seminormal life' in Kennedy's (1941, 9) – that is, the months during which people in Britain tried to go about some of their usual activities whilst they followed the terrifying news from France and awaited a possible invasion. When the two books were published, the authors of course could not tell what would happen during the rest of the war. As readers, we know more than they did, yet both narratives retain the power to suspend us in that time of unknowing.

Writing, publication and reception

In the spring of 1939, *The Adventure of Christopher Columin* was published, and Thompson was planning a new novel. Her work on *The Gulls Fly Inland* may not have started in earnest, however, until after the birth of her third daughter in June 1939. During the following months, Thompson stayed at various rented cottages in Hertfordshire, Kent and Surrey; at first all her family were with her, but during the earlier part of 1940, her elder daughters were at boarding school and she had a nurse for her baby. This is likely to have been the period in which she wrote the novel. If so then the evacuation of Dunkirk, between 26 May and 4 June, would have happened while she was at work on *The Gulls Fly Inland*. This event also features in her short story 'Southgate Belle' which appeared in *Story* magazine for July/August 1941.

The novel was published in in the US by Little, Brown on 3 April 1941 and in London and Toronto by Heinemann on 24 August 1941. Reviews in the North American press were largely positive; in the briefer notices *The Gulls Fly Inland* was praised as 'a delicate book, charmingly written' (R B 1941), as the work of a 'gifted writer' (Niven 1941), and as 'good entertainment' ('The Gulls' 1941). In a longer review in the *New York Times*, Jane Spence Southron commended Thompson for avoiding 'the experimental extremes of her time, both in life and literature', and for making 'delicacy of perception and the less obvious subtleties of character her special province' (Southron 7). Southron concludes: 'It is a novel made memorable by perpetual contrast. Blitzkrieg and the true, quiet story of deep human emotions behind the headlines' (ibid 21).

In notices in the British press, the same words – 'delicate', 'subtle', 'perceptive' and 'charming' – recur. The novel's reception in Britain was broadly favourable, and it received the compliment of serious attention from prominent critics and novelists. Thompson's compatriots tended, though, to criticise the book for a perceived excess of sentiment. The novelist L P Hartley, in a review for *The Sketch*, suggested that Blanche's unsatisfied longing 'makes the emotional quality of the book seem slightly steam-heated', but he admired many other aspects of the book. The presentation of Tante Julie, he says, is 'a gay portrait, a dry-point etching', while 'the little sketch of the Strudwicks,

American millionaires ruined by the slump, is full of insight and tenderness; the villa on the Brenta is deliciously evoked' (Hartley 215). In the *Tatler and Bystander* Christabel Marshall, playwright and suffragist, enjoyed Thompson's 'word-painting' but found some of her descriptions 'over-fanciful' (St John [Marshall] 416). Irish novelist Kate O'Brien, writing in *The Spectator*, thought there was 'too much glamour' in the novel, though she also found an 'admirable, wise detachment' in many passages. She suggests that her opinion will not coincide with that of most readers: 'And now, having carped because a book which contains a great many good things is never as good as it keeps on hinting it could be, I can only concede that it is bound to be enormously liked' (O'Brien). And, clearly, it was. Many reviewers overflowed with enthusiasm. 'Let me give high praise to *The Gulls Fly Inland*', wrote the critic and editor Frank Swinnerton in his influential weekly column in *The Observer*, adding: 'the detail is unfailingly deft, and some of the observations are very penetrating'. He concluded: 'No other novel of the week shows comparable accomplishment' (Swinnerton). The reviewer for *The Scotsman* concurred: 'The quality of the writing is equal to the theme, and Miss Thompson has reasserted her claim, with this original study, to be considered as a novelist of exceptional worth' ('New Novels').

Considering that Thompson combined a serious literary reputation with commercial success and public prominence, it is astonishing that she has not, until now, been rediscovered. During the period since the 1980s, her Somerville College peers have all been republished and written back into literary and feminist history, yet no new editions of Thompson's work have appeared and no scholar has published more than a page or two about her. This is difficult to explain, although one factor may be that while she is forever associated with the 1920s because of her one bestseller, *The Hounds of Spring*, her finest work actually belongs to the mid-century period. Indeed, her granddaughter is surely correct in observing that *The Gulls Fly Inland* was 'among her best writing' (Dammann 2023).

At the end of her 1960 *Vogue* article, Thompson expresses regret over not accepting Jacques-Émile Blanche's portrait of her, writing wistfully:

> The fact remains that, now that I 'have walls,' I have, alas, no romantic portrait to hang on them. No evocation of the white Russian hat, the pale gloves, the palely, luxuriously loitering young woman, gracious in chiaroscuro aspic, to be admitted, and disbelieved, by grandchildren. (Thompson 1960, 37)

Whilst *The Gulls Fly Inland* is no autobiography, its images of Annabelle and Blanche might be read as a form of self-portraiture. The luxuriously loitering young woman of the thirties is certainly present in this narrative, even if she is ultimately forced on more painful exertions during the war years.

Works Cited

Anon, 'The Drama League', *Chicago Daily Tribune*, 13 January 1932, 15.

—, 'The Gulls Fly Inland', review of *The Gulls Fly Inland* by Sylvia Thompson, *Kirkus Reviews*, 1 April 1941.

—, 'Miss Thompson Forum Speaker', *Waterbury Evening Democrat*, 9 January 1932, 3.

—, 'New Novels: Romance Recaptured in Memory', *The Scotsman*, 28 August 1941, 7.

—, 'Snatches', *Evening Star* (Washington) magazine, 2 May 1937, 2.

—, 'Sylvia Thompson, Famous Writer, to Speak at N C', *The Carolinian* (Greensboro), 18 February 1932, 1.

Brittain, Vera, 'The Somerville School of Novelists', *Good Housekeeping*, April 1929, 52–53, 122–24.

Dammann, Susanna, untitled outline of Sylvia Thompson's life and work, provided in mss to Handheld Press, 2023.

GREC [Winifred Holtby], 'Parnassus in Academe: Novelists at Oxford', *Time and Tide*, 28 December 1928, 1271–72.

Hammill, Faye, 'The Frantic Atlantic: Ocean Liners in the Interwar Literary Imagination', *Symbiosis: Transatlantic Literary and Cultural Relations*, 24.1/2, 2020, 157–77.

Hartley, L P, 'The Literary Lounger', *The Sketch*, 24 September 1941, 214–15.

Kennedy, Margaret, *Where Stands A Wingèd Sentry* (1941; Handheld Press 2021).

Niven, Flora, review of *The Gulls Fly Inland* by Sylvia Thompson, *The Vancouver Sun*, 12 July 1941, 38.

O'Brien, Kate, 'Fiction: *The Gulls Fly Inland*', *The Spectator*, 5 September 1941, 244.

Powell, Violet, *The Constant Novelist: A Study of Margaret Kennedy, 1896–1967* (Heinemann 1983).

R B, review of *The Gulls Fly Inland* by Sylvia Thompson, *The Saturday Review*, 12 April 1941, 21.

Ryan, Eilish, *Rosemary Haughton: Witness to Hope* (Sheed & Ward 1997).

Southron, Jane Spence, 'Life in Wartime: *The Gulls Fly Inland*', *New York Times*, 6 April 1941, BR7, BR21.

St John, Christopher [Christabel Marshall], 'With Silent Friends', *Tatler and Bystander*, 17 September 1941, 414, 416.

Swinnerton, Frank, 'New Novels: Some Love Stories', *The Observer*, 24 August 1941, 3.

Thompson, Sylvia, *The Adventure of Christopher Columin* (Heinemann 1939).

Thompson, Sylvia, 'I was a fool', *Vogue* (New York), 15 January 1960, 36–37.

Thompson, Sylvia, 'Round About The Occult', *The Graphic*, 10 October 1931, 25.

Thompson, Sylvia, 'Success', *Britannia and Eve*, April 1931, 50–51, 114–15.

Waugh, Alec, *A Year to Remember: A Reminiscence of 1931* (1975; Bloomsbury 2011).

Works by Sylvia Thompson

Novels

The Rough Crossing (Basil Blackwell 1921)

A Lady in Green Gloves (Basil Blackwell 1924)

The Hounds of Spring (Heinemann 1926)

The Battle of the Horizons (Heinemann 1928)

Chariot Wheels (Heinemann 1929)

Winter Comedy (Heinemann 1931; US edition as *Portrait by Caroline* Little, Brown 1931)

Summer's Night (Heinemann 1932)

Helena (Heinemann 1933; US edition as *Unfinished Symphony* Little, Brown 1933)

Breakfast in Bed (Heinemann 1934)

A Silver Rattle (Heinemann 1935)

Third Act in Venice (Heinemann 1936)

Recapture the Moon (Heinemann 1937)

The Adventure of Christopher Columin (Heinemann 1939)

The Gulls Fly Inland (Heinemann 1941)

The People Opposite (Michael Joseph 1948)

The Candle's Glory (Michael Joseph 1953)

Novellas

The Empty Heart, Hearst's International, May 1945; (Gordon Martin 1945)

All Our Lives, Woman's Home Companion, July 1948.

Play

Golden Arrow, with Victor Cunard (Heinemann, 1935)

Additional publications

Essays and stories in 40 periodicals, among them *Good Housekeeping, Vogue, Red Book, Town & Country* and *Time and Tide*. She also wrote an introduction and notes for a book by her seven-year-old daughter, Elizabeth Luling: *Do Not Disturb: The Adventures of M'm and Teddy, etc* (Oxford University Press 1937).

Further Reading

Beauman, Nicola, *A Very Great Profession: The Woman's Novel, 1914–39* (Virago 1983).

Berry, Paul and Alan Bishop, eds, *Testament of a Generation: The Journalism of Vera Brittain and Winifred Holtby* (Virago 1985).

Christie, Laura, 'Thompson, Sylvia 1902–1968', *Encyclopedia of British Women's Writing, 1900–1950*, ed. Faye Hammill, Esme Miskimmin and Ashlie Sponenberg (Palgrave 2006), 251–52.

Ouditt, Sharon, *Fighting Forces, Writing Women: Identity and Ideology in the First World War* (Routledge 1994).

Troyan, Michael, *A Rose for Mrs Miniver: The Life of Greer Garson* (University Press of Kentucky 1999).

Waugh, Alec, *The Fatal Gift* (W H Allen 1973).

Part 1

Inaction is difficult to bear.

Since I am forced into inaction, here, I shall write. Not, as I have written in peace-time, brief things for magazines of intellectual elegance. But retrospects, more or less as a journal.

✳

I shall write about Vernon.

And about Annabelle, his sister, and her marriage with Pierre.

I shall write about my aunt, Julie de Montal. (It would be difficult to have known Tante Julie, and not to write about her.) Also about my father, Anatole Lancret.

I shall describe, with affection, Hugo Fenchurch, whom I have from time to time almost loved. And I shall write of Cécile Dubois and of old Pauline with tenderness.

And of Leonora, Vernon's wife, I shall try to write with comprehension.

But shall l be able to write of Vernon? Shall I make him distinct? Or will someone, reading these pages, protest: 'But I don't "see" him at all.' I should like to be able to describe him, as Clouet or Holbein painted, with a tranquil and luminous art. I should like all the subtleties and contradictions of his nature to be explained with the greatest simplicity, so that the simplest reader would say: 'Yes. I understand why she loved him.'

And of course I must write about myself, Blanche Lancret, if I write about these others.

October 6th, 1939

There is time to write here. But there will not be too much time, I hope. In this big mediocre villa on the edge of the cliff, I am living alone; except for Annabelle's latest baby, Camilla Blanche. Annabelle wrote to me: 'If you are not yet fixed in any war work; and would help me? ... ' I crossed to England in reply to her letter. Pierre is mobilized. She is evidently bewildered as well as unhappy without him. For the moment my 'war work' is evident. I am to be mother to the baby here, while the other children are nursed through chicken pox by Annabelle in their home in Sussex.

Annabelle and Pierre bought this house some years ago when their eldest little girl, Amaryllis, had been ill and had to come to a seaside place. There is a lawn below my window, then a high box hedge; then the grass on the cliff. Then the sea, and on its horizon dark, castle-shaped battleships gliding straight across like ships on the stage that slip along a wire.

Annabelle telephoned last night; first to speak to Nurse and know how the baby, Camilla Blanche, is. Then she asked: 'Have you heard from Vernon? I hear Leonora is planning to come over to nurse in a French hospital.'

As well as the baby and her nurse here, there is Bridget, who comes all day and cooks and brings with her an enormous 'Old English' sheepdog whom she calls 'Darrlin'.' And there is also a woman who comes for the mornings only, called 'Mrs Drew'. She is extremely talkative, in cockney, which still I only half comprehend. She is thin, dressed always in dark green, and her face, with its red nose and gay brown eyes, has no precise age: but from the fashion in which she speaks of her (third) husband, 'Jo', I imagine she has not passed the age of amorous pleasure. Every morning she cleans the nickel taps in the bathroom to my bedroom, praising herself while she does this, so that I shall hear. The day that I came she told

2

me that she had worked for Mrs Morel (Annabelle) while she was here in the summer. And then there followed a long history, from which I understood that Annabelle had written to her (Mrs Drew) asking her to continue to work while I was here with Nurse, and Baby. She finished: 'I see to it that I get along with Nurse.'

Bridget said to me also the next day: 'I get along very well with Mrs Drew'. But it was almost her only reference to domestic matters; for she speaks most of the time of dogs and literature; and sometimes of her husband (who works in some superior situation in a bank in Margate and who also, it seems, loves dogs and literature). I think Bridget works here partly because she values money, but also because she loves Annabelle and Pierre. It seems that she came first to work for Annabelle when the Chinese butler-housemaid whom they had brought with them ran away. Bridget told me that she 'likes foreigners', and that she would like to meet Chinese people; and had I read *The Good Earth*? She is a good cook. She has pink cheeks and white teeth and hair striped russet and grey, and there is about her a perpetual high-spirited *insouciance*, except in questions relating to animals, especially dogs. It is because of 'dogs and cats' that she is furious against Hitler. When the raids come, she said, she is going to play the music of Wagner to Darrlin' so that he shall not hear the bombs, so she keeps a portable gramophone in the kitchen next to her gas mask.

October 10th

My father, Anatole Lancret, was Professor of Greek History in the Sorbonne. He used to take me on Saturdays to the Guignol in the Tuileries. He explained that it was really the legend about the Devil, who amuses himself by playing tricks on people. When things happen wrong, I still see Polichinelle battering about the stage of my life. After the Guignol he used to take me to visit Tante Julie in her *appartement* in the Rue Saint-Honoré. She often wore a dress of rich lace, moulded over pale pink satin that was fitted over her swelling and curving figure. Her auburn hair brooded in two lifted wings above her pink-powdered debased-classic features. Her green Breton eyes looked down on my clothes, especially my shoes, with an appraising expression, guessing their price. But when she smiled her eyes twinkled green between the beads of mascara. She always gave off a delicious fragrance, or rather aroma, especially when she was moving to and fro in her suite of over-crowded little *salons*, dusting ornaments with her handkerchief, and smoking, and talking in her deep voice, only her square underlip moving, and glancing in the different gilt mirrors as she passed them. My father always called her 'Semiramis'. *'Bonjour, Semiramis,'* kissing each of her hands in turn. Sometimes he called her 'La Tigresse'. Her fingers all had square ends, He said the texture of her hands was like vellum, and so her hands often remind me of the vellum binding of the Ronsard I have that had belonged to my mother.

Tante Julie is the half sister of my dead mother. She was eleven years older. My grandfather, Charles Valéry, had married first his Breton housekeeper, then the well-born little Mademoiselle Choiseul, a Renoir young woman in a fringe and 'bustle', who was my mother's mother. Most men marry their housekeeper last. But Grand-père Valéry always arranged things contrarily. He was a huge man who drove his own desires through life, like a team of stallions. Both his daughters, Tante Julie and my mother, grew up in awe of him. My mother was timid anyway; and he used to dominate Tante Julie in his quarrels with her. Once, when Tante Julie was eighteen, he whipped her but gave her champagne afterwards. He treated her like this because he had bred her from a servant. Towards my mother's mother he was ironical and polite, it seems. Evidently he married her out of a caprice of snobbishness. It was Julie who grew up into the kind of woman he liked; mixture of peasant and *poule de luxe*.

But Julie admired my grandmother (that is to say, her stepmother) extremely. 'A lady very correct, very elegant,' she describes her. Julie was a ten-year-old in a tartan dress and black alpaca pinafores when she got this stepmother, 'very correct, very elegant'. 'She used to embrace me every night on the forehead,' Julie says. I imagine this Mademoiselle Choiseul was a dull girl with the false distinction given by anaemia, and was married to my grandfather for his money. When my mother was born Julie felt a peasant's pleasure in the baby sister, Jeannette, and a respect for its costly laces and muslins. 'She was like a doll from a most expensive shop — thy little Maman.' Tante Julie remembers the price of the perambulator. Grand-père Valéry had a villa at Nice and arranged for my grandmother to live there, while he stayed in Paris. *Boulevardier* fits him. It was he who bought the *appartement* in the Rue Saint-Honoré; and left it to Julie when he died.

So my mother, *'cette petite Jeannette'*, grew up at Nice, hugged, slapped, and indulged by Julie; and received by her own mother once a day in the *salon*. Julie says my grandmother paid calls every afternoon in a private carriage, holding a parasol of beige silk. When my mother was twelve, Julie married de Montal and went to live in Paris. Tante Julie always says of de Montal that he was *'beau garçon'*. But in his photograph on her *table de nuit* he looks like a waxwork villain with false black moustaches. After this my mother was lonely. For my grandmother was not affectionate or gay, and children need one or the other quality, and prefer both. When she was eighteen my father came to the villa, a very young professor with an introduction to Madame Valéry. He told me himself how he was talking on a terrace with my grandmother, when my mother came up some stone steps to them; that she wore a straw 'boater' and a cloth skirt and bolero of a pale blue that made her face sallow, and that she was too thin, and shook hands with him without smiling. Then two days later when he dined there she was in pale pink and looked fragile and had a smile that came suddenly, curving one side of her mouth more than the other. Evidently my mother then fell in love with this young professor with black eyes and yellowed white flannel trousers. (He says: 'I dressed myself *à l'anglais* in those days, as far as my income would permit; and it did not permit it.') My father said that Nature and Solitude trapped my mother into a sensation of love for him. When he came to say his good-byes she was alone, and burst into tears; and so he 'saw at once that she had been confided to him by Destiny'. Behind this decision of my father's is much of his character: quick sympathy, and a disregard for common sense — 'the most *bourgeois* of all the senses'. His concessions to 'Destiny' were partly weak will, partly applied poetry. He thinks it is pharisaical to manage your life, and that there is grace in misfortune, and that 'all the curves of success' are *'grossier'*. He married my mother because she was sad and thin and not pretty and had a boring mother. He took great trouble to marry her; getting permission from Grand-père Valéry — who would permit anything that angered his wife!

During the four years of my parents' marriage my father's feelings for my mother changed evidently from tenderness to passion. (She died of pneumonia in the winter of 1908.) I remember her only once quite distinctly. She is seated at the round table in the *salon*; the lamp is on the table, its opaque glass a shade like a moon; in its light she lifts her face and smiles at me from under the brim of a hat with a pale blue ostrich feather. I see her face now; and now I see that it is a very young face, with a dimple near that corner of the mouth that smiles more than the other.

After her death we moved from Passy to the Rue Vaugirard. My father kept his professorship. But in other ways his habits changed. He and my mother had gone often to the theatre and when they came back he made a little supper (he is an excellent cook). And they used to talk and laugh in the room with the red wallpaper, next to mine. All the talk and laughter in my mother's life were concentrated in the years of her marriage. After she died my father ceased to go out, but used to read most of the night. Later he took to that habit of wearing at home the white cotton turban and a full-skirted dressing-gown of brown brocade. (That is how his friend, Jacques Blanche, has painted him.)

Tante Julie was living in New York most of the time during my mother's marriage. She had left de Montal and gone to live with a man called Rourke, a publisher. I suppose she was accepted in New York as his wife. While she was there she met John Strudwick (Vernon's father). Rourke had published Strudwick's *Studies in Metaphysics*. This explains how one of the Strudwicks of Boston could have met Tante Julie socially. She even went to Boston once, with Rourke. She says Boston was *'une ville fade'* (a savourless town). But that 'les Strudwicks' had a very fine house.

When, later, I went to stay in the Strudwicks' house on Beacon Street, I saw how much that alliance in it of great riches and high culture must have impressed my aunt. And I tried to imagine her, seated at their table, her glance appraising its abundance of heavy bright Early American silver and shining white napery; seated no doubt on the right of Mr Strudwick, her character as ill-assorted with his as if they were two animals in a fable of La Fontaine. I envisaged her also, her and Mr Rourke, the publisher (all she ever said of him: *'Il sentait les cigares'* — he smelled of cigars), in the blue guest room — which I had also when I stayed. A large room whose four-poster had curtains of a white chintz patterned with cornflowers, and in whose book-shelf, over by the big fireplace, I discovered several volumes of Henry James, each volume dedicated to Mrs Strudwick — 'To Mrs John Strudwick from the Author'. Also an entire set of the works of Mark Twain that had been given to Vernon 'on his twelfth birthday' by his aunt, Emily Strudwick, whose bust, by Rodin, is in the library downstairs.

✕

It was perhaps the increasing physical delicacy which prevented my father fighting in the war of 1914 that gave him, also, a sort of apathy about ordinary life after my mother's death. In any case his mental absences increased. And, when I was fourteen and the war was just finished, he decided to leave Paris.

For Paris, since my mother's death, had become, for him, only her mausoleum. And even as a little girl I noticed how he would say, in the gardens of Bagatelle: 'Jeannette liked this view from here', or, in the Trocadéro Gardens: 'This one was the favourite of Jeannette', pointing to one of those immensely vital stone elephants with lifted trunks (gone, alas, since the *Exposition* of 1936). And on our Thursday afternoons, if we varied our visits to the theatre or to the museums (by what Vernon calls a 'flâneur around'), he would discover memorials to my mother equally in shop windows of the Rue de la Pais and in the little *marché* at the top of the Rue de Passy ... pausing outside Hedjar to exclaim: 'Ah that is the *sirop* that she preferred', or outside the window of the Nain Bleu to say, with a sort of ironical reverence: 'It was here that she bought thy doll, Fanchon' (the reverence being for my mother, the irony for death, which has no power over dolls). And on the Quai aux Fleurs we would wander from stall to perfumed stall; and he would say to some bulky woman standing between a tree of Daphne and bank of narcissus: 'You remember how Madame Lancret loved these?' And the woman — a true Frenchwoman, combining real feeling with realism — would talk to him of my mother, shaking her head, and sell him (but never I think at much profit) some flowers to take home.

And thus, my mother, the Jeannette who died at twenty three, became for me, not the Greuzâtre girl in the photograph on my father's writing table, nor the *'pauvre petite Jeannette'* of Tante Julie's reminiscences, but a creature delicious as a fresh fondant, sophisticated but simple as a wax doll, flitting, to and fro in Paris, adorned with pale blue ostrich feathers, buying here a sirop of exotic sweetness, there a toy, and on the *quais* such sheaves of flowers that she must drive home with them in an open *fiacre*. For 'she loved to drive', said my father.

'She would take that rug trimmed with mink that thy Aunt Julie sent her from America, and say to the coachman, "Now circulate." … And thus we would continue to drive for two or three hours.' He added: 'She was not adapted to be the wife of a professor. She was a spendthrift in all simplicity.' I think that her spendings were caused by the gaiety that came to her after marriage, when life suddenly became for her a feast, at which, as a woman entertaining her lover, she desired that no little luxury should be lacking.

It was through such memories that my father bequeathed to me, when he retired to Italy, to his villa on the Brenta, a Paris whose main arteries were the shopping routes of my young mother. But after he went I discovered a second Paris, the restricted and more or less monotone Paris of a schoolgirl whose daily route lay between my aunt's flat, facing the Tuileries, and the Couvent des Oiseaux, off the Champs-Elysées, where I went to school. And partly I think because of the anaemia of my own system at that time I ceased to see beauty or to feel any emotion for the city through which I carried my daily satchel. (It was a period such as may happen in a marriage, when the first delight is over, and the *grand vin* of tenderness is not yet distilled from Time.) When I crossed the Rue Saint-Florentin at half-past eight in the mornings, the Place de la Concorde stretching before me on my left had an immense bleakness, and I forgot its lighted fountains which we used to visit on our Thursday evenings; the Rue Royale had too much traffic, the little bay trees outside Maxim's were no longer my special acquaintances, each with its own character; the flower sellers seemed importunate and the Avenue Gabriel was merely a stretch of pavement whose length was aggravated by a daily apprehension of being late. And even on my return walk in the afternoons, Pauline beside me (for though I was permitted to go alone, she always fetched me in the afternoon), even when it was spring and we made a detour through the Champs-Elysées, hardly observed the trees and the lawns, and often passed, unseeing in one of those dull obstinate moods of adolescence, by that very tree of magnolia which was to bloom with such unforgettable white beauty fifteen years later, in my 'third Paris'.

My third Paris ...

For, as my father gave me one Paris, and my schooldays another, Vernon gave me still another; and the routes of the third Paris are those we followed together: those narrow streets of the seventeenth century around the Place des Vosges; the alleys between poor yet so distinguished façades near the Luxembourg; and those three radiations to Saint-Cloud, to Versailles, to Fontainebleau ... In this Paris, which is the one I have still in my heart, there are corners made significant by our moments of brilliant feeling as by sudden effects of floodlight.

For example there is that moment outside the Post Office

in the Rue d'Anjou, when he kissed my hand, suddenly, and said: 'I shall never be able to leave you.' It was a beautiful midday; and I believed him. And it is this belief of mine that remains, like a stone garland, deliciously defined by that midday sunshine in the Rue d'Anjou.

And at the very centre of my third Paris there is that stretch of the Seine where, only two years ago, I stayed with Vernon in that *appartement* that belonged to the Strudwicks on the Quai d'Orléans, between the Pont Marie and Notre-Dame. We stood on the balcony in the mystical light of four o'clock on a May morning. Quiet was lacquered over the river, and over the houses on the opposite *quai* whose shutters were still closed. Only occasionally, there was a far-off rattle of lorries, or the rumble of wagons arriving in the Marché, over there on the Left Bank. We stood watching this lovely morning beginning over Paris; and we were startled and moved by it, as if we had surprised a flower opening ...

October 21st

This morning I was just beginning to write a chapter about my father, after he left Paris (I was writing in bed), when I heard distant sirens and realized with annoyance that it was an Air-Raid Warning. I got up and went to the nursery. Camilla Blanche was in her bath, gazing in astonishment at her own toes. Nurse asked if she should finish dressing Baby? I said yes; and then went downstairs. Bridget, in the kitchen, was playing a Wagner record on the gramophone while Mrs Drew was stirring a saucepan on the gas oven.

I went on to the verandah and now one could hear guns far away. But the sky was empty and very pale blue. Soon Nurse came down and arranged the pram ready for the baby. She said: 'Has the All Clear gone yet or had I better keep Baby indoors?' She said that Bridget was playing the gramophone so loud that Baby would never get off to sleep. Her face was a little discoloured, and she said: 'Shouldn't we go in the shelter on the cliff, Mademoiselle?' But I said no, it was too damp, and if the raid came near we would go into the dining-room, which has inside walls. I returned to the kitchen where Mrs Drew was now seated at the table, her gas mask beside her cup and saucer. She looked exasperated by the music with which Bridget mingled a chant of reassurance to the dog — 'They've gone, a-all gone, Darrlin', Them German aerreplanes'll soon be gone, my Darrlin'.'

I attempted to make her realize that the aeroplanes were not even visible. But, without ceasing her loud chanting, she gave me to understand with gestures that nothing must divert the animal from the sort of *café chantant* that she had arranged; for he was sitting with a bowl of milk between his dishevelled paws. Mrs Drew asked: 'Can I make you a cup of tea, Miss?' But I shook my head and left them. Nurse was in the hall, carrying Camilla Blanche, who turned her mother-of-pearl face slowly towards me, and then gave me one of her smiles that are grotesque yet infinitely charming. But then, as she heard the music coming through the kitchen door, the dimple vanished from her cheek, her eyelids, fringed with those gilded brown curled lashes, lifted again, her shadows of eyebrows grew level, and she was, once more, extremely serious because of the music of Wagner in her ears.

Nurse said: 'I've got her gas helmet ready.' But she had hardly said this when we heard the All Clear.

November 1st

I forget how my father found his villa on the Brenta. I rather think it was through a friend, a professor in the University at Padua. In any case it was exactly what he needed, a low-built stucco house, whose gardens were bounded by the canal. He rented it cheaply from an Italian woman whom I never saw, and who had a bigger property, in which she lived, outside Rome. So in my holidays, except the Christmas holiday, which was too brief, I used to go to Italy; accompanied on my journey by a certain Mademoiselle Cécile Dubois, an old maid, sallow and respectable and sad, whom Tante Julie employed from time to time, sometimes to shop for her, sometimes to write letters, or recover cushions. She always described her as *'une personne de toute confiance'*. When she escorted me to Italy she wore for travel, winter or summer, a dark green and black plaid cape with a black velvet collar, and as soon as we entered the train bound her head in a scarf of faded sky-blue chiffon which, swathed above her frightened-hare eyes, made her nose curve out like the beak of a bird.

I think she enjoyed the journey. She used to take every possible meal in the *wagon-restaurant*; and her manner, timid with my aunt, became, once I was in her charge, arrogant towards the officials on the train, and suspicious towards all our male fellow travellers. I was at the age to notice her peculiarities rather than to understand them. The pale blue cotton kimono that she wore in our *wagon-lit*, which smelled of camphor; her nail brush whose black bristles grew visibly more bald over the years of our journeying; her knitting 'for her nephew, Marcel'; her long prayers at night, kneeling against the twin berths, and the hasty modesty of her washing in the mornings — all this I described to Vernon, only a few years later; and it was he who said: 'But, Blanche, you aren't being *drôle* a bit, you're telling me a tragic novel!'

That was, perhaps, what my father felt about Mademoiselle Dubois. He always treated her with the greatest respect, and even gallantry. He brought flowers to the station to greet us both: mimosa at the beginning of the Easter holidays, and numerous bunches of roses when we arrived soon after the fifteenth of July. When he presented them to Mademoiselle

Dubois he always kissed her hand, and then we went out of Padua Station, and while we waited for our luggage Mademoiselle Dubois always, even on a cold arrival in April, made the same remark: '*Ah, le beau soleil d'Italie,*' and blinked, lifting her beak to the sky. Before leaving the train she had taken off her blue veil and put on a hat which was either always the same black felt or one of a series. It usually had a big black satin bow in front, and this gave her a sort of funereal plumage.

During the Easter holidays she used to remain with us in the villa; but making little tours, encouraged and paid for by my father, of course, to the towns of North Italy. She would return from such expeditions crying delighted adjectives; but also looking tired and a little bewildered. And I think now that the beauty of the places she had seen must have troubled her imagination; and, perhaps, hurt her by intimations that she only half understood, of all those riches of the heart and senses which she had never known. I think that I comprehended this when she returned after an absence of several days, and my father asked her how she had liked Venice. And she didn't reply at once — we were all three seated by a log fire, and it was evening; and then she said: '*C'était trop belle, Monsieur*' ... too beautiful. '*Venise était trop belle.*' And her flying, disturbed glance seemed to say that she had been overwhelmed, not altogether happily.

But in the summer holidays she remained one or two days only, to rest, and then went back to Paris. And only returned to fetch me at the end of September, ('What did she do during that time?' Vernon asked me. I said I supposed that she remained in that *petite chambre* to which she occasionally referred and whose address, I suppose, Tante Julie knew. 'How did she live? What did she live on? How did she spend her time?' Vernon demanded. I didn't know ... I shall recount Vernon's friendship with Mademoiselle Dubois later.)

Once she had gone back to Paris, my schoolgirl character and my existence with Tante Julie, became far off; and I became part of my father's existence, in which clocks and the calendar had been abolished, and only the sun and the seasons were permitted to assert the passing of time. Indeed, nothing could have been less like my other life in the Rue Saint-Honoré. We breakfasted separately when we had woken and rung a bell for Mario to bring coffee. We lunched in the cool shadows of the hall, where mythological frescoes, pink and yellow and grey-blue-coloured in some places, crumbled to blankness in others, had the quality of half-remembered dreams ... Our lunch usually coincided with the opinion of the sundial in the rose garden, that it was midday ... In the evenings we dined, on the loggia, after sunset. During the day we read, and talked, and wandered in the gardens, separately or together.

The talk of my father was extremely diverting. And as in all diverting talk, there was gossip. But it was generally about people long dead: foibles of Emperors, casual words of Kings dead ten centuries, and curiosities about the more recondite early Saints and Classic Courtesans. As he talked, those people turned their profiles and one saw that they had two eyes and two corners to their mouths. Sometimes he did speak about living people, but with such a tolerance and detachment that it seemed that the Clemenceau or Gide, Mademoiselle Yvonne Printemps or Trotsky whom he mentioned was already dead. I remarked at this once, and he replied with one of his impatient accusations of people who think only in dimensions. Then he would discourse, about 'reality' and 'truth', and 'past' and 'future', with a ripe and gilded pedantry that accorded well with the garden with its ancient fig trees and its stone fountains whose carvings were eroded by four centuries of midday suns.

I used to imagine that he must have talked so with my

mother — Jeannette — when he first met her in the gardens of Grand-mère Valéry's villa at Nice; that they perhaps went to and fro on gravel terraces, adorned with jars of cactus and *Lauriers-roses*, and she (in her pale blue skirt and bolero) received his smiles, that he would turn and present to one suddenly and irrelevantly like little bouquets; and give him, in return, that singular charming little flower which was her own smile on one side of her mouth.

November 3rd

I was already seventeen, and had just made the second part of my Baccalauréat examination, when Tante Julie received a visit from Mrs Strudwick, who was passing through Paris on her way to a villa the Strudwicks had rented, at that time, at Arcachon. Having heard from Mrs Strudwick that her daughter, Annabelle, was at an English school, Tante Julie wished intensely that I should go there. So she obtained the consent of my father, which arrived on a postcard, and in the following September I departed for England.

I was accompanied by Mademoiselle Dubois as far as Dover. There I was met by a Junior Mistress, exactly the type of young Englishwoman I had expected, that is to say with a charming complexion, and a good-natured but brusque manner. She had come in a hired car to meet me, and we stopped, before leaving Dover, and she went into a teashop where I could observe her through a plate-glass window, drinking many cups of tea, and eating a quantity of little cakes. I think her name was Miss Landon. But she is possibly merged in my memory with several of the other young mistresses, who were all equally amiable and mediocre, and frequented teashops whenever they had the opportunity.

When I arrived the Headmistress, Miss Churston, impressed me, for she was an Englishwoman of a different class and earlier generation; a dignified, stout woman with white hair, who had visible authority, but also that gay sense of proportion which the English call a sense of humour. She dismissed the mistress as if she had been a valet, greeted me kindly, asked after the health of my aunt, from whom, she said, she had received such charming letters. (I knew that all my aunt's letters bargained to have the fees lowered on the ground that I was the daughter of a poor professor. I am afraid now, knowing that Miss Churston had a fine and futile distaste for money, that my aunt may have succeeded.)

Miss Churston took me to a sitting-room full of chintz where there were several girls of about my age. One of them was Annabelle Strudwick, who came forward at once to receive me.

Annabelle wasn't at all 'Bostonian', according to Tante Julie's account of Boston (*'des gens plutôt cultivés que élégants'*). Annabelle was *élégante*, even at sixteen; and vital and frivolous. I had never seen such beauty in a girl before. Frenchwomen aren't uncompromisingly beautiful in the way American women can be. Nobody ever argued whether Annabelle was beautiful or not.

I first saw her brother, Vernon, when he came from Oxford to see his sister; and I thought: 'He is like Annabelle would look if she were more excitable and more clever!' I thought this when he came into the hall at Pegwell House. I was going up the front staircase. (I was seventeen and so I was allowed on the front staircase.) He was lean for his height, and his eyes were dark and soft-lidded; 'Spanish' eyes like Annabelle's.

His look is always either excited and intensely aware of the people with him or else distant, fixed on the horizon of his thoughts.

He did not see me. He said to the parlourmaid: Miss Annabelle Strudwick? I didn't know English well enough then to notice his accent, which is like Annabelle's, pronouncing each word with a consideration that English people do not use towards their language.

Later that afternoon Annabelle came into the senior sitting-room where I was writing a letter to my father, and asked if I would come out to tea with her and her brother. While she was speaking the afternoon sunlight was on her face, which was firmly perfect like a ripe fruit. She said that we would have tea at the Grand Hotel, and that Vernon had a friend with him, an English boy. She said: 'I have Miss Churston's permission already for you.'

I went upstairs to my room and changed my school white blouse and brown skirt for the little navy blue dress that Tante Julie had bought me. It had narrow white piqué frilling around the high neck, and at the cuffs. While I was fitting it at Callot's, where Tante Julie got her dresses then, she said: 'At least you have a well-proportioned figure.' And the *vendeuse* said: 'Mademoiselle is slender, which so many *jeunes filles* are not.' I used to treasure such remarks, because they reassured me, a little.

When I went down Annabelle was in the hall and introduced me to her brother. We shook hands and looked at one another.

Then we all went out to a white sports car. Vernon's friend was waiting in the car, smoking a cigarette in an ivory holder. He was fair with prominent blue eyes, like a Norman. He had the most beautiful kind of English manners, making you feel as if you were his first cousin whom he had known always, but respected as if you were an heirloom. Vernon said: 'Mademoiselle Blanche Lancret, may I introduce Mr Hugo Fenchurch to you.' Hugo began at once to talk to me in French with an excellent accent. He said that his father had the pleasure of knowing mine. We all drove into Margate, Vernon driving, with me and Annabelle on the front seat, and Hugo on the 'dickey'. The wind blew against our faces, and the sun lit up everything, and I noticed some white lilac already out in a garden of one of the little villas we passed. Hugo's drawling voice kept on talking to me in French from the dickey. Whenever I turned to reply I found him regarding me attentively. Vernon drove. I noticed his hands, and what long fingers he had, and how his hands grew beautifully out of his wrists, as Annabelle's did.

(It is curious that I met Vernon and Hugo first, on the same afternoon.)

November 17th

As I look out of the window now I see that there are the same kind of waves, flat, curving, and grey-blue, with thick white fringes, exactly as there were that afternoon. Only then it was spring, so that the sunlight had more green in it; and now it is autumn, and the light is ochre ... Nurse has just been in to ask if I would like Baby in the drawing-room, after tea. I told her that I should. The baby, Camilla Blanche, is my god-daughter. She is five months old, but is so far advanced that she does not feel there are thirty-four years and ten months between us. By mutual looking we awaken her mother's smiles; and when I talk to her, reciting any words, prose or poetry, or the phrases of the advertisements, she answers with the same kind of sounds, which is friendship.

I asked the Nurse as she was leaving my room: 'Are there any letters?'

'No, Madmaselle Lorncray.'

Nurse is a pleasant girl who wears dark green linen dresses and white aprons and is well trained in the education of infants. Every morning she does 'her washing' in the nursery bathroom, and one passes a smell of warm soapsuds, and her voice singing out of tune: 'You are my Heart's Delight'.

(If I had a baby I would not have a nurse. Only a girl to do its laundry. I would behave like a peasant or a Madonna and let it sleep in my arms.)

No letter from Vernon. But the American mails are delayed now. His last letter took three weeks.

November 18th

After tea, in England, is children's time. Already Camilla Blanche enjoys this privilege. To-day, I impersonated 'Maman' and Nurse brought her to me, in the drawing-room, having dressed her in fresh white muslin and a little pink satin-quilted jacket (that Annabelle had made for her).

Camilla Blanche sat on my knee. She was like a huge white muslin and pink flower. She looked long and with profound admiration at the fire; impressed by its gold and red, delighted by the dancing of the flames. Its light made her cheeks like those of a nectarine.

The fire occupied her attention for several minutes. Then she turned her face to me. (Sometimes she is like Annabelle, because her eyes are dark. But she has some of Pierre's expression. She laughs, as he does, suddenly, with the most mad and delicious abandon.) This evening she laughed like this when I sang her '*Trempe ton pain, Marie* ...' Also she has moods of excitable curiosity, as Pierre has.

At present, human hair astonishes her: she feels it, with amusement. She stares at it. At my brown hair (which is piled up in a few curls on the top of my head). Evidently the crescent and tendril shapes of those curls surprise her. She stares. She murmurs with interest. (She has, of course, no idea that the same kind of thing is beginning to happen on her own head.)

While I was singing '*Sur le Pont d' Avignon*,' she smiled graciously. And transfixed her attention to my eyes. We look often into each other's eyes; like two people regarding each other with curiosity from their front doorsteps. Only her curiosity is rather about my façade (my eyes shine, my teeth are so amusing between my reddened lips); while my curiosity is prying and complicated: a real provincial desire to know what goes on behind *her* façade, what becomes of the impressions that are going in, all the time, at her eyes? Why is she so amiable to pearls, lights, frills, toes and to everything that is scarlet? What is her real opinion of Bridget's Wagner records which she listens to with an air of severe surprise? And her expressions, that move like shadows behind the curtains of a lighted room, are they the shadows of thoughts — or rather of memories? For sometimes I am sure that her mother-of-pearl face is grave with a sensation of remembering; and that, as she begins to be aware of flames and toes, and frills and flowers, of scarlet and her delight in it, and of voices and milk and warmth, of the alarms of solitude, and the great sweet reassurance of a caress, her small heart feels 'this' (the flowers, the alarms, the scarlet, the wireless) — 'this is Life — again!'

November 19th

I return to that first meeting with Vernon.

That afternoon there was a *thé-dansant* at the Grand Hotel. We thought it would be amusing to go. Vernon danced smoothly like an American boy, and I danced jerkily as French girls did then. So we stopped soon, he saying: 'Let's stop. I do so want to talk to you.' We went out into a lounge full of palms and wicker chairs. And by the time our tea was brought, we were talking, there was an excitement in both of us. That feeling came whenever we were together in the first years. Different feelings came later, and different excitements; but not that one.

Not that first astonishment of the heart and senses.

That first meeting — 1 remember so many details of it, in that stale hotel. How when our tea was brought and set on the wicker table with its pink glass top Vernon was asking me which part of Paris I lived in, and I told him the Rue de Rivoli. There were five buns, no longer young, on the plate. I took one. He said that he and Annabelle had been in Paris in the Easter vacation the year before, with their mother. He said: 'Was it your aunt we went to see — the Baronne de Montal?' And that was the first time I saw one of his 'double' expressions. This one was great politeness veiling an amused curiosity. I said, yes. And that I lived with her, but no doubt I had been away in Italy with my father.

Just then Annabelle and Hugo Fenchurch joined is. She said: 'Oh, you're having tea here?' What Annabelle says is often self-evident, but she gives the sentence to you like a present, prettily tied up with a ribbon of your favourite colour. Meanwhile Hugo had heard the name 'de Montal', and said to me that his father had had the pleasure of meeting the Baron de Montal when he was once in New York. I said my aunt had divorced de Montal while they were in New York. While I turned to talk to Hugo I was aware of Vernon, without looking at him, as one feels the sun.

While Hugo was talking to me I made a wrong estimate of him; for that evening I said to Annabelle that he was 'cold and worldly'. A very youthful sort of judgement! Now I look back on my friendship with him. It is not accurate to call it friendship. But there are many relationships between love and friendship which have no official description.

After we had tea, we went back to dance. I with Hugo this time. While we were dancing he asked if I knew Otto Behrens, who, he thought, was a friend of my Aunt de Montal. I said I did not remember meeting him: that I rarely met any men at Tante Julie's. Then he said: 'My father admired your aunt very much when he met her.' Then he went on talking.

I listened but also was watching Annabelle and her brother dancing. Together, they looked obviously American, their jaw line so well defined from below the lobes of their ears, their foreheads having a special candour, and their nostrils cut upward. Vernon had a fine-shaped head, and Annabelle a pretty one; and I wondered if that indicated the kind of difference in their dispositions. But 'fine' is misleading, perhaps, about Vernon's character: because it seems to indicate a kind of nobility of outlook. He never had that. His father and mother have it! But it is not in him. He has not what Hugo calls their 'moral attitood'. In that he is not American, in the best sense. On the other hand what is very American in him is his great eagerness of heart. (Incidentally he is unBostonian, in that he lacks all sense of the past; and all interest in history except as a basis of the present. Vernon's real interest in history begins with Bismarck whereas Hugo is bored by everything that has happened since the death of Byron.)

November 25th

That evening at school while I was talking to Annabelle in our dormitory she put on her nightdress and sprayed Coty's Lilas Blanc behind her ears and under her chin. She always scented herself before getting into bed, 'to get into practice for a husband,' she said. Her nightdresses were of white cotton then, but very fine and trimmed with real Valenciennes. And all her appointments were luxurious: her brushes of tortoise-shell, and her face towels and sheets that she brought to school had monograms on them, and each of her padded blue satin dress hangers had a scented sachet on it. I remember that even then her dressing-gown was white, and her slippers quilted satin, white, lined with pink: while I had a *pensionnaire*'s dressing-gown of thick ugly deep blue wool and black felt slippers, all chosen by Tante Julie at the *Printemps*. Also Annabelle always had flowers on her dressing-table, in a Venetian glass Vernon had bought for her when their parents took them to Murano. Beside it were photographs of her mother and father. They both had that well-nourished but noble air that one finds often in Royalty, and in the type of rich family that is always fulfilling obligations. When I met Mrs Strudwick later, I was impressed by her unquestioning self-respect; and saw how Tante Julie had come to describe her as *dévote* — a mistake in fact, but not in spirit; for Mrs Strudwick would certainly have gone to early Mass every day as a matter of course and given money to the Church, if she had been a Roman Catholic.

(I have never discovered what Mrs Strudwick thought of Tante Julie, because her way of disapproving is to minimize the existence of things or people she disapproves of. I only know that later, when I stayed in Boston, she told Annabelle that I did not resemble my aunt. Incidentally, I suppose it was Mrs Strudwick's power of blinding herself to what did not please her that, during that first visit of mine, made her altogether ignorant of Vernon's being in love with me. Mr Strudwick *père* saw it; though he never could comprehend why Vernon could prefer me to Leonora or rather to what Leonora represented. For Leonora was handsome and always very practical and good at sport, and her family were 'prominent' in Philadelphia.)

Mr Strudwick's photograph, on Annabelle's dressing-table, had a small 'snap' stuck in the frame of him on a polo pony when he was younger, and resembled Vernon exactly in features, though never in expression.

Annabelle asked me, that evening, how I had liked Vernon, I remember that while I answered that he was 'very *gentil*' (she and I, and later Vernon, often spoke an 'Englefranc' of our own), Annabelle took up a pair of scissors and snipped herself a thick fringe. But I did not realize she was doing this, although I was watching her in the glass. For my mind was still seeing Vernon. Then, suddenly, I observed the fringe, and how she was suddenly like a young man of the Renaissance. She said: 'Vernon thought you *gentile* too, Blanche, *chérie*. He said you were half-way between a Lemur and a Stephanotis. He's a funny *garçon*, Vernon … Did you think Hugo was a *gentil garçon*?'

I asked her if she liked Hugo, and if she would like to marry him. Because she always thought about each young man as if she would like to marry him. She said: '*Heavens*, no!' That he wasn't her type.

She was always saying this and that boy wasn't her type, and talking as if she would only marry the most superb of men: and then she married that green-eyed delicate ragamuffin, Pierre Morel! She got into bed, Lilas Blanc wafting, and soft brown chunks of her hair lying on the floor, and took a tube of cuticle cream and started rubbing it in, intently; and it was then she said:

'He said you were bittersweet.'

'Who said it?'

'Vernon.'

I was pleased, in my heart: though I thought it was a little banal, as a description.

December 2nd

(A letter from Vernon to-day. Leonora has sailed for France, it seems.)

What is peasant in Tante Julie has always caused her to rise early in the mornings; what is *demi-mondaine* explains that in those early hours between six o'clock and eleven, when she takes her bath, she wears always the same pink or white satin negligée, trimmed with lace and garnished with ribands, which, without being dirty, is never absolutely clean.

Looking back I see her in one of those negligées, beneath it a transparent nightdress that used to embarrass me in my childhood by its unconcerned revelations; but the cotton handkerchief around her 'head of Semiramis' is crisp, neatly knotted, and secured by one of her many diamond brooches. She used to go through the series of little *salons*, dusting in the wake of Balthasar, frequently addressing him in a thick, rumbling morning tone, her underlip square with ill-humour, her slippers thudding on the parquet; and in the kitchen, as she supervised the filtering coffee on the stove, she would snap orders at the obstinate Pauline, and pry into her cherished copper pans to see if any needed retinning, the perfumes which emanated from her luxuriously-tended body mingling with the aroma of the coffee; and indeed for me, the essence of Tante Julie is always that mingling of the delicious bitterness of coffee with a warmth of Molinard's mimosa 'friction'. Also I see her emerald and diamond rings on the sink board, and her white square hands peeling onions under the cold tap!

She was alternately taciturn and quarrelsome, before eleven. But after her bath (a ritual which began with those intimacies of cleanliness unknown to most Englishwomen, and progressed to all the refinements of fragrance, of *maquillage*, of coiffure) she was entirely gracious, contentment simmering in her, her eyes, her mouth, her nostrils intimating 'that serene avidity of all sensations — even of a Baba-au-Rhum' (my father's comment). And, at midday — corseted now beneath a dress of, always a little excessive, chic, her hair marvellously arranged and copper-shining, but still her *pantoufles* on silk-stockinged feet — we would lunch. And our luncheon however simple, would last an hour — often more, while Tante Julie drank cup after cup of sweet black coffee, and sipped her liqueur glass of *anis*. (When I ate seedcake for tea at Pegwell House, my senses recalled Tante Julie's lingering over our luncheon in the little *salle à manger* with its red brocaded panels whose windows overlooked the Rue de Rivoli, and the Tuileries opposite.)

Tante Julie, at these lunches, would talk: some of it the gossip of a concierge — about the people living in the apartments above and below; also about fashions and furniture, anecdotes about her buying of them, and about food and her servants, and about men. Her anecdotes about men were usually tempered to what she liked to consider my 'innocence of a young girl': this she treated as a wilful child her doll, cosseting it one moment, banging it about the next. There was one phrase which ocurred as the finale to many anecdotes. '*Mais enfin, il était très bien, très correcte.*' (*Correcte* I came to learn meant that he had treated her well financially.) There was one, '*ce bon Robert,*' who had given her the ruby earrings that she wore always on Sundays to go to the Mass. I think she must have been with Robert in Brazil after she left de Montal — before Rourke.

Balthasar never permitted us to remain at table later than two o'clock. Then he would come in, in his clean white jacket put on always at midday, with eau de Cologne on his wrists, set the gold box of toothpicks before Tante Julie and say that Madame la Baronne must take her *sieste*. And Tante Julie would rise and go slowly, picking her teeth as she went, to her bedroom, where for half an hour precisely, she sat upright on the chaise-longue. For the real *sieste* was not in the grain of her character, any more than in old Pauline's, who during the same time was also sitting upright on her kitchen chair, her white hair sleek as sewing silk, her white overall, as always, without a crease, reading *Le Petit Parisien*. Only Balthasar slept, crouched forward on the kitchen table with his head buried in his arms.

✕

My aunt liked Vernon when he first came to see me, principally because he was one of *'les Strudwicks'*. She remembered him from the visit he made to her, with his mother and sister, the spring before. She said that he resembled his father, but that he seemed to have more *tempérament*.

She invited Vernon to dinner, and we had bacon-and-eggs and champagne (Tante Julie's whim at this time). Afterwards we went to see *Ruy Blas* at the *Comédie-Française*, because Tante Julie considered it suitable for a young girl. She slept several times during the performance, a gap between her lips, and her ear-rings flashing light from the stage.

Vernon said to me that *'Madame, il fait grand vent et j'ai tué cent loups'* was just what a love letter ought to be. (In fact his letters to me have been equally precise. He dislikes letters; he said that they are like a mouth talking without eyes. He has never used the word 'love' in writing. And rarely spoken it. I asked him once — two years ago — at the Gare Saint-Lazare, at the boat train, to say it. The noise of the crowd, the porters, were round us, he had my hands in his. 'Say "I love you".' But he only repeated my name in a whisper.

But as to that evening with Tante Julie. Vernon wanted to take us on to supper in a restaurant or café. But Tante Julie would not hear of it for me, so we went back to the *appartement* and she sent Balthasar out to Prunier's and he brought back oysters and slices of *foie gras*, and made us Turkish coffee.

(Pauline was away — doubtless for the First Communion of one of her innumerable little nieces at Lille.)

While Balthasar was serving us he joined in the conversation with that air of profound respect subtly flavoured with arrogance. For, even in those days, Balthasar, half Frenchman and half Oriental, combined his reverence for all forms of prosperity, and his own valuable genius for service, with a pride at being chosen by the Spirits to receive and distribute their special news.

While he was occupying himself with the coffee, pouring it into those little green cups in gold stands that Tante Julie claimed had belonged to Napoleon III he looked often at Vernon. I thought that he must be admiring him. Balthasar's dark glance begins closely attentive as a child's, and then slides off its object as if suddenly indifferent. The day after that supper he said to me: 'That Monsieur Strodouique is not for you, Mademoiselle Blanche.' I did not reply, and could not imagine how Balthasar knew that Vernon Strudwick inhabited my imagination.

A few days later he said to me: 'They have told me that you are following a wrong path, Mademoiselle Blanche.' Whenever Balthasar said 'They' he meant the Spirits who communicated with him. He said that when he was dusting the chandelier in the *Salon Japonais* (the smallest of the three salons) 'They' had knocked in the corner behind the silk screen, and so he had seized pencil and paper at once, and written their message. I asked him to bring it to me. On a torn-off sheet of yellowish shelf paper was 'Tell Mademoiselle Blanche Lancret,' in that pointed non-individual writing which is Balthasar's; then a series of pencil marks, as two-year-old children make them; then 'avoid Monsieur Strodouique.' Then he handed me the paper. 'Mademoiselle, you had better keep it.' I was secretly angry with him; but I took the paper so as to terminate the matter. As I left him he said: 'Mademoiselle is angry. But They are always right.' (Later They were to consider Hugo Fenchurch *l'homme qu'il faut pour Mademoiselle Blanche,* and to spell his name 'Ugo Fangeorge'.)

On a Sunday soon after this Vernon telephoned and asked if he might come to tea.

When he came he was not the person I had expected. Since then this has often happened. (Hugo calls it the 'Railway

Station Deception': the version of your beloved that you go to meet and that never arrives.) When Vernon came for tea he talked about Socialism; a subject so little sympathetic to my aunt that perhaps I caught her antagonism. He wore a grey flannel suit, square at the shoulders; and was doctrinaire and impersonal. In making a catalogue of Fortresses of Non-Thinking, he instanced such girls' schools as Pegwell House and turned to me and asked if I was going back there. I said: 'Yes, for one more term.' He said that he was sorry to say Annabelle was also. Then we had an argument: but during the argument our emotions began to approach like two dancers gradually possessed by the same hardly audible but insistent rhythm. And when Tante Julie left us to go out, to Mass, he had become the person I had expected him to be an hour before; that is to say partly the boy whose grace and humour I admired, but above all an influence which made me feel alive.

He questioned me for more details about my life. And I told him that I lived partly with my father on the Brenta, and partly with my aunt in Paris. He said it sounded such a lovely existence, but he supposed there was a 'not belonging' side to it, that must be a little sad. This was precisely its sadness, so that I felt, at once, towards him that intense gratitude one has for being really understood.

Vernon has always used his eagerness and his sensitiveness to understand people. Often, when I have criticized or mistrusted, he has comprehended, and liked.

December 6th

Annabelle and I left Pegwell House the same summer term. (It must have been the year after Vernon and Hugo Fenchurch came on their visit from Oxford.)

I suppose that I have always had a 'delayed reaction' to

events that are happening to me. (Many people do so; and this is often an explanation of what seems to be courage in danger, or indifference in sorrow.) I can feel now the sadness of leaving my English school, which affected me only at the last moment when I was in the hall, waiting for the taxi which was to take me, with Annabelle, to the station. When Miss Churston (the Headmistress) came out of her sitting-room to say good-bye to me, I could hardly reply to her; because suddenly she was part of that atmosphere of easy justice and unthinking security which was characteristic of the school. (It was she who demanded in the girls those shy but charming 'good manners'; and who told us to put glycerine on our hands at night, and never to employ the words 'serviette' or 'mantelpiece', but to say 'napkin' or 'chimneypiece'.)

I see again the façade of the school with its latticed windows and chintz curtains. And I feel again the desolation which was in my chest, like a cold hollow, as we waited on the railway platform. Beside me Annabelle was crying and attempting to read *Vogue*. In the train we went into the restaurant car and she ordered tea. This calmed her, although her eyelids remained red. But to me the yellow squares of buttered toast and the tawny tea became identified with all the beloved Englishness that I was leaving; and, although I drank the tea, I could not eat the toast.

It was towards the end of this journey (to London, where Mademoiselle Dubois was to meet me) that Annabelle invited me to come to stay with her family in Boston. She said I ought to try to come for the Yale-Harvard Game, in the autumn. She said: 'We'd all be *ravis* to have you, Blanche'; and she mentioned that Vernon would also want me to come; saying this with a sort of affectionate teasing. (He was leaving Oxford this year, and was returning with her to America, though his career had not yet been decided upon.)

When we reached Victoria, Mademoiselle Dubois was on

the platform. She wore her checked green-black cape, but by her grey cotton gloves and blue (artificial) rosebuds on the front of her hat-brim she acknowledged that it was summer. She greeted me with her customary, a little timid, affection. She had stayed the night before at the Grosvenor Hotel. She always did so when she had to come to London because it was in the station, and she was afraid of losing herself if she went further, in the London fog, which she suspected to be there at all seasons.

I introduced her to Annabelle.

After Annabelle had driven off to the Burlington Hotel where her father was staying, I must have said something to Mademoiselle Dubois about her. For I recollect that it was while we were going in the back entrance of the Grosvenor Hotel (to have our lunch there) that she said 'Yes, yes, it is an extraordinary beauty,' in a hurried subdued way, as if the mention of something so definite as Annabelle's loveliness were, on her part, even a little indiscreet.

December 10th

Vernon said: 'I know bittersweet is banal. But there isn't a better adjective for explaining you, Blanche.' This was in Boston, the first time when he said this. We were walking along the Esplanade beside the Charles River, in a wind that froze our faces. 'It's what makes you exciting,' he said.

'Isn't Leonora exciting?' I asked, more to seem flirtatious than because I was really thinking about Leonora Peck, a girl who was staying in the Strudwicks' house party for the Game, and who was evidently attracted by Vernon. He said: 'She's pretty,' but not thinking about her either, I thought. Then we looked at each other, our eyes swimming in the wind, his eyelids reddened; and he told me that I looked 'frozen up'. Perhaps that is why he only said then that we had 'best be going back' ... instead of what was in his thoughts.

So we went back to his car that he had left on Embankment Road and drove back to his parents' house.

The staircase rises from the black and white marble floor of the hall, and is of oak, and has an old, fine balustrade of twisted ironwork. Leonora was leaning on the balustrade talking to Mr Strudwick (Vernon's father), who had just come in and was sitting on a carved oak chest, taking off his rubbers. She was wearing a yellow polo-necked sweater.

December 11th

Next day we went to the Yale-Harvard Game. Many young people came to the Strudwicks' house beforehand, for an early lunch. But I only recollect that one of them was called 'Tad' and that he was very tall and had that frank, 'college-boy' charm; and that Leonora flirted with him in the American-girl fashion; that is to say she gave him orders in a loud voice, and looked into his eyes, her lips parted in a wide smile, whenever he approached her. After lunch Vernon drove us in his roadster out to the Stadium: Leonora got in beside him, and I was with Tad at the back. I had already a prejudice against Leonora that whole weekend; but I don't think it was because of Vernon. In the car I watched her profile, turned toward him while he drove. She wore a white wool turban which made her black hair and olive skin look remarkable. She always had vitality; and that day she seemed electrified by the intense bright cold; and she was talking and laughing, while my lips were so stiff I could hardly pronounce words.

Outside the Stadium there seemed to be all the cars in America abandoned on the rough ground: as if their owners had arrived at Eternity and would not need them any more. All the people streaming into the Stadium bought red or blue flags and buttons. Mr Strudwick had been at Harvard, so we bought red flags and buttons, except Annabelle, who was engaged, for the moment, to a boy at Yale (whose name she also has probably forgotten by now).

When we were in our places I found myself between Mr Strudwick and, I think, Tad. I was extremely interested and astonished by the sight of those forty thousand people, all the women in fur coats, and many of the men also in square-shouldered yellow fur coats and wearing immense gloves like paws. I did not notice that Vernon had changed his place until I found him beside me (that is to say I felt suddenly a sensation of intense warmth mixed with a beautiful nervousness); and I realized that my heart was beating faster, and only then I turned and looked at him, and discovered that he was looking at me. And then he said: 'Please put on my gloves.' And I did. They were nutria fur gloves, and they were warm inside from his hands.

I said: 'But you will be cold,' and he replied that he wanted to be. And we both felt that there was meaning in his reply, although I don't think we knew precisely what it was. And outside our secret, sweet emotion, there was the loud, blurred noise around us, and the great arena below, and the white bitterness of the air.

Mrs Strudwick began to talk to me, in her excellent French that made few concessions to accent. And then the first wave of cheering possessed the crowd, because the Game was beginning ...

Never had I imagined a spectacle of such magnificent savagery. The players, their heads belittled by close-fitting bonnets, their torsos enlarged with padding, had the air of gorillas in red or blue fancy dress. And, like the most disciplined gorillas, they played a game in which slyness and brutality seemed to have equal importance: crouching in heaps, or dispersing to run — still crouching but with formidable speed, clutching at each other with long arms, then seizing a ball resembling a large nut and running with it ... while, on each side of the arena, the Cheer Leaders (a sort of chorus of Nijinskys and Massines in white trousers) danced and leaped and pirouetted in the air, their frantic arms inciting the spectators to roar with them either '*Hah!* — *Vahd!*' or "Yale! *Yale!* — YALE!' while from time to time there burst out from either side of the Stadium the lunatic music of two brass bands playing the two tunes in conflict. From time to time one of the players was carried or hobbled from the arena, and another picturesque gorilla took his place. (At one moment I said to Vernon that this would not be possible in Europe. To which he replied that he supposed we preferred the 'gentler arts of war'.)

In the Interval the two bands played, but then in succession. And I remember that the Yale team trotted back into the arena accompanied by a bull-dog; and everyone around us had got out hip-pocket flasks and was drinking out of them (there was Prohibition at that time). Vernon had a flask and offered to give me some whisky. I was amused; and told him I had never tasted whisky in my life. I was surprised to see that Annabelle and Leonora were sipping it out of flasks of their own; and that Mrs Strudwick, although she did not drink herself, did not forbid this, but seemed entirely occupied by the Game.

In the second half of the Game snow fell and dusk began with it, and the bands played louder, and the little 'Massines' danced more madly, and exhorted us through megaphones as they leaped and pirouetted among the snowflakes; and the cheering waxed, wave upon wave, and the snow fell thicker, and as the sky grew darker torches were lit in the arena, flaring above those crouching and speeding creatures in the Game, and bronzing the rank upon rank of spectators who kept up an incessant and hoarse, mad roaring of 'Harrvahd! . . . *Harr–vahd!!!* . . . Yale! . . . *Yale!* . . . YALE!!!' And then, in the final moments of victory (which was for Yale!), the front ranks of the crowd gathered and broke into the arena, the teams seemed to disappear, and apoplectic *pères de familles* and shrieking businessmen seized torches, or began to wrench up the goalposts, stamping and roaring as they did so; while beside me, Mrs Strudwick, shaking snow off her sable coat, said placidly: 'Well, that's too bad about Harvard and now, Vernon dear, let's try to get to the car before it gets wrecked like last year.'

December 14th

(Annabelle has telephoned to say Pierre had a weekend leave in Paris, and saw Leonora there.)

That evening there was a dinner party for about thirty young people at the Strudwicks' house.

I wore a white picture dress that Tante Julie had given me in the summer, from Lanvin. It was so much prettier and more inspired than the dresses of the American girls that I was consoled for feeling so quiet in comparison with them all. Leonora had an ice-blue dress, very *tailleur*, that made her hair look black and her teeth still whiter. She was next to Vernon at dinner, opposite me, across the long big table, with all its flowers and silver and linen. On the silver was the Strudwicks' crest with the motto below, *Altiora Semper*. There were many young people there with names that I had begun to recognize as Bostonian. The only older people there were the Strudwick parents, who were at dinner but did not come with us to the dance given afterward at a Country Club outside Boston somewhere.

When all the girls were waiting in the big hall to leave for the dance, after dinner, I felt detached and therefore a little shy. Perhaps I was depressed by watching Leonora with Vernon at dinner. But I am not sure. For at this moment, although I had a very special feeling about Vernon, I had analyzed it to myself as admiration and interest. Anyway, the girls talked so loud, and all knew each other; and they were all so sure of themselves. And they all had wonderful fur coats, and 'overshoes'. Then Annabelle came downstairs, and came to me with a pair of her own 'overshoes' and made me put them over my silver slippers, saying: 'Blanche isn't prepared for our savage climate.' Then she put her arm through mine, and kept it there while she manoeuvred me easily into a conversation. And she was so warm, physically and mentally, beside me that I felt easier, and more gay.

Then the big front doors were banged open from outside, and all the boys came in with snow on their shoulders, having fetched their cars. Vernon came direct to me and said: 'Blanche, I haven't seen you all evening, you and Annabelle are coming with me.' His dark eyes sparkled with pleasure and eagerness. Only the three of us went in his car. I sat between him and Annabelle, the hood of his roadster making a sort of coupé. As we drove into the countryside, the headlights blazed on the road ahead with its high snowdrifts on either side and its hinterland of fir trees weighed down with snow. Vernon talked all the time he was driving, with a special warmth and excitement in his voice, and said some things that were really witty. And from time to time he broke off in talking to ask me: 'Are you all right, Blanche?'

We arrived finally at what seemed to be a big low-built house of white wood with a charming portico. Inside the dance had begun. The rooms had all wooden panelling. There were many small rooms, all thick-carpeted and extremely 'heated'; and the dancing was going on in a long double hall with a band playing at the far end.

When I came down from the cloakroom Vernon was at the bottom of the stairs. He didn't say anything but 'Come and dance.' We had danced badly together at that hotel at Margate. But now our steps seemed to understand one another. While we were dancing I began to feel a sort of wonder in my senses; I felt how intensely I enjoyed dancing with him, and what an enchanting occasion this was; and he asked me why I was laughing. I said: 'I don't know, I suppose I am happy!' He didn't answer. But I had a sudden sensation that his feeling, so close to me but locked up, was quite different from mine; and this startled, and troubled me, but not altogether unpleasantly. And we went on dancing. But when he spoke to me again he said 'You look sad now.' But I said 'No, I am not sad.' And yet I was, in a strange and delicious way that I had never experienced.

But when we stopped dancing and stood apart, he wasn't looking at me, but towards the band, clapping for the music to continue; and after a moment I became myself again. And we went into one of the smaller rooms where the buffet was and found Annabelle there, with Tad, and Leonora Peck and her partner.

But it was either then, or a little later during the evening, that Leonora, ignoring me altogether, addressed herself to Vernon and made a sort of 'false' scene, because he had not cut in on her yet. She was smiling with the greatest assurance as she spoke; and yet I could feel a purpose below her manner; though I thought this 'purpose' was only a technical and characteristic one, to keep Vernon attracted. In any case she took him away, to dance with her. And I suppose I danced with a series of other young men. I remember noticing Vernon several times, while he danced with Leonora, and cut in on other girls, and thinking that he always looked so much 'alive' and so much 'himself'.

Then, later, he cut in on me and we began dancing again. And this time he began to talk while we were dancing, in a low voice, and in this manner that seemed to me strange because it was intimate, and yet he avoided meeting my look.

He began by talking about my dress, and how it looked 'different'. He said: 'Wherever you are "Paris" is written up.' He continued on this 'Paris' theme. He said I was a sort of 'miniature *ville lumière*.' He said that whenever he looked at me I looked 'so different'. He said, too: 'Blanche is "your" name. It was invented for you.'

But I wasn't happy, as in our first dance. I couldn't understand if he was flirting with me, out of high spirits, or if he was just 'in a mood' (I knew already that he wasn't always *equilibré*). Anyway the idea that he was flirting with me hurt me. Although I should have been amused and pleased, with anyone else.

But as soon as we stopped dancing we went into one of the small rooms. It was empty. He left me and came back carrying two glasses and a bottle of White Rock: and he got out his flask. I said I only wanted water, and he tried to make me consent to have whisky, but I said that I didn't like the smell of it. I think it was at this moment that I realized that he must have been drinking all the evening. I realized. And was startled. And then I was shocked. And because I was shocked I was angry. But my anger came slowly; and it probably did not show in my manner.

If I had been an American girl, I should not have been surprised or shocked. I should without doubt have been at least a little intoxicated myself at this period of the evening (especially after the Game in the afternoon). But although I had seen much wine drunk, and seen people talkative and gay after a dinner, or observed Tante Julie become more confidential after her second or third cognac after lunch, I was astonished that young people of the milieu I was now in, and, above all, a boy of Vernon's breeding and personal distinction, could be really drunk in my presence. (If he had been in the company of other students, or with women of another kind, I should have considered it quite natural.)

In any case, while I was realizing this, and while I was becoming, slowly, angry, he continued to talk to me. And some of the things he said were lovely, and would have moved me deeply if I hadn't also been observing, now, his eyes, and voice, and the slight quavering of his gestures. (I was most angry from a sensation of betrayal, which proves how far already I had unconsciously 'idealized' him.) He said: 'I wish I were more — apt, with words, Blanche —' And he said 'Blanche, my dear,' in a tone that almost did move me. I remained silent. But he didn't notice the pauses between his own sentences. He looked at me. My expression can have given him no idea what I was thinking, and feeling. He began an exposition of how he had thought of me often, since we first met. He recalled the evening in Paris, at *Ruy Blas* with Tante Julie. He quoted, I think it was a Sonnet of Shakespeare, in such a manner, with such a mixture of diffidence and intensity, that again I would have been moved — if I had not been obsessed by the idea that he was drunk, and that therefore everything he said must be without meaning …

Then he said my name … 'Blanche?' And I stepped back from him; although he was standing quite still. And when I did this, it was as if I had hit him. And almost in the second in which I moved back he … I don't know how to describe it — but his face changed. His expression changed.

Perhaps the meaning of my movement sobered him. Or he wasn't as drunk as I imagined; only excited and more easily expressive. Anyway he turned and went out, leaving me in the little room. I remained, still trembling with a sensation that seemed to be fury. Then I went back to the crowd, and I found the good-natured Tad and told him that I didn't feel well and would he drive me back. I had an idea in my head of packing and leaving as soon as I got back to the house.

But, in fact, I didn't do this. I left on Monday, as it had

been arranged. (I was to visit New York with Annabelle before sailing.)

But Vernon was not there during Sunday. I didn't see him before I went. Mrs Strudwick told me that he had left a message for me saying good-bye and that he was 'so sorry' not to see me. It appeared that he left early Sunday morning to drive Leonora Peck down to her home in Philadelphia; and wouldn't be back in Boston until after I had sailed.

December 17th

The day that I returned from America I found Tante Julie sitting in her black, astrakhan coat at the deal table in the sewing-room, telling her own fortune by cards. She leaned back to receive my embrace, and patted me on the shoulder. But her smile was vague; and I had the impression, probably from the more golden colour of her hair (which she wore at this epoch no longer in wings above her brow, but shingled with a fringe of thick curls in front) and also from the fact that she was evidently in full confession to Pauline (who was ironing), that Tante Julie was once more in love.

The expression of Pauline, however, told me nothing. Her features (which seem always to be ingrained with flour, and have the same whiteness as her hair and her overall and her cotton stockings) did not even disclose more than a flicker of pleasure at my return. Indeed, all that she asked me was: 'Mademoiselle has lunched well?' But if Pauline said nothing to me, it was clear she had said something to my aunt. Something discouraging or critical — for a cup lay smashed beside Pauline, below the ironing-board, while the saucer and spoon were on the table next to Tante Julie's gloves and bag.

Meanwhile my aunt said to me that she was trying her new system. 'One sets out first the card of one's own colour ... the

Queen of Diamonds ... All those on the left represent what is already past; those at the head of the Queen of Diamonds what will happen immediately ...'

I sat down in a chair opposite her. I had a feeling of consolation, from the smell of ironing, and from the sight of old Pauline, and from the sound of Balthasar humming *'Parlez-moi d'amour'* in the dining-room, while he was laying the table. And I was, somehow, relieved of some of my inward unhappiness by observing the hair of Tante Julie gilded for conquest again; and hearing, outside the shutters, the sharp bleat of taxis down in the street; and by seeing the exquisitely applied patch on the elbow of Pauline's overall — which little patch seemed to me 'France', as definitely as the rain at Cherbourg had been French rain, falling from that north French sky equally well disposed, in its variable beauty, towards peasant and painter ...

I suppose Pauline went into the kitchen next door to prepare dinner. For we were alone when Tante Julie gathered the cards together, and remembered that I had come back from America; became suddenly welcoming and tender, asking me questions about the crossing and if I had had a good cabin, and then about the Strudwicks, and if Madame Strudwick was still so handsome? But she asked me no questions about Vernon; although I had prepared myself for the pain of her doing so, and I had decided to say that he was engaged to a Society girl.

Then Tante Julie told me that she had amused herself well, lately. And asked me how I thought she was looking? I told her that I found her *'en toute beauté'*; which was true: for the look of her green eyes was softer, and less inquisitive than when I had gone away. And her skin looked warmer; she had never painted it much (in contrast to her eyelids, which were always greased dark brown, like the backs of beetles), but now it had a glow which suffused and obliterated the lines at the corners of her mouth, as if she were lit by footlights. And when she laughed, it was a sort of gay, abrupt purring.

(She is a woman who does not laugh from amusement, but from physical causes; and she smiles less often than she laughs; and when she smiles it is either deliberate, to please, or in response to flattery. Or it is that altogether different smile, which is evoked in her by babies or any very young, or very small creatures, that gives her face an expression of desirous tenderness. I have seen her, with this expression, holding in her arms one of those chinchilla rabbits she had at Nice, which she sold at an excessive profit.)

The next evening Otto Behrens came to dine.

I was in the Salon Rose, writing to Annabelle. I remember I had written the sentence '*Ma tante* has a new beau. She says he is "un gentleman",' when Balthasar announced: 'Signor Behrens.' (Balthasar always believed, or pretended to believe, that Otto was Italian. Either he didn't think Otto's German-sounding name was creditable to my aunt or else he thought Signor sounded less commonplace than Monsieur! Once at a cocktail that Tante Julie gave, Balthasar announced him as 'Count Behrens.')

At all events Otto Behrens was extremely cosmopolitan. It was a quality I perceived in his first entry. It was impossible to say whether he looked distinguished in an English or a French or an Austrian way. With him entered an atmosphere which was partly of Russian *eau-de-Cologne*, partly of the first nineteen hundreds at their most chic, most Edward VII!

In that first moment, when he advanced towards me holding out his hand, I observed how his, then grey brown, moustache embellished his aquiline features, browned by fashionable suns. And in the same moment I was charmed by his brown bird-lidded eyes which shone clear with his natural goodness of heart, For unlike many worldly people he loves his world. And he is only a snob with the permission of his affections. He said to me once, of a friend of his: 'I can't say that I am not delighted she is *duchesse*; but if she were not a charming *duchesse*, I would not frequent her.'

We began to talk, and I wondered that he should have become the special 'friend' of Tante Julie. For I knew, by now, that my aunt, though never actually *demi-mondaine*, did not take part in any reputable social life; and did not desire to. I did not understand then her greatest distinction, which is that she lives according to her own values; and of all the artificial values respects only money and fashion. (My father, explaining this negatively, said: 'Semiramis is never snob and almost never hypocrite.')

While Otto Behrens talked, I asked myself, too, why a man of such a fine taste should be attracted by my aunt; who seemed made much more for a type of mountebank like de Montal, or an unclassable businessman with charm, as Rourke must have been. I could not realize then how much the Collector in Otto Behrens, and his taste for 'period', made him choose Tante Julie, at first. A phrase of his own, which he employed years after when he was discussing her, explains this. 'She is so *fin de siècle*.'

In fact she was born in 1874, and her best years have been in this century. Indeed, one may say she was at this time, when Otto first knew her (in 1925), only perfectly matured. For she is of the species of woman that has most flavour, most 'body', in her forties; and who still, in her early fifties, has rich qualities that warm the senses ... I can imagine that chuckle that she has, sonorous and coquette, accompanied by a sudden laziness of those bistred eyelids and a melting and darkening of glance ...

While we were talking Otto Behrens asked me about my visit to Boston of which my aunt had told him. He said: 'She has a great affection for you.' Also he said: 'You have the same eyebrows.' He asked if my mother had resembled her.

I told him that Tante Julie was the step-sister of my mother, and about our family, and about Grand-père Valéry, who had married first a *bretonne* — the mother of Tante Julie — and then my own grandmother. I think he must have asked me questions about us all. Relationships always interested him. Later, when we knew each other very well, he told me that he had been amused to find me — as Tante Julie had boasted to him — *'tellement une Young Lady.'*

During dinner there must have been more talk about our family, for Tante Julie sent Balthasar to fetch the little photograph of my mother which is always on her night table in its embossed silver frame. Otto Behrens said that she looked more gentle and more fragile than me, but that there was a great resemblance. And Tante Julie said that I had a smile exactly like my mother's, more at one corner of my mouth. Then she said, as always when we spoke of my mother: *'Ah, cette pauvre Jeannette,'* and her eyes filled with tears and she took Otto's hand and made him bring his chair next to hers, and her affectionate regrets for my mother mingled with sensuality in her. Then I could see, though his response retained a cool and stylized gallantry (because of my presence), how much she pleased and satisfied him; and yet, at the same time, a certain curve of the lower lip and a glimmer of amusement between his eyelashes betrayed the amiable irony of the man of the world toward his own caprice. Tante Julie was wearing a silver dress, and her brass-gold head and jewelled throat and her bosom decorated with purple cattleyas came out of her dress as out of a cornucopia. Otto, in his grey suit, looked as if he were visiting her incognito. As they drank their cognac, his manner became more and more gay, and her profile, turned toward him, more amorous. I think she forgot my presence. But he didn't; and there was skill in the fashion in which he conversed with each of us in a different manner. Probably it was his mind that suggested to me that I was too tired to go out with them for supper. Tante Julie put on a silver-fox cape and a little hat of *violette-de-Parme* tulle which matched her dress. She said good night to me, saying: 'Sleep well, child,' and kissing me on both cheeks while she kept Otto's gloved hand drawn through her arm. He said, as he went, that he would come one day to escort me, if I would permit him, to visit his collection of porcelain.

They went out taking with them an atmosphere of ripe expert enjoyment. The ripeness, the savour, coming, perhaps, from her: the expertness from him. The atmosphere of Boston seemed very far away.

Tante Julie did not return until the next evening, when we had one of our informal suppers together, she in her old rose-flannel dressing-gown. Pauline made us a little grilled sole with steamed potatoes and my aunt drank whisky *a l'eau* and was vague in her manner, asking me questions and not listening to my answers. After supper she went to her room and made me sit with her while Pauline put her hair in *bigoudis*. She told me they had been to the Boeuf the night before, and that it was very chic there. She hummed bits of music and made little grimaces at herself in the mirror. 'What an air I have! ... Look at the double-chin I am getting ... And my eyes ... my eyes are terrible! Aren't they, Pauline?'

Pauline, angular as a chicken bone, blanched as an almond, who had been intent only on the rolling up and bending over of the *bigoudis*, whose only sound had been the whisper of her sleeves against the body of her starched white overall, answered: 'Madame needs sleep — that is all.'

December 20th

A letter from Tante Julie. The strokes of her handwriting are like purple blades of grass, and three words fill a line. 'I drive out every afternoon in a carriage that I have hired, which is

now in the fashion, since there is no longer petrol … Otto
came yesterday … the poor boy is in a very bad state; this war
devours his entrails.'

I can see them, down there in the sunshine of the Midi
which is not blacked-out!

When she drives out she carries her parasol of beige silk.
(Memorial to my Grand-mère Valéry which makes her feel
très correcte, très élégante …) And Otto … *'le pauvre garçon'*
(Otto with his pearl-grey waistcoat, his carnation, his
walnut-coloured features between his pale Homburg hat and
his pearl-coloured walrus moustaches); does he drive beside
her along the Promenade des Anglais, staring from under his
melancholy eagle's eyelids at his loved horizon of dark azure
… feeling himself, as old people do when war comes, suddenly
very old, and defeated? I should like to write to him. But
what shall I say? 'Otto dear, how is the little Bavarian Cérès
on the terrace? Is she still so pretty?'

December 21st

I remained in France for more than a year after that return
from Boston. During that time I had an ordinary life of a
young girl. I went to lectures on Art, and Literature, at the
Museums, and at the University. I enjoyed little gaieties with
friends, and in the summer I went to visit my father, and
one summer to some friends who had a house in Switzerland
on the lake, near Lausanne. They were musicians, and had
many artistic friends, one of them the playwright, Georges
Charnaux. Altogether the people I knew were chiefly 'artistic',
and a few families who had been friends of my parents when
my father was still at the Sorbonne. Tante Julie allowed me
to meet those of her friends who were, more or less, *comme il
faut*. On the other hand, she was aware that her reputation
prevented my being accepted in a certain world which she

would have liked me to be in. I know she would have liked me to marry into *la Diplomatie*. She often said so. Once she proposed to my father that he should return to Paris, and engage a distinguished lady who would live with me and conduct me into the World. She had unreal and rose-coloured notions of respectable Society into which she, herself, had no desire to enter.

During this period I only heard about Vernon in occasional letters from Annabelle. She said he had gone out West for a time, and then come back and gone into the family shipping business. (Have I said that the Strudwicks owned the Green Star Line?) Then I had a letter from her telling me that she was planning to spend at least a year studying in Europe. A few months later she wrote that she and her mother were coming over, and that she was going to take an apartment in London. And she said that Vernon might be in London, later, also; because there was a question of transferring him from the New York offices, where he then was, to the London offices.

I was pleased about Annabelle's coming. About the coming of Vernon I felt, more or less, annoyance. There remained in my mind a vague anger with him about that episode at the dance at the Country Club; and also shame that I had permitted this episode, at the time, to cause me so much emotion. Therefore I expected my meeting again with Vernon to be embarrassing, or nervous, and yet to have a hidden sensation of pleasure.

But when we did meet — at my aunt's (for the Strudwicks came 'through Paris' to London) — Vernon appeared full of frank pleasure at seeing me again, And I behaved in the same way. It was a duet of frankness and unemotional friendliness. A dull duet. A stupid duet.

(And yet when he had left, with his sister and mother, I asked myself if it had been, not a duet, but a duel?)

December 22nd

When Annabelle was a girl she never supposed she could fail in anything she decided to do; and whatever she did seemed to her absolutely (never relatively) successful. All the same she was never conceited or selfish; and during all the years women have flattered her, and men have admired and tried to make love to her, she has responded with equanimity, and sometimes with impatience, but never with vanity!

After she left our English school she went to Vassar College, in America. And it was after this that she studied Seventeenth-Century Art in Europe. She took three years to do so. And at the end of the time she wrote a thesis, for her college in America, I believe. And after that time she believed that she knew everything about Seventeenth-Century Art in Europe. (Until she married, when she ceased to desire to be 'intellectual'.)

While she was studying in London collecting material in churches and museums, she took an apartment in the Adelphi Terrace (since torn down). It was not luxuriously furnished; its chief charm being the view of the Thames, and admirably panelled walls of the eighteenth century. Therefore Annabelle stored most of the furniture and bought her own. And when I stayed with her there, she had created an atmosphere of luxury combined with learning. There was an abundance of books; and we ate off beautiful English porcelain she had bought. There she first had the four-poster bed, hung with white brocade, which Mrs Strudwick disliked; saying of it: 'How nice it would look if it was single, my dear!'

Mrs Strudwick had been staying with Annabelle just before I went there, and then proceeded to Greece and Egypt in her brother-in-law's yacht. I was surprised that she could leave her daughter to live unchaperoned; for I, then twenty-one, a year older than Annabelle, had only obtained the permission of Tante Julie to go and stay in London by saying that Mrs Strudwick would be there. And I did not dare to tell her that while I was staying Vernon used to come, and often slept on the big Charles II settee in the library. In fact, he had his own flat too, in Kensington, and used to go every day to the Green Star Offices in the Haymarket.

While Annabelle was living in Adelphi Terrace, Hugo Fenchurch went there frequently. And it was he who brought Pierre Morel. Pierre, *parisien*, was then studying painting in London. He said always that he went to the Slade School. Hugo brought him to one of Annabelle's little dinners.

At those little dinners of Annabelle's we were all very gay, and at the same time so nervous and enchanted by our hidden feelings.

For we were all in love.

All, except Hugo perhaps. Or rather, Hugo was, but in a way that I understand now, but didn't then. For he was in love in the fashion of a poet in the act of writing a sonnet, not as a man desiring a woman. And I think that while he was with us, with Annabelle with the green-eyed, shabby, moody little Pierre, with Vernon … and myself, his fancy was probably seduced by each of us in turn; and the poet in him (who has never written) felt the beauty of Annabelle, the pathos and sensuality of Pierre, the eagerness and subtlety of Vernon, and — in myself, what?

December 30th. Still 1939.

Annabelle has been here. I thought I should be alone for Christmas because Annabelle had decided to leave the nurse and baby here, as the final quarantine (of the Czech servant she had there in Sussex) was not yet over. But at midday on Christmas Eve there arrived in a Ford van Annabelle and all the children, and a Christmas Tree, already decorated

and swathed in a sheet, and immense boxes of food, and
bundles of holly and chains of coloured paper; and within a
few hours the house is decorated, and full of noise. Bridget's
gramophone is playing all the time; the children are running
in and out of all the rooms; Annabelle herself, looking thin
and pale (she is so sad without Pierre, quite apart from her
anxiety for him) but somehow gay all the same, is running
upstairs to adore and embrace Camilla Blanche still another
time, whirling into the kitchen to plan once again with
Bridget the festive dinner of the next day — hurrying again
into the drawing-room (until her arrival so orderly in my
bachelor quiet!) to continue her arrangement of all the little
piles of parcels tied up with different-coloured ribbons, and
placed in different corners … It was 'too horrible' — at home
without Pierre, she said. Also they could not have had me
and the baby with them.

Before we went to bed it was midnight. She was just putting
the last of the little red and pink and blue candles on the tree
when I said that it was already Christmas Day. She stopped,
with a blue candle in her hand, and said with an expression
of sadness that made her obvious remark extraordinarily
moving: 'Just think of its being Christmas, in such a world.'
And then she added: 'Think of all the heartbroken people
there must be in Germany, too.'

New Year's Day, 1940

To-day a cable from Vernon. Hardly shorter than his letter
for Christmas.

I do not know at what moment Vernon and I told each other
we were in love. Neither he nor I can ever remember: because
what we felt was that sort of miracle that happens before
one's eyes, and yet one does not see it until it is complete; like
the making of frost flowers on a window-pane.

I don't think we even spoke of any feelings until after, long after, our love had explained itself by that most classic, most simple of all the gestures of passion, a kiss (that gesture whose beauty survives, always, its million debased interpretations).

It was 1928. We were in my father's house in Italy, in the big room that has those pale half-vanished frescoes. My father must have gone out, probably to Venice, for we were alone, and we had come indoors because it was raining. It must have been late September or early October, for there was on my father's littered writing table a bowl of those late-blooming small yellow roses whose smell is sweet like a taste. Big logs lay smouldering across the ashes, and Vernon went and stood close to them, under the stone canopy of the fireplace. I see him now, standing there, with one hand raised back over his shoulder to the edge of the stone canopy, as if he were upholding it, the other held down towards the flames. He is in profile. I am on the broad stool by the writing table. One can see the rain on the windows and smell the little yellow roses; and this subdued gossiping of the raindrops, and the perfume that is like a sweet taste, are mixed together in the room.

He doesn't move. His arms, his inclined head whose features are pale-bronzed, his long thigh and bent knee, do not move. I can hear the footsteps of one of the servants, felt soles crossing a marble floor in another room. And still the rain on the fragile panes of the big windows ...

And then, without turning his profile, he does what I have known for a long minute before he was going to do ... he holds out his hand. And then he says 'Please come'; as if he were afraid, himself, to come to me. And I went. And then he took me in his arms, and we kissed each other.

Whatever I were to write of this would be inexpressive, and mediocre.

All that I can explain is that, for me, in those long seconds, the rain on the window-panes became imprecise, and the room, and the silent house, became very far off outside my closed eyelids.

January 2nd, 1940

Before this afternoon we had, each of us, experienced various feelings about the other. But from then we began to feel for each other the greatest warmth and emotion and tenderness; and to confess this, myself more often with words, and Vernon by caresses that were most sweet when they were unexpected, Sometimes he was silent and quiet beside me for a long time; and then took my face between his hands and looked into my eyes.

Whenever we were together, at this time, we were in a great light. We saw each other with a wonderful clearness; and everyone else, that is to say my father, the servants, the occasional visitors, were indistinct, as if out of focus. We used to go in the gondola on the Brenta Canal or walk along the white dusty roads of the country between the festooning, tall vines. Or we remained in the house or in the garden; talking or reading. If my father was very much with us, I don't remember it. I think probably he left us alone, understanding his rôle as a shadow.

I don't think either of us slept well. The sustained sensation of beauty that I had was like a spiritual breathlessness. I was in an altitude in which it was impossible to take a deep calm breath. From time to time this exalted condition made me gay as I had never been before. And Vernon, too, had moods of the most fantastic, the most delicious gaiety, and we were sometimes altogether foolish together, laughing about nothing at all, like children in perfect health. One day, when we were shopping in Venice, we were in such a mood, and we strolled about arm in arm, and I remember how in a certain glove shop in the Merceria our folly pleased the merchant, and he looked from one to the other and laughed too; comprehending, no doubt (as a good Italian), the profound cause of our gaiety.

But also we were grave; moved, beyond any expression, by the fact of each other's existence.

I don't know if Vernon stayed a few weeks or many. I know that during this time we realized that he would have to go back to Boston, before we could get married, so as to explain to his family, and make practical arrangements. (I imagine my father's consent was already understood; but I was to tell Tante Julie when I got back to Paris.)

I suppose he must have stayed several weeks for the weather was cold the day he went. I was to drive Vernon (in Father's old Lancia) to Mestre. Then we decided I would drive him even as far as Milan.

In Milan we spent the time that was left in the Brera, instead of in the station. We wandered round arm in arm, linked more closely as the minutes passed. We looked at the pictures without attention. But I remember that the beauty of the rose and gold in one of the Veroneses seemed horribly sad.

When we were by the Booking office I said: 'Now I understand about *partir c'est mourir* being true.' He said: 'Banal?!' ironically. But then he told me to go, and not to come on to the platform.

After this I had his letter from Paris, where he had seen Tante Julie. He wrote that she seemed rather *souffrante* and he added in a postscript: 'Why did she try and make me think you were in love with Hugo? Just out of temper, or does she want you to be?' Evidently he hadn't told her we were engaged, and I should have to do that. This letter was very long, as if he felt he was with me while he was writing. But its only phrase of love was at the end, when he wrote: 'How frighteningly happy you make me.'

But almost immediately after this I got a telegram from Otto Behrens telling me that my aunt was ill, and asking me to come at once to Paris.

I left at once. During the journey I was thinking about Tante Julie, but I couldn't help thinking also that I should be able to see Vernon again before he sailed.

When I arrived Otto was at the *appartement* and told me that Tante Julie had had peritonitis; and that she had been operated on the night before, and was still very ill. I saw from his manner how dangerously ill she was. We sat in the Japanese Salon together, and he told me he was going back to the hospital at twelve o'clock. (It was still early. I had travelled by night.) When Pauline came in, her white overall looked crumpled, and I saw that she had been crying. She brought me some coffee and stood beside me while I drank it. She said how Madame had suffered; and that she would not call a doctor at first; but they had telephoned to Monsieur — she indicated Otto ... And Madame had kept on taking aspirin and *cognac-a-l'eau*, and only at last when the terrible pain was too strong she had permitted the doctor to come ... And Balthasar had gone out, to church, to pray for Madame.

I said I would accompany Otto to the hospital. He tried to dissuade me but I insisted, because I was possessed by an anxiety to be near Tante Julie. I had the idea that if only I could be near her, I could somehow protect her from her great danger.

Just as we were going out of the door of the *appartement* I turned back to ask Pauline to telephone for me, and leave a message for Vernon at his hotel (the Hôtel de Bourgogne) saying that I was back in Paris, as Tante Julie was ill. Pauline said, ah, yes, Monsieur Strudwick had been to visit Madame only the day before she was ill. But that he had told her (Pauline) that he was leaving for America. I told her: 'His boat is not sailing until to-morrow. So be sure to telephone to him.' As I said this Balthasar came in. He said that he would telephone for me. He was still in his overcoat and the black felt hat with the straight brim that he always wore in the street. He said to Pauline and me: 'I have been to church to pray for Madame.' And then Otto, who was already in the lift, asked me to come at once.

We went downstairs and got into Otto's car. While we were being driven to the hospital, Otto said; 'If she dies, I shall have no more desire to live.' Even in my own condition and shock and fear I was surprised by these words. I knew he had great warmth of heart. But I had not supposed him capable of any sort of extravagant emotion, because the snob part of his character made him seem shallow.

When we arrived at the hospital a nurse came to the waiting-room where we were and told us that we could not go in to see Madame la Baronne. But that during the afternoon it might be arranged that we should go in for a few minutes, although Madame la Baronne would be drugged, and would not know us.

So we waited; and Otto insisted on taking me out to lunch near the hospital. There was a *brasserie* almost opposite. I don't remember if we talked or not; only that while we were sitting there a woman came in who was selling violets and that Otto gave her a fifty-franc note and took a bunch for me. The woman stared and repeated: 'Monsieur is very kind,' and offered to give us a second bunch. But he didn't hear her, and she must have noticed the pain in his expression, for she went away, muttering automatic blessings.

Later in the afternoon we saw Tante Julie. She was in a small room and there was a screen, its wood frame filled with blue and white check material, which was between her bed and a high window. Everything else in the room was white and in transparent shadow because the blind was drawn half down. There was a nurse beside her. I had expected her to look terribly ill; but not to seem to be someone else. Her hair was plaited back tightly from her forehead, which I had never seen; and her cheeks, usually pale, had red marks on the cheek-bones, and her eyes were nearly shut but showed in dark slits, and she seemed to have no eyelashes, as she had no mascara on them. She was unconscious, but breathing very fast. I was seized by a feeling of terror. But I don't think it was Tante Julie's death that I was afraid of, at that moment; it was illness itself, its ugliness, and above all its power, which terrified me. Tante Julie lay there, in its power. The absolute whiteness of the room, the silent nurse, the heavy smell of anaesthetic, the 'things' on the metal and glass tray, dressings and so forth (which I only half looked at), all this was part of illness ... I saw that pain had been conquered; but that illness was a different enemy from pain; more hidden but more real.

The nurse indicated to us to go. She came outside with us into the corridor. She said in a low voice that she would telephone in the evening. To a question of Otto's, made in a low voice, she answered that she could not tell yet. The smell of anaesthetics was all along the corridors, and it mixed with the wet perfume of the violets in my coat.

I could not stop crying all the way back in the car. I was crying from fatigue and intense anxiety; and from shock too, because I hadn't realized before how the most simple certainties (such as Tante Julie's gold-dyed hair and magnificent bosom and husky gossiping) are perpetually menaced.

When we got in Pauline took me to my room. She had lit a wood fire and she helped to undress me beside it, and then she brought a foot bath and made me sit with my feet in it. It was then that I heard the telephone and sent Pauline to find out who it was; I could hear Balthasar's voice answering. I thought that it must be some dreadful message from the hospital: or it might be Vernon. But I thought it was the first.

Pauline came back and said that it was only the manicurist of Madame. Then I asked if Monsieur Strudwick had telephoned. Pauline went to ask Balthasar, who now came himself to tell me that he, Balthasar, had telephoned to the Hôtel de Bourgogne, and had left a message, as Monsieur Strudwick was out.

After this Pauline insisted on my getting into bed; and she gave me a tisane and aspirin. And I suppose I slept.

Otto must have been staying in the flat for I was waked by him in his dressing gown. He was telling me that there was better news of Tante Julie. He said: 'There is hope.' I saw it was morning, because now Balthasar came in, in his black alpaca jacket, and asked me where he should serve the coffee for Monsieur. He said to me: 'Better news. "They" told me that Madame la Baronne will recover.' By this time I was altogether awake; and relieved for the moment of the worst anxiety. I wanted to know if Vernon had not telephoned again last night after I was asleep? Balthasar said that he hadn't. Then he added, as he was going out, that Monsieur Fenchurch had called yesterday while I was at the hospital. But I hardly realized what he was saying, because I was looking at the clock beside my bed, and saw that it was after eight o'clock. I went to telephone myself. I suppose because I was altogether in a nervous state, as I waited for the reply, my heart beat quickly and there was an intense although indefinite fear in my thoughts. When the concierge of the hotel answered he said that Monsieur Strudwick had already departed for Le Havre by car. He added that Monsieur had intended to go by the boat train later this morning, and had changed his plans at the last moment.

I was astonished, and agitated beyond reason. I could not imagine why Vernon, who must have desired to see me, should have left Paris after he had heard I was here. (I knew he must have had, before he went, the message Balthasar left with the concierge of the hotel saying that I was in Paris.) I went back to my bedroom, and then I wrote a message to be radiographed to the boat, saying 'Why didn't you come?' and informing him that Tante Julie was a little better, I gave the telegram to Balthasar to send for me.

In the next twenty-four hours I received no radiogram in answer.

I heard nothing from Vernon until I received that letter written from his home in Boston.

I haven't got the letter now. I destroyed it after I had read it. I burned it in that log fire that Pauline lit for me, every day, in my bedroom because all this time she considered that I had '*l'air bien souffrante.*'

The letter was only one page. It didn't look characteristic. The writing was unusually cramped. He wrote that the fact that I had refused to see him confirmed the two other facts that he had learned about my coming to Paris. He said that during the voyage he had realized that it was 'providential' that he had discovered 'all this so soon'. He added that he could only suppose I had been afraid to see him, because I was intending to write to him, and explain. But there was no need to write because any letter that arrived with my handwriting on the envelope he would tear up right away.

The same day that I received this letter Pauline said to me, did I want my carnations in the *salon* kept any longer? I asked: 'Which carnations?' (I had really noticed nothing visible quite distinctly since Vernon went.) She said: 'Those white ones that were sent with the yellow roses to Mademoiselle the night when Madame was so ill.' I said I knew nothing about them. Pauline looked so surprised at this and said: 'But Balthasar took them in, and, since it was late and Mademoiselle was already asleep, he unpacked them and arranged them. He should have informed Mademoiselle.' Pauline looked, as she always did, pained by any failure, in Balthasar, to fulfil his duty. She asked if Balthasar had not given me any note or card from the box.

I went at once and found Balthasar. He was cleaning the silver. I asked him why he had not told me about the flowers. He pretended not to remember. And he was full of apologies, blaming himself in a monologue that lasted while he searched for a card that had come with them in his pockets, in the drawers and cupboard in the pantry, and then among his receipts which he always kept safety-pinned together on the window sill above the sink. Then he said: 'Mademoiselle, I regret … I must have lost it.' And then he added with an air of reassuring, almost paternal affection that, in any case, there was no doubt they were from Monsieur Strudwick. He repeated this. I left him, polishing silver candlesticks, his movements expressing great devotion to his duties.

I knew that the flowers must have been from Vernon.

But why had he sent me flowers, and then that letter?

I think that people often change the course of their lives by their least characteristic gestures.

Vernon is not jealous, and it is absolutely the contrary of his nature to believe that anyone is behaving badly.

But because Tante Julie, when he visited her on his way through Paris, hinted that Hugo was in love with me, and because then Balthasar told him that I would not see him, and in the same telephone conversation informed him — untruly — that Hugo had made me a visit that same afternoon, Vernon went back to America convinced (he has told me since) that for me, it had been only 'the usual romantic episode in Italy'; and that once returned to the North of Europe I had realized this.

He says that he can't remember anything about the voyage back. That probably he was drunk most of the time.

When he arrived in New York Leonora was on the dock. She had learned from Annabelle that he was coming. And he never received either my radiograms to the boat or my cables to Boston. And the two cables which he sent to me, one from New York, one from Boston, both of them saying that he was coming back to France to me, immediately, never reached me. He says he wrote one of them on the dock itself, and Leonora gave it to a Western Union boy to send. And that when he got home to Boston, and had still no message from me, he talked over the matter with Leonora, and she advised him to cable again. He says he remembers distinctly, in the middle of all that nightmare, how he sat down at the writing table in the library, and took up the receiver and telephoned the cable company. And that Leonora went out of the room as soon as he began to dictate the message.

✳

For some time I believed that Tante Julie had deliberately caused Vernon to suppose that I was in love with Hugo.

But now that I have a perspective of ten years, I can see that Tante Julie's influence on what happened was more than she meant it to be. What she said to Vernon about Hugo was only an expression of her hidden, but not specially obstinate, wish that I should marry the son of 'un Lord' (namely, Hugo). And I am sure that Vernon, as a rich young American, seemed to her an excellent second choice. If Balthasar had not mixed himself up in the question, her casual words would have had no more effect than to make Vernon feel more sure of me — knowing that I preferred him to Hugo.

What remains to explain is the point of view of Balthasar. I couldn't explain it to myself; nor for a long time afterwards. But now I see three motives which, in fact, explain it easily enough. First Balthasar has, in his character, a liking for power in itself. He and Pauline, herself a precise and tranquil tyrant, have always had a combat of wills — in matters even as who should give the tip for the delivery of wine;

and beneath his deft and sometimes almost servile manner he has always attempted to become a kind of impresario to Tante Julie, influencing her whenever possible, and without seeming to do so, in small matters, such as her choice of glass and table linen for some special dinner, and also in her acceptance of visitors and invitations. 'Madame X has telephoned and desires that Madame la Baronne will lunch with her to-morrow, but I have said that I will ask Madame la Baronne, but that I think she is not very well and is not going out very much at present!' The telephone is one of the weapons which he uses most frequently to exert his power, delaying the delivering of messages or slightly altering their emphasis while leaving their words the same. I have no doubt it was not the first time he had enjoyed, for the pure pleasure of strategy, influencing a love affair; only the others had been those of Tante Julie. And his second motive had without doubt, although unconsciously, a sexual explanation. He felt himself in charge of me, as of Tante Julie. He liked discriminating between one lover and another, and had a certain sadistic interest in the cheating of desire. (I can see him, telephoning, obsequious yet authoritative, in his white afternoon jacket and pin-striped trousers; telephoning to Vernon ...)

And for the third motive? It derives from the typical *valet de chambre* in him; for the lackey, which he is, much more than he himself imagines; for, like many servants who have been for a long time with a family, he sees himself as 'a character'. He is snob. (Who should be a snob, if not the chic sort of servant, who lives by the cult of appearances?) Thus for him, much more definitely than for Tante Julie, it seemed desirable I should become the wife of an English milord. I remember once his remarking to me that one had told him that the father of 'Monsieur Fangeorge' had a beautiful chateau near Surrey. I don't know if it was 'They' who told him. I think not. He had, though I didn't know it then, other, and more embodied familiars.

Perhaps the analysis of those motives makes Balthasar seem a sinister personality, which he was not. The worst one can say is that self-interest made him a little unscrupulous.

It is possible even that this self-interest, quite simple in itself, was his whole motive. And that all he intended was to assure himself, in case Tante Julie should die, of a good situation in the chateau of a milord near Surrey.

In fact it would be absurd to make a villain of Balthasar. For by the time Vernon reached New York he had decided to return to me by the next boat. To his temperament a voyage to New York and back was no more than quitting a room in a sudden violent mood, and returning a few minutes later. He did not return because Leonora influenced him to hesitate.

Part 2

Otto took Tante Julie, after her illness, to her beloved Nice. And it was while they were there that he bought her the property of 'Les Délices'. Once possessed of it, she decided not to retain the *appartement* in Paris. And for several weeks (I was with her then at Les Délices) she could not decide whether to sublet it at the biggest possible profit, or, having removed her own furniture, to permit me to live there. She was quite openly disturbed at the difficulty of such a decision, and the lace-curtained salons and glassed-in loggias of the villa resounded with crescendo cluckings as she argued with herself. For she would exclaim at one time at 'the unheard-of folly' of not making the profit that the house agents, as well as her own notary, had assured her she should make; and her glance would challenge me and Otto. At another time she would call me to her long chair or sofa and take my hand, and draw me down and pat my cheek while she demanded of herself, and sometimes of Otto, whether the principal thing in life for her was not the assured future of *'cette pauvre petite'* … the daughter of Jeannette.' All the more that she (that is, myself) had a father so stripped of all paternal sentiment, so egoist, so miserly … And more remarks about my father's avarice (she could never comprehend that he had little money since he had many books of great value). Then she would recall to her own mind the importance of money, and the obligation one had to make such little profit as one could.

Otto, however, solved the problem of the *appartement*. He bought the lease from her, and presented it to me. When he told Tante Julie this she wept with affection and nodded and smiled with satisfaction; and called the chef and changed the menu for dinner so that it should accord with champagne.

She had her doubts, after, as to the propriety of my living in the *appartement* alone. But she consoled herself with arguments about the independence of the young girl of today, adding one of her favourite sayings: 'Men are no longer the same.' Also I would have *cette brave Pauline* to look after me. And it was still possible that I should marry, she said. And asked me where Hugo Fenchurch was. I said that as far as I knew he was in England.

✳

During this time that I was at Nice with them, my ordinary behaviour coincided automatically with ordinary events. But I could not sleep at night without some sort of bromide or tablets; and I was very thin, so that Tante Julie noticed and used to urge me to eat twice of everything, which was impossible for me, because my intense secret misery caused me a perpetual physical sensation of sickness, above all when I had to eat.

I must have been many weeks at Les Délices with them when Hugo Fenchurch arrived to see us. It seemed that he was staying at the Hôtel Grande Bretagne with some friends. Tante Julie was excessively welcoming to him and invited him to dine the same evening.

She wore rouge for the occasion (as she did sometimes since her illness). And had told me that I must wear a pretty dress. (We had both reverted to our habit of dining in dressing gowns. For Otto was away in England, staying with his sister, who was married to an English Baronet called Sibthorpe, to enjoy an event, mysterious to us both, called 'Newmarket'.)

It was as clear to Hugo as to me that my aunt looked upon him as a *prétendant*. During dinner he made for her the kind of conversation she loves about Society People. He proffered her, with his flattering courtesy, little scandals one after another; and she responded with little scabrous bouquets of her own gathered from her dressmaker, her *coiffeur*, her *manicure*. And so, strophe and antistrophe, they recounted together many details of the economies, the debts, the perversions, of well-known people in well-known places; adding, to embellish still more, little details of humble parentage or physical malformation. And when their power to exaggerate, or minconstrue, failed them, they exchanged sly hesitant smiles, and little silences as filled with malice as an eggshell with egg.

In Tante Julie all this was no more than the concierge twist in her character, with which I was familiar, and which, I knew well, had nothing to do with the real disposition of her heart; this type of curiosity being a sport which she practised now and then. For towards her real friends she has been always generous in conduct and in understanding. To that grey rheumatic Violette once so much *belle fille* and star of operettas; to the milliner Suzette and her husband in that bleak *appartement* in the Rue Mozart; to those men friends, no longer rich or gay or *gentil garçon* (of whom Pauline has spoken to me sometimes), 'Madame la Baronne' has remained loyal and affectionate.

But as to Hugo, if at that time I had the least inclination to love him (because I so much needed warmth, and because I desired also to forget Vernon), this kind of talk that he made with Tante Julie prejudiced me against him. For I observed his expressions, and phrases, at the time; and after remembered them and the strange provincialism (essentially a lack of real self-respect) which his malice revealed in him.

All the same after dinner when Tante Julie left us, he changed entirely, and I found that I was able to speak to him about Vernon going away. He said he had heard that Vernon had married one of the Philadelphia Pecks, and why? He said: 'Vernon's madly in love with you. *What* happened?' I told him the details; and that I didn't understand why Vernon had gone. Then I recollected, as I was speaking, that Balthasar had told me about Monsieur Fenchurch calling while I was at the hospital. So I mentioned this and asked why he hadn't come again. Hugo said that he had never called at all, at that time, and could not have done so, as he was in California, on his way to China, that autumn. Then he got up and walked about the room, looking like an English milord of the nineties, drawn by du Maurier. His blond moustache, his poached dark blue eyes, appeared in each gilt-framed mirror in turn. He asked me if Balthasar disliked Vernon. I was surprised by this question. I said that I thought Balthasar (who always had opinions, and was conceited about them) had some vague prejudice against Vernon, on my behalf. Hugo said that Balthasar, half Oriental, probably liked influencing events 'in a silent-footed way'. Also that there was 'something of the eunuch — that is to say protective and impotent jealousy — in all menservants of his sort who had worked for women of ...' I remember Hugo's hesitation — he kept both his hands in his trousers pockets and hunched his shoulders in the superb dinner jacket he was wearing ... and said finally, 'for women whose fortunes were influenced by the men who frequented them.' Then he became agitated, and angry one minute with me, the next with Vernon. Evidently his emotions were extremely troubled for both of us. When he was going he held me by the shoulders, and kissed me hurriedly on both cheeks, said: 'Blanche, darling, *something* must be done.' We were on the steps outside the front door: he put on a Homburg hat the silhouette of which showed against the stars and the palm trees that were pale gold ghosts in the light from the open doors.

I said nothing could be done. I knew this. I knew also that when Hugo got back to his hotel a new mood would relieve him of this agitated one.

January 10th

(Poor Hugo. His heart has always assumed responsibilities which his nerves rejected. Yesterday he writes to me that he has ten *évacué* children living in his house in Sussex. He offered to have them. He buys them toys. Mostly — he writes to me — he detests their presence. But, in his letter, he describes the Christmas Tree he has trimmed for them himself.)

※

I was twenty-three by this time. And I knew that Tante Julie, like many people, imagined that I had not married Vernon because I considered Hugo Fenchurch a better *parti*. Like most people she attributes motives which she would have herself. Of the immense vulgarity of a choice as between money and a title it would have been impossible to convince her. And if I had attempted to explain what I felt about Vernon, she would only have comprehended that what I felt for Vernon was a physical passion; and she would, I think, have advised me to marry Hugo, and to have Vernon as 'a rich lover'. (The English phrase 'fallen between two stools' might have suited her thoughts about me, at this time.)

January 15th

When once the lease of the *appartement* in the Rue Saint Honoré was mine, I began to change its interior.

I do not think I should have done this if Tante Julie had not moved all her furniture, including even the mauve and gold enamelled door handles. (My strong tendency to accept might have fixed me in my aunt's 'frame'.) And (according to Hugo's theory!) I should have become more and more adjusted in character, and finally in appearance, to *japonaiserie*, red velvet portières, Louis XVI chandeliers, and satin brocade let into the Louis XV panelling of the walls.

But, once the *appartement* was empty, Hugo took charge of the decorations; and one of his young men of taste undertook the work at small expense.

Once I was well established in the *appartement* a life more gay and *mouvementé* and agreeable than I had anticipated developed around me.

I had supposed that I should not be able to dominate my essential unhappiness. But as every day became filled with interests (I took up painting at this time, encouraged by Otto) and the number of my friends increased, I found that I could escape from thinking about Vernon. But I do not mean the pain itself went away. It was only that the life I lived was narcotic.

Perhaps it was a secret, but quite undramatic despair about achieving any happiness of my own which made me become, at this time, more interested in other people, and probably more sympathetic than I had been formerly. And I made many new friends, some of them extremely brilliant and interesting. This caused Otto to tease me about my 'Salon'. And I did indeed establish a 'day' (Wednesday). But only so that people who really were my friends should know they could find me that day. And I always discouraged people I didn't like from coming, however amusing or famous they were. Incidentally Georges Charnaux was impossible to discourage, because he is so thick-skinned. My friends asked me: 'Why do you have Georges Charnaux when you dislike go-getting people?' I was definitely impolite to him often; because it exasperated me to see him slowly presenting his blond 'rat face' round the door as if it were a delightful surprise for me. But he did not notice this: and later, when he married the self-satisfied little Russian dancer Natasha they both adopted the habit of coming to my Wednesdays.

As well as friends there were, of course, men who admired me, or were in love with me. Certain ones imagined themselves more in love, I think, because they found no response in me at all; neither in my senses nor in my vanity. I remember two specially, who really loved me. I see now that I was cruel in showing my indifference; for somehow I did not imagine they would suffer about me as I did about Vernon, One of these, a charming boy, used to come every day at one time and demand I should marry him. (Tante Julie would have been delighted for he was a diplomat and went to Rome soon after.) But to me his love was only a mirror in which I observed that I was charming and desirable. And all the sentiments which I evoked in men at this period were only mirrors in which I looked at myself, perhaps a little reassured, but without any special interest. For I was never a flirt.

During this time Annabelle seldom wrote to me. (I know now that it was because she did not know what to say about Vernon and myself. He had not told her any of the circumstances. She had been in California with her young aunt, Mary Strudwick, when she received, quite simply, a telegram from Vernon, from New York, saying that he and Leonora Peck were married.)

... So when she did write, her letters were friendly, but without personal news. Then one day I answered my telephone and heard her voice, telling me she was in Paris. I felt her hesitation, though, and told her to come at once and see me. She said: 'Guess why I'm in Europe?' And then she told me that she was on her way to England to be married to Pierre Morel, and that her father and mother were already in London.

When she arrived to see me I had the impression that she had grown more interestingly beautiful. (Indeed, in each new phase, it has seemed as if Annabelle's appearance had been painted by a 'greater' artist; and this is because life itself has brought out in her more feeling and more intelligence.) I remember that when she came that afternoon her young lovely face had such sweetness and such warmth. But the joy I felt in seeing her was in contrast with other feelings in me. For she brought the 'realness' of Vernon with her. And her pronunciation of words, and her dark, long-lidded eyes, were his also. She must have felt or observed in my expression what I was feeling, because she said suddenly, holding my hand, 'There's a lot we've got to speak about, Blanche-*chérie*.' But then she began to consult me about her trousseau, and asked me if I would shop with her. She said she was staying at a hotel (she did not mention the Hôtel de Bourgogne, because Vernon always stayed there, but I guessed it was that). So I insisted she should come and stay with me; and it was I who said that we could 'revive Adelphi Terrace'. She said: 'Are you *sure* you want me, Blanche?' She was very moved. And after a day or two, when we came to speak about Vernon, I discovered that she had been, and was still, very distressed about Vernon's marriage; but that she had supposed that I had 'changed my mind', and broken off our engagement, and that he had married as she said 'on the rebound'. When I told her about his letter she was astonished. She said: 'But he must get a divorce, Blanche-*chérie*, right away.'

Then she said that anyone could tell that Vernon wasn't really happy. But I changed the subject of our conversation by making her talk about her approaching marriage; and she said that Pierre was *such a gentil garçon* when you knew him well, and that his having led what her mother called 'a life of dissipation' would make him a good husband because he would enjoy the 'contrast of being good'. (This view amused me at the time. But she has proved to be right.) She also said, for the hundredth time, that it was 'wonderful being in love'. And certainly she looked like an advertisement for happiness. She said that I must come to London for the wedding. On a later visit — or perhaps during one of the shoppings I did with her — she told me that Vernon and Leonora were soon coming to Europe, as he was now to be in the London office of the shipping line again, anyway for a year. And repeated that 'he and Leonora should get a divorce soon.' But in this idea she counted on Vernon being more consistent than he is. And she did not comprehend that Leonora, in her own mind, spells certain emotions and certain ideals with capital letters, and then respects them. One of these emotions is Love: and one of the ideals is 'the Sanctity of Marriage'.

January 25th

To-day I have a letter from Tante Julie. She has a new gas-mask container combined with a handbag. She has been told that the Queen of England has the same kind. There is still no shortage of food: She is 'very content' to read that these *sales Nazis* are already half-starved. Did I hear that the wife of Georges Charnaux was one of those drowned when the *Athenia* was torpedoed in September? What a horror! The poor little woman was on her way to New York, it seems. She adds: 'One cannot doubt that God will avenge himself on Hitler.'

Poor Natasha Charnaux. Even Charnaux must feel his grief spontaneously.

There is also a note from Otto. He thanks me for my letter. He recounts that *mot* of old Pauline about her gas-mask. 'It is very well, Monsieur Behrens, for my head. But what will become of my feet?' (*Que deviendra mes pieds?*) But he ends: 'When this war is done the whole world will be in tears.'

Yesterday, the day after I got Tante Julie's letter, I saw in the *Observer* a paragraph about Georges Charnaux, referring also to Natasha's death; also that Georges is working at the Ministry of Information in Paris.

Georges belongs to the family my father used to call 'les Profiters' ... I have somewhere the sketch he did of Monsieur et Madame Profiter and their children — Monsieur Profiter in a top hat and all the family with very small eyes.

January 26th

A few days after Annabelle's visit I wrote a letter to Vernon, in which I said only that I had heard from Anabelle that he and Leonora were coming to Europe; and that I hoped very much to see them if they came to Paris.

It was a short friendly letter. When I wrote it I didn't feel as if I were writing to the Vernon who had been with me at my father's villa.

In fact that time seemed as far off as my childhood. And as little part of my present life.

His answer surprised me by its quality of definite coldness. He said it was 'unlikely' that he would be in Paris. And he did not mention Leonora.

✕

But it was Leonora who telephoned to me. She said that she and Vernon were staying a few days in the flat (owned by this time by Mrs Strudwick) in the Quai d'Orléans. Her voice was just as definite and full of life; and immediately I imagined her as she had been that night at the dance after the Harvard-Yale Game in her ice-blue dress. She asked me if I would lunch with them. I refused. But I said that I had some friends coming in towards six o'clock ...

Vernon told me after that Leonora had insisted on telephoning to me. That he had not intended to see me. But once she had arranged to come he began to feel he must see me again, although only for a few minutes and in a crowd. (It was three years since we had seen each other.)

I was expecting those friends who had already learned the habit of coming to see me on Wednesdays. Before any of them came I was so nervous that I chose a moment when Pauline was putting the plates of sandwiches and *petits-fours* in the white *salon* to go to the passage outside the kitchen and take a glass of the brandy which she kept always in a cupboard there. This made me feel unreal, but just as nervous. I felt a little more reassured when my friends began to come, because they were part of my real world. But I kept watching the door.

✳

As to Leonora, her features, and her assured manner, her figure with the narrow 'Egyptian- looking' hips, the sustained clear metallic note of her speech, were even more defined than at that weekend of the Yale-Harvard Game. She was like a drawing in which every line is traced to its conclusion. It is perhaps this absence of any doubts and implications in her which makes her remarkable, but prevents her having beauty.

She advanced towards me with a smile which advertised the whiteness of her teeth and the blackness of her eyes: and her frankness towards me had brightness but no warmth. She told me about the motor journey that she and Vernon had just made in the North of France. I thought that this was to make me comprehend their intellectual and artistic companionship (they had been to Bruges, and then visited the Chateaux of the Loire.) But evidently, from that scene that took place four years later between her and Vernon and me in New York, she did not have any hidden intention, and had not the least idea that there had been even a flirtation between Vernon and myself. Also I did not realize at this time that she was incapable of imagining that marriage with her was not, for any man, a sort of absolute good fortune:

and that if anyone had told her that Vernon had been in love with me, she would not have believed this.

While I was talking to her I felt all the time as if I had a slight fever, each thing in my familiar little *salon*, as well as every sound, having a different emphasis than usual: and my own responses to what people said to me seemed right only by chance, and if they had been incorrect I should not have cared, or have felt entirely responsible for them.

I remember that I said to Leonora: 'Would you like to make the acquaintance of Georges Charnaux?' And she, knowledgeable as always, answered: 'Charnaux, the playwright?' with approving enthusiasm. So I beckoned to him (he was doubtless in the middle of a little group telling some witticism) and said: 'Charnaux, my friend, here is Madame Vernon Strudwick who is an American admirer of your plays —' and while he was kissing her hand and beginning his repertoire of glances from his thick-lidded pale-blue eyes, I heard her explaining that she had spent much time in Paris, where she felt nearly as much at home as in America; 'perhaps more so'.

I suppose she must have remained for a long time in conversation with Charnaux for when finally I found myself with Vernon, he began our conversation by saying Leonora and my 'rodent-faced friend' seemed to be getting along beautifully together. And I thought: 'He is in love with her, for he is jealous!' I said: 'You are not very nice about my friend Charnaux. He is the man who wrote *Cauchemar.*' (The piece that was then being played at the Théatre Edouard-VII.)

After this we only spoke for a few moments, asking each other conventional questions, and not looking directly at the other for more than the necessary second in which the question was pronounced.

When he and Leonora were going she said to him that Charnaux had promised to lunch with them, at Le Vert

Galant, the following day. But Vernon announced that he had a business engagement; and I thought perhaps he is not jealous, all the same? Because Vernon is direct; and if he had not wanted his wife to lunch alone with Charnaux he would have given her no opportunity to do so. But I could not be absolutely sure about this.

January 30th

I have been reading what I have written since I began. So far I think I have made better portraits of people I have loved less. Balthasar, with his wits and his emotions amalgamated (so that he cannot distinguish an impulse from a feeling), is defined better than Otto. Leonora, though only sketched, is clearer than Annabelle; and Hugo, that egoist so full of sensibility, detaches himself better from his background than Vernon.

Whatever I have written of Vernon seems true, but like a conventional photograph; not evocative. Have I made it apparent that physically he is restless but graceful? In type like an American crossed with a Spaniard, his bone structure fine, his eyelids sensuous, his look dark and eager. His mouth, sometimes so Bostonian, the upper lip long and reflective, and the under lip kind and determined, is at other times the most Latin of his features: expressing sweetness and sensuality, impulsiveness and, when he begins to smile and his nostrils give a sudden little arching, the most indulgent irony. I don't think I had defined him visually.

Perhaps I have only added up little characteristics, but failed to explain him.

Could anyone, reading this, answer such questions as 'Has Vernon a strong or a weak character?'

I don't think Vernon has a strong character; because he has the weakness to see all sides of a problem. Equally he so tries to comprehend people's conduct that he sometimes fails to condemn it when he should. For instance, our lives would have been different if he had permitted himself to observe Leonora, instead of trying to explain her 'idealistically'.

Is he clever? Not as 'thinkers' are clever. For he is capable of immense intellectual excitement; but not of sustained study. He has a big appetite for learning, but he satisfies it in snacks.

He belongs naturally to the species 'patron,' since he has a passionate and flexible admiration for the intellectual or artistic expressions of others. And he has been brought up with the conscious belief that Learning and Art were his heritage (*Altiora Semper!*).

And perhaps that answers another question: Does he lead a 'good life'? In a purely amateur way, yes …

Yes: but I add 'sometimes'; because it is characteristic of him to distrust theories of living. He is unconscious of how he profits by his parents' theory of living (*Altiora Semper!*). He said to me once: 'The classical, good life wasn't adequate, as a standard. That is why Christianity had to carry an amendment.'

I said: 'Are you getting a 'moral attitood', at last?'

He didn't defend himself. It's possible he didn't hear what I said, for he had one of his expressions of the most courteous inattention, and came and took my hands in his, and looked at me for a long moment with a tenderness for which he made no attempt to find words.

February 2nd

Annabelle had her wedding in London at St Margaret's, Westminster. The Strudwicks had a small reception afterwards at the house of a Strudwick cousin in Hill Street who is an English Countess. Her house was very much like the Strudwicks' house in Boston inside; so that one had the feeling that Annabelle was being married in her own home: especially as the wallpaper in the big bedroom upstairs, where the ladies took off their coats, had a blue sprig on a spotted white ground exactly like the one in the guest room on Beacon Street. Also Mr and Mrs Strudwick seemed to have imported a sort of 'straight-backed' atmosphere which did not prevent the food and champagne being excellent, and the flowers — jasmine and red roses everywhere — maintaining their own atmosphere of perfumed celebration. And the guests seemed to be mixed in the same proportions of Puritanism to luxury, and one saw everywhere sables, pearls, and dresses whose hem and shoulder line failed with the most subtle yet absolute assurance to be chic. And magnificent *couleur de rose* Englishmen in top hats and American old gentlemen long expatriate (with beige cheeks and English homes furnished from Italy).

Suddenly I caught sight of Vernon. And he began to come towards me in the crowd. Or else I thought so; for he was coming in my direction, But then some acquaintance stopped him; or else he chanced to let himself be caught in conversation. And meanwhile whoever it was that I was talking to must have left me, and finding myself alone, and realizing that I was suffering, quite suddenly, from a kind of 'illness' of unhappiness, I decided to go.

On the doorstep I found that Hugo Fenchurch was beside me. He said: 'Let's go to a movie.' He was carrying his umbrella with the Malacca handle. We walked across Belgrave Square, our long distinct shadows — Hugo's with its top hat — moving before us on the warm pavement. While we were walking along Grosvenor Street he asked me if I would come for the weekend to Pryde (which was then his father's house, but is now his). He said there would be 'no one there' except his family. I accepted. The idea of going was a distraction. What I wanted was to be distracted, and to be kept moving.

February 3rd

Pryde is one of those Dutch seventeenth-century houses which still blossom red in the green English country; incidental memorials, as are the coins of the realm, of an — profoundly laic — intolerance of the Roman Catholic Church.

Moreover, nothing is more 'English' than what is called 'William and Mary'. And although it was Pryde that I discovered once on a journey in Holland, it was Pryde with the appearance of having its face washed every day, and without, it seemed to me, that *patine* of poetry with which the English countryside climate overlays its houses.

Surrounding the pomegranate-coloured house were lawns and gardens of a beauty which can only be sustained by that constant tenderness and expenditure which also are something especially English. For in England, for the great as for the simple families, the garden is a heritage; and, I think, often for the clumsily worded English an expression of their real grace and sweetness of spirit.

At Pryde lived the father of Hugo, Lord Coldharbour, and his two aunts, Miss Tanagra Fenchurch, and Mrs Adare, a widow with three dogs.

Mrs Adare, who welcomed me on my arrival, emanated friendliness and unrest. She had the same rather bright and prominent blue eyes as her nephew, Hugo, was thin and wore bright-coloured sports clothes and had her white hair set in a quantity of twisted thick curls and so 'blued' that her head recalled an arrangement of blue hyacinths. It was she who escorted me to my room, talking the whole time very loud; a habit perhaps made necessary by the fact that her spaniels, two brown and one black, were always barking around her feet.

Hugo addressed her as 'Posy,' and seemed to have a profound affection for her. He told me that she had been married to the governor of some island, a 'great bore', and that she had had a virtuous youth and become a little *détraquée* in her late forties, and that she had a house in Morocco and lived at Pryde when she was in England.

In contrast to the cordiality which she displayed to me all that weekend, showing me the garden, inviting me to come for walks with her and the dogs, diverting me with stories about her servants in Morocco, her sister — Hugo's younger aunt, Tanagra — was so reserved as to seem disapproving. She was often in her room, and did not come to lunch or tea. At dinner she appeared, and ate twice of each course, and looked extremely handsome, her grey hair piled elegantly on top of her head, and her Greek features undefeated by time. She had a deep voice, and spoke chiefly about international politics, arguing with Hugo thoughtfully, and with such gravity that at first I did not realize how often her sentences contained charming wit. But she would become silent whenever her brother Coldharbour had one of his outbursts of temper, which happened during my visit certainly once at every meal.

And this brings me to the description of that remarkable man of violence, distinction, and greed. Physically he was big and tall, and still blond at sixty-four, with a moustache curled at the ends, hair brushed up above ears dark pink like the lips of snapdragons, a deep dent in the centre of his chin, and azure long eyes brilliant with self-will and entirely empty of gaiety or humour. He had the same skin as Hugo's, firm and delicate, but rosy where Hugo has (with the help of sunburn oil) achieved a very light brown. And although he and Hugo were of the same type their differences impressed me, on seeing them together. For one thing Lord Coldharbour had stupid-looking hands (though manicured as carefully as his moustache ends were curled). And whereas Hugo has warm good manners, his father's manners, although automatically courtly, were in some way desiccated, and by betraying his fundamental lack of real personal interest gave exactly the impression he most dreaded to give — of old age.

Towards me he was extremely gallant, telling me anecdotes of well-known people he had known or encountered; showing me the gardens, taking me to see the farm and a golden pheasant that lived in a humble wooden hutch in the woods. He told me that he had known and admired my father, and asked about him, but without waiting to hear an answer. As I sat on his right at meals (at a table far too long for our small party) he was politeness itself, flattering me with small attentions and having bottles of special wines opened. But it would be precisely such a matter — the bringing by the butler of the wrong wine, for instance —that would detonate one of his rages, When his ears would darken, he would spring heavily to his feet, shake his fists, knocking over a glass or his own chair, begin to pace to and fro in an invisible cage, alternately roaring like a lion with his head bent down and, at the end of sputtered sentences, lifting his magnificent head and giving gasped hysterical shrieks like a woman, and then turning on his heel to pace the cage again …

After two such outbursts, on which I could not bring myself to comment, Hugo surprised me by remarking quite calmly that the butler they had was 'a fool and made Father furious'.

And afterward I observed that while Lord Coldharbour was in full rage Hugo would continue with some discussion, and Mrs Adare's loud voice went on, and only Miss Tanagra retired into one of those withdrawn silences that seemed to be part of her character.

It was only the last day of my visit — I think on Monday morning — that I found Miss Tanagra alone in the little panelled breakfast room, and we had some conversation; part of it in the room, part in the gardens, which she suggested we should 'go round'.

I cannot remember what we talked about except that, for a short time, it was about the *entente cordiale*. But I know that, while we walked in the fresh morning shade of yew hedges (which in one part of the gardens at Pryde constituted a sort of walled city inhabited by roses), she was gracious and even amicable, eating little ratafias out of an oval silver-plated box, and, this I recollect, telling me the names of each of the roses, and often pausing, bending over some especially lovely bloom, touching it with two caressing fingers as if it were a child's face. While we walked one could hear a drowsy booming of foghorns in the Channel, which is five miles to the south of Pryde.

What pleased me in Miss Tanagra was the distinction of her profile — like a Greek medal and, in contrast to her sister, Mrs Adare, her absolute lack of interest in herself, which evidently caused her to wear the same dark blue dress (or dresses of exact similarity) every day, and to accept (this Hugo told me) whatever jewels and coiffure her maid arranged for her. (Fortunately, the same excellent maid had been with her for years, accompanying her, this Hugo told me also, on her expeditions to Persia and South America in search of plants; and from time to time to the Visitors' Gallery of the House of Commons when there was an important debate upon Foreign Affairs.) At the beginning of my visit I had had the quite wrong impression that she suspected me, with antagonism, of wishing to marry her nephew. During our walk in the gardens I realized that she would regard such an event benignly as an Anglo-French alliance.

As for Hugo, he was so extremely charming during my entire visit, so amusing, so sympathetic, so evidently devoted, and interested and observant of everything about me, that just as one feels on one certain poignant day in April 'at any moment it will be summer', I felt 'at any moment it will become love'.

※

I have written little of my father. In fact I did not see him often during the years I have described so far, that is to say from the time that Vernon married Leonora and I had the *appartement* in Paris until after that weekend that I spent at Pryde, with Hugo's family, It was in answer to a letter I had written from Hyde that I got a telegram from him saying he wanted me to come to Italy and visit him. I was glad of this command, as it offered me another change of scene.

In my letter I had described Hugo's family, and said also that I thought Hugo himself might become a 'charming habit'.

When I arrived at the villa I found my father feeding his white pigeons by the sundial. He was wearing his same straw hat, whose crown is onion-shaped like the dome of Santa Sofia, and whose brim is so wide that at midday my father moves about within a pillar of shadow — and it seemed to me that if he had changed at all, it was only in the way that stone or marble changes, by the gradual bleaching in one place and discolouration in another. Thus his beard was whiter, his white linen trousers more greyish, than when I had left him, and his hand, moving, in that gesture of enchanting antiquity, to scatter seed, seemed of a browner parchment — perhaps in comparison to the gold white of the pigeons that were making their greedy little obeisances about his sandalled feet.

I joined the pigeons, but pecked at his cheek. Then he set down the bowl of maize and embraced me and, still holding my shoulder, read my face, very slowly and with the most careful affection, as he reads one of his old manuscripts ; and I felt that he was deciphering all that I had felt since Vernon went away. But he made no comment except: 'You have become beautiful, Blanche. You used not to be.'

And then we walked arm in arm in the garden, the brim of his hat scratching the right side of my forehead from time to time, and I listened once more to his conversation, his grave voice, with its sad cadences, his witty comments, his little ironic reflections; and poor Mademoiselle Dubois's *'beau soleil d'Italie'* drenched my neck and arms and back and entered my veins, changing my blood into liquid sweeter and richer and more slow; so that by the time we sat down to lunch in the cool among the fugitive blue and rosy and gold pallors of his frescoes I felt as if my spirit as well as my body had been chemically changed; my clothes felt cool against my warm skin and the centre of my emotions which on the journey had felt depression was now filled with gaiety. But it was gaiety; not happiness. For in the evening when we sat in the library by the fire of great logs, the time when Vernon and I had been here together became present in every detail; and, like a negative where one photograph has been taken on another, Vernon in his open shirt and sailcloth slacks would be superimposed upon my father, sitting opposite to me in his dark-blue velvet jacket. Vernon's voice traversed some sentence of my father's, and from the open windows, through which the spring night was clear and the cypresses moonlit, came the whispering of rain on the panes, and the autumn scent of yellow roses.

When we were going up to bed my father called me to look out with him from the oval window that is half-way up one of the corner staircases of the house, And as we looked north toward the Alps he asked me what had happened. And I told him.

Then he said (I remember how dryly he said it, and this dryness helped me, for I was crying) that he thought that what had happened was less surprising than I seemed to think; that I emphasized too much the conduct of Balthasar, whose little machinations — like those of Iago on a bigger stage — could have had no effect if Vernon had not been capable of jealousy. He added that there were so few cases in which love did not contain the instinctive violence of jealousy; and that the first symptom was that the sufferer ceased to reason and could only feel; and, as in cases of madness, often behaved deliberately in ways which endangered his own life.

I remember that while we were still at the window, a mist lying above the surface of the canal that was polished with moonlight, he asked me what Leonora was like: and I answered that she had, like many American women, a traditional admiration for herself and a corresponding will to be worthy of her own admiration.

I think it was later on during my visit that he spoke of Hugo; and said he thought it would be imprudent to marry a man for whom I felt neither desire nor admiration, and seemed to cherish rather as a piece of furniture, 'more rare than beautiful, more elegant than comfortable'. In the same conversation he went on to speak of my mother. He said that it would have broken her heart to imagine that her daughter should not make a 'marriage of love'; for she had, he said 'the most romantic, the most sentimental, the most passionate heart' out of which 'little sentences of delicious tenderness grew like jasmine'. And then he looked at me and said: 'How old are you now, Blanche?' And I said: 'Twenty-seven.' And he said: 'Now she is younger than you …'

And I remember that in fact she had quitted life with an irresponsibility which seemed to accord with the fact that she had been, in that year of hats and ribbons and ostrich feathers: and fat uncertain aeroplanes in the sky, only twenty-three years old.

Sometimes I had wondered why my father, who was only thirty-seven when she died, had not married any other woman after. But I think that my mother had ended by being, in his imagination, the only complete expression of a woman he could love; so that beauty, smartness, and wit in other women seemed, in comparison to my little mother's lack of all these, excessive and therefore uninteresting.

I had, at one time, a schoolgirl's fancy that he would remarry with Tante Julie. And I think now that it is possible that, at one time, there was between them a relationship which comforted him and which she understood. And after, in the years in Italy, there must have been Marias and Rosas and Maddalenas who, like the returning delights of those long summers, reassured his senses. But, profoundly, he cherished, not the memory, but a real existence of my mother. And on this visit to him that I have been describing I discovered on the marble console table in his room a little glass jar with a lid, in which he always kept a supply of fresh crystallized violets, for which she had a special little greed, though he himself disliked the taste.

February 16th

I had let my *appartement* for a time while I went to Italy.

I stayed with my father for three months, and on my return to Paris, as the tenants wished to take it for another fortnight, I went to stay with Annabelle and Pierre in their new house on the further side of the Bois.

When I think of Annabelle and Pierre as they became later, when they had lost or spent most of their money, I am amused to recall those first years of their marriage, enriched by all that was most arrogantly luxurious in Annabelle; by all those 'Princess-Royal' assumptions which characterize the women of rich merchant families. Assumptions — almost noble in their simplicity — about the comfort and beauty and deference and responsibilities to which they are born. And disporting himself among this luxury was Pierre with his grace of thought, his spontaneous disorder, his ribald laughter, his incurable habits of Bohemian poverty, such as cleaning his own shoes and hiding from tradespeople; Pierre, reading a dozen books at once, and then abandoning them about the chairs or sofas; beginning to paint yet another fresco, so that anywhere, on the spacious pale-painted walls, there were the pink ghosts of goddesses with immense behinds, and coral-red trees and phantoms of dancing elephants. At those perfect meals ordered by Annabelle, at the table marvellous with glass and flowers and lace, over which she presided with her gay and undoubting serenity, it was Pierre who rejoiced loudly in some specially exquisite dish, his fish-shaped *eau-de-Nil* eyes twinkling, who would seize a flower from a vase as a buttonhole, who would sing aloud, or argue, or walk around the table and kiss Annabelle on the lips; or, at other times, when they had to dinner people of worldly importance, he would be silent for the entire meal, crumbling his bread, his look abstracted — his thin body and his pointed ears, his fat eyelids, his curled-over under lip, giving him the appearance, as Annabelle said, 'of something off Notre-Dame'. In any case, then as now, whatever his mood was, she found it lovable. And when, on one occasion, he had offended a Personage, and Mrs Strudwick, who was at that luncheon, remonstrated with her daughter, Annabelle only said: 'Yes, Mother. But he hasn't offended *me*.'

Indeed, Annabelle had always that loving and beautiful serenity. I used to think it was only the result of her being young and without anxieties; that it was, in fact, a lovely but slightly unimaginative complacency. But later I saw that it was in her character; and that, indeed, her serenity became more gay when they became poor; as if, in losing her inherited wealth, her whole nature had been relieved of an inherited high 'seriousness' (that nineteenth-century weightiness of thinking, conserved in certain American families, which as a girl Annabelle had applied equally to her choice of a thesis and the cut of a swimming suit).

February 20th

At this time, when I went to stay with them, Annabelle was making plans of an intense seriousness for the furnishing of the nursery. It was early September and the baby was to arrive in November. All that was Struckwick dominated her in this matter, and at least three times during each day we would go into those two big rooms, shuttered from the sun, which contained already some white furniture of severe design and a cot delicious with laces and pink ribbons, to discuss the colour of the walls and curtains; and Annabelle would stand in the centre of the room, like a dark-haired 'Primavera' in one of her flowered peignoirs, saying to me that although pink was gay, blue was 'calming' ... saying that patterns, either of animals or of flowers, although delightful to others, might have the most profound effects upon the psychology of the child ... asking me if I did not think that frills on the curtains were 'unhygienic', and whether the (one) picture that Pierre had put above the chimneypiece — a banal and charming coloured reproduction of a Raphael Madonna — would not unconsciously give the 'child mind' a 'fixative' about mothers being more important than fathers ... and so on. She discussed all this with an expression of intense sweetness, and was not at all disconcerted by my mocking at these theories. She would ring the bell and her maid would bring stacks of patterns of stuffs for the curtains, and she was always drawn to pale curtains with still paler arabesques and stars upon them; but Pierre, when he joined these conferences, Pierre in sandals, in red sailcloth trousers, with a body like Massine and his 'English pipe' in his mouth, would lounge against one of the bare walls, exclaiming that there should be wallpapers with flowers, and curtains with flowers, and good solid mahogany furniture which smelt of wax — and 'lots of pictures, as little artistic as you like but gay and full of stories.' I was of Pierre's opinion. It was he who had bought the cot with ribbons and laces, bringing it back on his sports car from the Maison de Blanc. And in the end it was Pierre's nursery which received the baby — Amaryllis — even to the smell of wax on the furniture. For the most profound influence in Annabelle was Pierre; and what was Boston in her, even then, was more a question of habitual gestures of thought than part of her real character. During this time that I was with Annabelle I don't think she referred at all to Vernon. On the contrary, she invited other men to the house, especially those who she knew were my admirers, such as Raoul de Grignan and Charles Wentworth, who was then the *Times* correspondent in Paris, and was as brilliant as he was physically attractive, and consequently invited everywhere.

February 21st

It was very hot that September while I was at Annabelle's and many people were away in the Midi or on the other coasts. All the same there were enough of our friends in Paris to make possible those evenings when we dined on the loggia, and talked and laughed, the ends of cigarettes becoming red, and each of our voices in the night containing a kind of liquid echo.

Such evenings were so strangely enchanting, and the long hot days in the shuttered house were so unreal, that my normal existence was cut off from me; and, like someone drugged, I desired nothing more than to continue in this half-dream, half-sleep.

Charles Wentworth came to several of those dinners. Then,

one day, he arrived about midday in his car and took me for a drive. I think it was to Fontainebleau.

What I remember distinctly is that there was a thunderstorm while we were having lunch in the courtyard of a little hotel; and our table had to be moved indoors; and that he said to me that he was going to take his holiday in the Adriatic, and asked if I would go with him.

He took my hand while he was asking this. And, as I have said, there was something physically exciting about him, and also, in the same moment, I thought about Vernon with Leonora, and I said, yes, I would go.

He said we would motor to Venice; and then take a boat.

On our drive back he did not even take my hand and this amused and pleased me.

When he left me he said: 'I am leaving on the twentieth. May I come to your *appartement* on that morning and fetch you?' (I had told him I was returning to my *appartement* on the fifteenth.)

In my decision to go with Charles Wentworth there were, I suppose, two principal motives: first, to give Vernon (even though he would never hear about it) a real cause for jealousy. Secondly, to fall in love, if possible, with Charles himself.

I have written my 'decision'. But I know well that it is out of character, since I have always avoided decisions, and rather accepted each new situation as if it were weather (my only decision being in not taking shelter when the weather became emphatic).

I saw approaching that twentieth of September, and my journey with Charles Wentworth. He was attractive, amusing, and we were to go to romantic places. And the double question of scandal and of virginity that my Tante Julie would have urged upon me, or — much more real — my own former point of view (when I could not imagine love except with Vernon), no longer counted. Tante Julie would not know; my own world would only have their purely imaginary idea of my love affairs confirmed by a real one; and, for myself, it might be at worst a distraction, at best the beginning of something real.

When I woke up on the morning of the twentieth, my valises ready packed, on the floor, reminded me that toward eleven o'clock Charles would come to fetch me: and I lay for some time considering this fact without excitement. What I remember principally is a slight feeling of depression, such as one has in facing an unavoidable duty. On getting up I put an extra amount of perfume in my bath, and occupied myself even more than usual with the details of my *maquillage* and dressing; and, at the end, I looked in the glass at the image of a young woman, more or less beautiful, and without doubt elegant. But all these preparations were like the arrangements for a reception that one is going to give, not to one's friends, but to one's acquaintances.

Charles was a little late. While I was waiting I stood at the window and looked into that part of the Tuileries Gardens which belonged as much to my *appartement* as, behind me, that oblong still-life, given me by Hugo, of a dead hare and some peonies and pears, which surmounts the high doorway between the front salon and the dining-room. I stood looking at the trees, whose leaves, while still green, quivered now and then in a breeze that was like a presentiment, and seemed to steep themselves in the sunshine with an intensity of delight that contained despair. I watched the children running or hesitating, and remembered the Sundays when my father and I, having quitted the Guignol performance, would come down that same gravel walk toward this *appartement* to visit Tante Julie. I saw again my father's black felt hat with the curled-up brim which he only wore on Sundays, And I relived, between one moment and another, a whole series of afternoons of my adolescence, when after my day at school I obeyed, more or less sulkily, Tante Julie's order to 'take the air a little', and, crossing over in front of those windows, I would enter the gate and walk, toward the Orangerie one day, towards the Louvre another, my steps nearly always slowed by a sadness that was caused by a mixture of anaemia, boredom with my schoolwork, discontent with my own appearance, and intermittent agitating desires to write poetry and to fall in love.

Perhaps something of that sulking, half-unhappy, half-exasperated schoolgirl relived in me as I waited. Certainly there was that left-handed feeling that belongs especially to adolescence (and which derives from the assumption that there is, without doubt, a right-handed feeling that one should be having).

Then, suddenly, Charles had come into the room behind me; he said my name; and when I turned and saw him, my state of mind and emotions changed. I can envisage him now, exactly — how gay and handsome he appeared, and, withal, a little nervous. I saw for the first time a shadow in his so much admired dark eyes, which was infinitely becoming. I remember he had a tie of a purple-red, and that against the extremely pale turquoise paint of the room his sunburnt features and brown hair seemed to be of the same bronze, and that altogether he was so admirable at the moment that I was suddenly satisfied with the idea that he was to be my lover (as if, having bought a picture in a sale room, having had perhaps doubts, I found that when it came, my impulse could justify itself to my taste).

He took both my hands and kissed them; and mixed with his assurance of technique, I could feel in him a real emotion ... and (no doubt like other women before me) it was that which renewed the interest of my senses. Then he went to my room to fetch my valises. (I had sent Pauline to the country, to her nieces near Lille, the day before, finding myself unable to make such a departure before her eyes, yet sure, in my conscience, that she knew exactly why I had forced a holiday upon her.) And then we went downstairs to his car; the concierge helping him to fit in the cases at the back, and receiving a *pourboire* large enough to make him suppose nothing. When we had turned a corner into the Rue Saint-Honoré Charles gave me a pair of dark sun glasses to put on, and he put on another pair; and I laughed at him for having this double disguise attached, as it seemed, to his car. He smiled too; but said that it would be stupid if we met Annabelle or Pierre. He added that it would 'shock' Annabelle. (This was true; but not the way in which he meant it.) And that Pierre was so gossiping. (Quite true. He said once of himself that making little scandals was his 'knitting'.)

As a consequence of the dark glasses we passed through a Paris that was like an old print whose outlines have remained sharply black while the colours have become yellowed, and the sky green-blue as before a thunderstorm; and I remember the road to Fontainebleau, and the Forest of Fontainebleau itself, had this same appearance. Ordinarily I should not have thought about it, for I nearly always wear such glasses in strong sunshine. But on this occasion I felt a growing obsession to see the real sunlight as if it were in some way a reassurance ... And when finally we reached Sens, and Charles advised that I should keep on my glasses while he went into the hotel to see that there was 'no one of our friends there.' I sat regarding the dark and yellow Cathedral with nervous dislike.

I forget if we lunched there, at Sens. I think so. Anyway, I know that during our lunch Charles succeeded in charming me again — I think deliberately, because he evidently observed that I was in some way nervous or uncertain; but assuming that it was a state of mind natural to a girl in such an 'adventure' (although I am sure that he had not the least idea that he would be my first lover, since I had given in to his proposals with what must have seemed to be *sang-froid*). While we lunched he assured me that this would never be for him 'just an ordinary affair'; although, evidently, it did not occur to him that he might have made me a more honourable proposal. It was necessary for him to marry a girl with a *dot* — he had already told me this himself, with a mixture of chagrin and self-assurance. What I recollect precisely about that lunch is that by the end of it he had known how to make me say, what I had never said until then, that he 'pleased me'. Actually I said the French, '*Tu me plais,*' for we spoke most of the time in French. And the effect of my words was that he leaned back —we were still at table in the corner of a little hotel dining-room that smelt of the stone floor and of spilt red wine — saying, with a sort of astonishment: 'You really are … *delicieuse.*' After lunch we motored again (and we did not wear the sun glasses), and I felt a different person, possessed, above all, by a kind of delicious laziness, sleepy from the liqueurs we had drunk, and the light which seemed to be reflected from the white road and the white clouds; and I felt that my laziness was a slope of an increasing steepness, that had already marvellously deprived me of will, or even of any precise sensations except that of inevitability.

February 27th

The hotel where we arrived in the evening could not have been more agreeable, being a former small chateau built on rising terraces above a river bordered with poplars and willows. When we arrived the evening was calm and still light, so that we agreed to the proprietor's suggestion that we should dine out of doors on a loggia which overlooked the river valley. He — the proprietor — after detailing his menu to us, added that it would be moonlight — giving us to understand that he knew how to arrange everything for lovers; and this amused me, as if I had been watching all this in a play. And it was with this same sensation of being a spectator that I followed him upstairs to see our rooms, with the *salle de bain* between them. He addressed me as 'Madame'; and his perfect comprehension of our situation made him, not less respectful to me, but respectful in a more personal manner, since as a man he also observed me — with connoisseurship, as an Englishman observes an animal.

When he left us alone the room seemed really quite lovely because the walls were white and the windows tall, and it was filled with gold echoes of the sunset and the strong perfume of red roses. In the centre, as in a scene of a farce or a tragedy, was an immense bed, whose cover of a bright purple satin helped me to remain ... what? I was going to say 'amused' or 'detached'.

It seemed that the red roses, in two immense vases, one beside the bed, one on the writing table, had been sent in advance by Charles. And now, for the first time, he came to me without invitation, and took me in his arms, with a practised charm of gesture; and I shut my eyes, expecting him to kiss me; but opened them again because he was asking me something. *'Je te plais toujours?'* (Do I still please you?) I remember in the second that followed his question adding up everything in him — his looks, his charm, his voice, his wit, the shaping of his eyelids, his fragrance — and in the same second making myself feel an intoxication from the strength and the warm sweetness of his embrace. And I answered either by whisper or by expression in some way that reassured him.

At dinner he said little, at first: but then became sentimental, and drank champagne and quoted poetry, much of it verses that I love very much. And as the trees and the valley below us became dark and the sky more decorated, and as those verses of Donne, of Ronsard, of Shakespeare, of Verlaine, flowered in my thoughts, my mood changed too; and for a time I forgot Charles and felt nothing but that emotion that is caused by beauty, and that resembles pain. Then (the remembrance of this becomes so exact now that it is like the present), then I got up, and I heard my own words, as one does out of doors at night, saying that I would go up. And Charles answered that he would follow me. I went in; I remember exactly how the hall of the hotel looked as I passed through it, the tiled floor and the concierge's desk at one end, and grey armchairs disposed in groups and a console table supported by a gilt *sirène* on which was placed a TSF in a cabinet of shining yellowish wood. In my room the curtains had been left open — the whiteness of the bed was in full moonlight (more as in a tragedy than a farce), and the fragrance of the red roses was very strong. I went to the window — perhaps to draw the curtains, or perhaps just automatically, and as I did so the effect of the framed sky was like a final forcing open of a door that my whole mind had been resisting, to keep shut all the evening; and now, in giving way to the nocturnal resemblance between the tops of cypresses and the tops of poplars, I admitted the full force of those weeks when Vernon and I were at my father's villa. And in that hotel room, in which I was, finally, by this adventure that was half deliberate, half hazard, to deny Vernon's existence for me (and by the same gesture to refute the significance of love itself by the facile amusement and intoxication of a 'love affair'), I remained, transfixed, between the window and the moonlit bed, utterly possessed by this remembering of Vernon. Possessed by Vernon. Vernon suddenly real to me. And, like a convert, my mind and spirit were able to forget my conduct and circumstances up to this moment of conversion …

The scenario-morality which would have championed my escape at all cost played no part during the moments in which I now considered what I 'ought' to do. For it was still evident that both honour and a sense of humour demanded that I should become the mistress of Charles Wentworth; the contrary case being simply that — I couldn't.

If we had been in a *garçonnière* in Paris it would have been possible ... and even a little gay and delicious. In a lace-shaded lamplight I shouldn't have remembered Vernon.

But here, the night through the open windows was too beautiful, and Vernon too real.

February 28th

I note briefly, since I still feel its humiliation, the episode that followed. My attempts to explain to Charles, insisting on my own general characteristic of 'caprice'. The succession in him of incredulousness, which showed itself in a sort of amused but stubborn tenderness; then of annoyance, momentary violence, and final alternation of anger and an intense unhappiness and then anger again.

It is enough to say, to the credit of Charles, that the next morning he took me to a small station, and put me into a train for Paris, having insisted on buying my ticket. Since we met again in the morning he had been extremely courteous, though silent. Just as the train was moving out the hard detached expression in his fine eyes changed; and in the same moment I had a desire to be in his arms. Perhaps he saw this change in my look. In any case he turned away and walked out of the station.

I met him, hardly a month later, in the Champs-Elysées, accompanying an extremely pretty woman (I learned later she was the Contessa —, with whom he remained on intimate terms for a year or more).

March 2nd

There are *grisaille* periods in one's life. These occupy spaces in the calendar, but not in one's memory, which seems to retain clear-coloured impressions, made by one's imagination at the time of real experience.

There must have been three years between the episode of Charles Wentworth that I have just described and my going to America for the second time, which was in 1934. I know it was in 1934 because Tante Julie celebrated her sixtieth birthday that January; and she was born in 1874. I went south, to Les Délices, for her birthday; and my father even deranged himself and came from Italy to stay there. On the evening of her birthday we went to Monte Carlo where Otto had ordered, according to Tante Julie's wishes, a gala dinner for between thirty and forty guests in a private room at the Magnesco (which my aunt always patronized because the manager was a good friend of hers). The guests were a mixture of French, Americans, and English who inhabited the coast; the men mostly with puffy eyelids, heavy nostrils, and extremely good-natured; the women with the chic of experience, remarkable jewellery, and sunburn make-up. Differences of their nationality or talent were rendered more or less vague by the imprint they had in common of an existence of luxury without responsibility. They all were excellent friends with Otto and Tante Julie and arrived gay from cocktails and with small presents (some costly, some strikingly cheap). There were also several of Tante Julie's old cronies from Paris. One of them, a stubborn-nosed Député, the owner of a famous motor works, had known and, without doubt, loved her, when she wore the feather boas, the long corsets, the immense mushroom hats of around 1908, and who came now to salute her savorous *soixantaine* with sentiments that — during that evening of champagne and toasts and reminiscence — became almost love again … And there were her women friends of other days, actresses, models, little *bourgeoises* of imprecise respectability (some blooming and established, others faded by a succession of small difficulties and disappointments), who, in their unpretending dresses, brought to the celebration a vivacity of spirit and tenderness of real affection which Tante Julie recognized — for it was they who occupied places near her at the long table strewn with cattleyas and afforested with silver candelabra. I was also near this end of the table: and to me, who had been living, in Paris, among people of critical intellectual restraints and of refinements of emotional complexity, the whole occasion had the brilliant and gay and noisy sanity of a Fair. There were many speeches; the owner of the motor works made a short witty speech; the little modiste got up to pay a tribute to '*notre chère Julie*' which ended in handholdings and in tears that blotted the mascara on to her thin, carefully enamelled cheeks. Otto got up, a gardenia in his buttonhole, to enunciate charming compliments which came so evidently from his heart; and Tante Julie, in a dress of purple *paillettes*, made a speech of thanks, in her husky voice, proposing toasts to her different guests, and lapsing one moment into emotion, which made her voice still deeper, the next moment into the chuckling narration of a bawdy story, and sliding from the story into the half-grumbling, half-singing of some refrain familiar to them all, her whitened features beaming with salacious, kindly high spirits. At one time during the evening the manager came in (a little man with the polish and physical agility of his caste); and Tante Julie invited him to sit beside her, calling him '*mon petit Napoléon*'. (I have learned since that this really was his name!) And as he was going she shrieked after him that he was not to forget to make her a special price for the dinner.

Afterwards we went on to the Casino. It was there, while

I was dancing with the owner of the motor works, that he began talking — I forget apropos of what — about Germany preparing for war. It was, of course, a commonplace of conversation in France by this date (though not in England, where it suited 'business' to think of Hitler as a rampart against Bolshevism). But Monsieur added various definite details. He had just come back from a business journey to Germany. He knew Thyssen and had stayed with him in his villa in North Italy.

✳

At the beginning of February I sailed with Annabelle. She had asked me to go with her because she wanted to visit her parents, as her father was not well. (He had retired from the management of the shipping line in 1931, after which Vernon and Leonora had left London and gone back to America, and were now living in New York.)

Pierre was to stay with the children, in England. By this time the process was almost complete that Annabelle called 'losing our money', referring to it with a simplicity but lack of real interest, as if they had lost a handkerchief. The house in the Bois had long been sold, and they lived, I think, mostly on the proceeds of 'Pierre's job in London', to which he went by train from Chichester, which was something to do with the importing of French wines. Some of the money from the sale of the house, and of all the beautiful and fantastic things they had collected, was used to buy the Palladian house in Sussex in which they were now living; a house with twelve bedrooms and a lake in a small park, which, Annabelle explained to me, was cheap to buy (probably true) and 'cheap to run if you didn't run it too much!' (The rest of the money had bought the seaside villa in which I am living now.) Annabelle has admitted to me that, at the time when they bought these two houses, they 'still had a little left' (that is, a corner of the handkerchief). In any case, by the time I was to go to America with her and went to stay with them for a day or two beforehand, they had one servant (the Chinaman) and Annabelle spent her mornings wandering in and out of rooms and up and down corridors with an electric sweeper and a duster which I recognized as a white and pink dress she once had from Schiaparelli. And at weekends Pierre occupied himself polishing the parquet in the hall and dining-room and drawing-rooms. One of his methods was to sit Charles Vernon, then three years old, on a white bearskin rug and, attaching a dog leash to the rug, pull it over the parquet like a sledge. This method pleased the whole family.

As our boat sailed from Southampton on a Saturday, Pierre was able to see us off. Although Annabelle would only be away for six weeks they both behaved on the quay as if they were quitting each other forever. Pierre was absolutely pale with unhappiness, and tears ran down Annabelle's cheeks without her making the least attempt to stop them. Pierre came to our cabin where there were boxes of flowers that he had ordered (and would never, I was sure, be able to pay for). When she saw these boxes, and I unpacked the top one for her which contained white liliac, she being unable to see clearly to cut the string, and also her hand clasped by Pierre — she was so touched that she threw herself into his arms, exclaiming that she would not go at all; and he, holding her, looked at me with his green eyes shining with tears, demanding several times, without listening for my reassurance, that I should bring her back safely. Then that appalling hooting that lacerates the hearing of even the most stolid traveller, and for those who are already sick with good-byes is like the final ominous screaming of distress — that sound forced Pierre to let his wife go, to catch my hand, to seize her once more in his arms, and to rush from the cabin; and Annabelle sank down on a trunk among the half-opened boxes of flowers, exclaiming that she would not go on deck and wave, that that was 'worst of all'.

I was touched but I was almost equally amused by such an irrelevant display of despair; and I said that, all the same, it was only for 'six weeks': to which she at once replied, turning her Amazon's head to me with an expression the least Amazonian in the world, an expression so full of violent tenderness and completely without humour, that six weeks was 'a thousand and eight hours'.

As she said this she had one of her resemblances to Vernon; something in the great warmth and depth of her glance, and in the speed with which it was flashed at me, then withdrawn, so that a second after her head was in profile. Also, this I reflected after, I discovered in this whole behaviour of hers, in this surprising lapse from her characteristic serenity into the most irrational emotion, a parallel to the strange way in which Vernon (always as assured and vital as his sister was serene and strong) had lapsed from his characteristic assurance into the most desperate jealousy and self-mistrust.

Annabelle herself offered me during the voyage an excuse for 'making such a scene', which was that she was expecting another baby in eight months: so that it was difficult she said, 'to tell when she was feeling sick or when she was feeling sad'. I remembered, without comment, that as a young girl she had told me that modern women approached childbearing scientifically and didn't let it 'dislocate their lives', but I did mock her a little about Pierre's tears. She said that he 'felt anxious' about her; and she added, with one of her absolutely unthinking perceptions that were like moments of cleverness, that Pierre was 'just as primitive in his feelings as he was hypercivilized in his tastes'. 'Hypercivilized' was a word employed by Annabelle, and by Vernon when I first knew him, to explain to themselves a certain sort of European point of view, not obviously 'decadent' (another term they used) but — here is Vernon's own amplification — 'implying a passion for beauty without any special belief in its ethical importance'.

Annabelle spent much of the voyage lying down in our cabin; for it was too glacially cold and impossible to lie on deck. She liked me to be with her, since what she called my 'fascinating talking' distracted her from feeling 'seasick one half-hour and baby-sick the next'. She did look pale and thin in the face, lying there in the last of her luxurious peignoirs, of pearl-white satin. (I have recognized since its superb unworn texture in the 'best coat' of Camilla Blanche!) Every day of the voyage there was a radiogram from Pierre, so that Annabelle wondered how he would pay the grocer this week. This led to a conversation in which she told me that the only disagreement she and Pierre had was that she wanted to adopt the ideal of paying the books every week, while Pierre considered that the only fashion for poor people to save money was never to pay anything until you were obliged to. She also told me that, although her family were paying her steamer fare for this voyage (we were travelling Tourist), they had sold the house three years before, and were now living in an apartment.

Being together on this voyage made us almost as intimate again as we had been at school and Annabelle spoke to me about her existence in general terms, as well as in particular; her conclusion being that she could not be grateful enough for so much gaiety and affection. And, with hesitation, she questioned me about my life. She 'had heard' that everybody who was amusing frequented me; that a dozen different people were in love with me; that, 'one said', I would marry this or that man. She mentioned a painter; she asked — amused — if it was true that my former *bête noir*, Georges Charnaux, had become a 'flirt' of mine, to which I replied that, on the contrary, he had now married that pretentious little dancer, Natasha, and that both of them came to see me regularly, for the same reason they frequented others — that is to say, out of self-interest. (Annabelle, who rarely had perception of character in strangers, said that Natasha had seemed 'rather sweet' and that Charnaux 'wasn't so bad' and 'awfully polite'.)

She asked me also if I had seen Hugo recently. And added that he had been to stay with them for a weekend, and — tentatively — that he had spoken of me with such admiration. And I felt it would be a relief to talk to her about my visit, with Hugo, to the fortune-teller.

March 8th

As I have not recounted this before I will tell it directly, just as it happened, about two months before this voyage; and before Annabelle had herself even decided to visit her parents. It was after my second visit to Pryde, which took place in the autumn. This was infinitely more pleasant than my first visit, although the garden, so resplendent and perfumed when I had seen it with Miss Tanagra, was now in slippers and curlers. Lord Coldharbour himself was absent, at Bath, where, Hugo told me, he went every year in the obstinate belief that its waters would prolong his life more surely than any 'foreign' waters. Without him the house was tranquil, and therefore, like a lovely face from which an expression of strain has departed, one could enjoy its loveliness.

Mrs Adare was back in her arranged Paradise in Morocco, although her three spaniels remained, under the care of Hugo's valet, a little man who looked like a prawn, his black lugubrious eyes bulging, his knees and feet of comparatively little consequence. His name was Pomeroy, and he was the son of a butler and one of those cooks who, as Hugo has explained to me, have in England the title of 'Mrs' without the necessity of losing their virginity; although the birth of Pomeroy seems to prove that in this case the title was merited in the most banal fashion. I had the impression that Pomeroy understood 'gentlemen' as completely as Balthasar understood women. And he was tender and disciplinary with dogs. I saw that he fed those of Mrs Adare in separate bowls exactly at 12.30 in a small courtyard below my bathroom window: and twice a day, early morning and late evening, he took them for a walk, and one saw his small dark form distantly walking in the park, having the touching air of a creature out of its element, so much one felt for him the need of a horizontal posture under water.

Hugo had been in Paris before this weekend, and I had come over with him, suddenly seduced, as happens to me from time to time, by England, or at any rate by the England which I have been able to enjoy — that is, which ignores a dozen Englands which either I do not know or do not wish to experience; industrial England, political England, England expressed in midland towns, in dockyards, in suburbs, in slums. The England which, when Hugo said: 'Why don't you come over?' possessed my imagination so suddenly, was an *ambience*, a fragrance, a series of visions: of orchard grass patterned with narcissus; of fields, alternate pale green and raisin-coloured, each existing tranquilly within four hedges, and therefore having, modestly but with absolute individuality, its own blossoms, its own birds, its own sloes and blackberries. And of trees, for at once my vision was of trees. For the trees in England are a poem which I do not know how to write, in which the metre changes from majestic verses — which are for the chestnuts, the great oaks and silver-muscled beeches — from fine couplets for the great cedars, to lyric passages which sing the spring of the fruit trees, the snow-showering wild cherry and the enamelled gaiety of apple blossom; I should like to write the magnificent and delicate forms of branches, the shadows and transparencies of leaves; to find the metre for the cathedral solemnity of woods, to evoke the whispering repose of copses.

Hugo said: 'Why not come over?' He said too, when he invited me to Pryde: 'You always say you love the country. No one really adores the country unless they adore it in winter.'

Very Hugo that. Comprehension of a general truth and the use of exaggerated verb.

So I went. I shut up the *appartement*, and sent Pauline to Lille. She was pleased to go to her nieces. (The older was now married, giving Pauline already two great-nieces!) But at the same time she did not like me to go to England, where she believed (like Mademoiselle Dubois formerly) that the fog made it impossible to see the *sac à provisions* that one was carrying. I knew that she envisaged me lost, forever, in the fog. She said that '*en Amérique*,' to the contrary, 'if one spoke the truth' the air was good, and added that 'for herself, she found the Americans very amiable, very generous, while the English, it was well-known, were a race of misers.' I had heard this before from Pauline; and imagine that at one time, at least, Vernon must have tipped her well; whereas Hugo never tipped unnecessarily, unless in some crisis in his private life when he felt that an act of his generosity might bribe the gods.

When Pauline was packing for me she remarked that Balthasar had claimed that Hugo was 'un milord' — which was not true? I told her that the father of Hugo was '*un Lord*'; to which Pauline replied dryly that, one knew it well, there were plenty of false titles — did not Mademoiselle Blanche remember all those 'Russian Princes' who drove taxis after the war?

Naturally I made no attempt to assure Pauline how unlikely it was I should marry Hugo. And, at Pryde, as my visit lengthened from a weekend to a week, and from a week to a fortnight, I found an opposite problem in my relations with the handsome Miss Tanagra; which was to make her understand that her encouragements to us, to Hugo and me, were quite wide of the mark … For she would divert her thoughts from the political situation to say: 'Why, don't you both take a stroll in the garden?' Or, lilting her fine, beautifully *coiffée* head from reading *The Times*, she would say: 'Hugo, why don't you take Mademoiselle Lancret to see' — some new chrysanthemum for which she had a special affection.

And alone with me one evening, she remarked that she hoped 'dear Hugo' would marry, since it would be 'the greatest pity in the world' if the estate were to go on to the son of a cousin of Hugo's — a family, she said, who were 'none of them gardeners'. She said this with contempt, but apprehension; and I thought there might be worse vocation for me than to ensure to Pryde a 'gardener son'.

I know Hugo also must have had moments when the idea of such a future for us both either diverted or touched him sentimentally.

But, even if I had wanted to, how to explain to Miss Tanagra, desiring a gardener great-nephew, what had only gradually and recently become clear to me, that a great-nephew would demand from Hugo either a sustained decision or a sustained impulse, and that he was incapable of either? That he was, in fact, in character, incoherence itself? That during a day in which he was pleased he was also displeased with the mad exclaiming displeasure of the egoist; that every mood was followed (as if he were three years old instead of thirty-four) by its reaction: gaiety succeeded by depression, optimism by pessimism, a phase of intellectual preoccupation by sensual obsession, his periods of expansive affectionate sympathy (his greatest enchantment) checked, as spontaneously as they set in, by fleeing to a nervous and often tormented solitude; and, in the same way, his friendships changed to enmities.

And the effect on me of this illness of instability in Hugo had been to make me very attached to and fond of him (it was impossible not to delight in his wit, and to feel his most delicious sympathy) but to preserve myself from any defined relation with him instinctively, and often against my own wishes.

Sometimes I had told myself that he would change, that he would 'cohere'; for, thinking what I desired to believe, he seemed in so many ways the only real alternative to what Vernon might have been for me; because, in default of filling my heart, he could entirely occupy my fancy. And on definite occasions — there was one during this visit, our evening's conversation in the Chinese Room — when our two moods coincided, there was such a sympathy between us that it was like love. Almost: because there was never, at any moment between us, enough feeling to make words unnecessary.

Anyway, I define the situation as it was that week. I recall how at the end of that special evening, during which the firelight made the birds on the wallpaper stir among the leaves, our own act of getting up from our opposite sofa and armchair broke the thousand filaments that had held us together during the preceding two hours. And it was then that Hugo, selecting a topic of conversation that would just fit into the time it took us to go up the staircase (and which would also give me to understand that the evening had had a significance), asked me if I had ever been to Madame Smith in Upper Grosvenor Place? I had never heard of her, I said, and guessed that she was a fortune-teller. We were now in the hall at the bottom of the stairs. As we went up he told me that 'a friend of mine' (a phrase he used always when he had to mention someone with whom he had consorted of another class, or in a discreditable relationship) — 'a friend of mine' had said that Madame Smith was 'absolutely marvellous' (English adjective of the 1930s that descended as far as the third social class!).

He proposed that during the days which I was to spend in London we should visit Madame Smith together.

March 11th

She was, one saw that immediately, much more Smith than 'Madame'. Hugo explained to me afterwards that in England one calls oneself 'Madame' if one sells corsets or foretells the future. (Why is this?)

In a jersey suit of white she rather resembled a white parrot. Or perhaps I think so because a real white parrot inhabited a cage in the one window in that sombre little room overcrowded with furniture and smelling of charcoal fumes and stale beef gravy. Anyway, she had a high-beaked nose, and black eyes and a white felt cloche hat, survived I suppose from the earliest 1920s, below which one saw a fringe the colour of marigolds, and pearl ear-rings ... And her hands were like little sad claws. She sent Hugo into a room next door, after he had made, evidently, the most distinguished impression: for as he closed the curtained door behind him she exclaimed that she was sure she had seen him before; she thought it was 'at Windsor Castle'. She added that she believed in 'race', at the same time taking my hand palm upward and powdering it from a tin of talc powder which stood on the table, astonishing me by remarking: 'No, my dear, any perfume would interfere with my Getting Anything, y'see!' — this being her answer to my thought that the talc powder would certainly be heavily scented! She pronounced 'Getting Anything' with an emphasis which is really over-expressed by capital letters; for during our interview she passed from the banal to the mystic with matter-of-fact facility, as if they were adjacent stations on the Metro. One moment she told me that my mother had died when I was a child, the next that she (Madame Smith) had spent Easter at the house of some very wealthy people 'near Brighton'; but I will write down now the 'facts' about myself and my future which later I recounted to Annabelle on the voyage. She said:

That I was still unmarried; but that I ought to have been married six years before.

That I was either an artist or a musician; or 'if I wasn't I ought to be'.

That she 'saw me' in a hot country in 'a wonderful garden'. Kenya perhaps? (I never answered her questions.) That a man, an 'elderly' man, was in the garden thinking about me. And that 'there was a lot to be said in some ways for older men.' But:

'No. That elderly man wasn't my 'true mate', (she had described my father even to his 'wide-brimmed rather green hat'!) I should 'have to wait'. Then I think she took the crystal and made me hold it, then took it from me and held it between her little claws, and I observed her rings of imitation emeralds and diamonds. When she was looking down into the crystal the lids of her eyes looked exactly like a parrot's, and she held her lower lip with her two front teeth. Then she said that I would have an invitation from a woman friend to go a long way across water; that she saw me on a big boat, surrounded by people and having a gay time. That she saw a man, whom I should meet on the boat; that she saw my cabin, an outside cabin — 'I see the porthole' — and a scene with a man, and tears to do with a parting; but 'even if that parting comes it won't be for long'. She added that she saw me wearing a fur hat, 'mink it looks like'. When I asked her to describe the man she was confused at first; then she said he was dark; then, with sudden energy, she said that a great 'turning point' in my life was nearer than I thought. And at the end she became very sure that there was a fair man who cared a lot about me; a fair man with blue eyes who would propose to me before 1937 (that is to say, during the next fourteen months). She also reverted to the significance of this voyage in my life, and told me that I should hear about it before Christmas. (In fact Annabelle wrote to me early in December.)

There was more, but not worth remembering. Except (I had forgotten to put it down) that twice she described to me a street 'in a foreign city' where the houses were very dark grey and had shutters and little balconies of 'ornamental ironwork'. But she admitted that she couldn't understand why she 'kept seeing' this street, rather a 'dreary street', she commented; and it was clear that her prescience of a sea voyage accorded better with her own personal view of romantic destiny, and her final encouragements to 'follow my heart' when 'the moment comes, my dear' — this said with intimacy as if she had known me since my childhood. She put my treasury note into her handbag of worn white crochet, without seeming to know what she was doing, and came to the door with me, talking and looking up into my face. (Her legs were short and she limped, or else her dreadful shoes hurt her.) But once she had slipped her hand around the curtain and turned the door handle her talk and her interest faded out, abruptly and absurdly, and she said, turning her head to glance at the clock, whose face seemed only just to survive drowning in the tide of ornaments, vases, photographs, shells, dried grasses in the chimneypiece — she said: 'Ask your friend to come in, will you?'

I remember how Hugo hurried in with a grave expression; and I did not wait for him, but went in a taxi to Quaglino's, where I was to meet a friend for lunch.

March 14th

When I was telling Annabelle about this in our cabin she asked me 'if Hugo had told me what Madame Smith said to him'. I said that he had come afterwards to join us at Quaglino's but that he refused to say more than that she had been 'extraordinary'; and he looked pleased and silky and cordial, like a cat that has had cream, and very affectionate in his manner towards me.

Annabelle said that she supposed I was impressed by all that Madame Smith had said now because the part about the voyage had come true. I said, yes, even to the 'tears and good-byes' in the cabin, although (typically) she had not been able to foresee that I was not personally involved.

Annabelle smiled. She was sitting at the dressing-table, and said that she was rather ashamed of that 'scene', but that it had been just the same last year when Pierre had had to go to France to the funeral of his grandmother at La Rochelle. Then she asked me if the fair man had proposed yet. I said no. Then: 'What about the dark man?' in a manner deliberately light; and I answered in the same manner that I had considered all the dark men on the boat and none of them pleased me. (And so we avoided — as we had to at some moment every day — mentioning Vernon.)

During the voyage, I think it was after I had had this conversation with Annabelle, a packet was delivered to me in my cabin, which contained Beckford's *Vathek*, a present from Hugo which had not been delivered to me before (through some miscomprehension, having been sent to the cabin of a 'Mrs Landon'). I showed it to Annabelle, who said, with amusement but affectionate interest also: 'That proves he *is* thinking about you.' By this time she had long renounced her idea that Vernon and Leonora should divorce; in fact, while I was staying with her in Paris during that September when I met Charles Wentworth, she had said to me that 'Vernon and Leonora seemed to be settling down, and that Leonora was really a very fine person'; a phrase which certainly had its effect at the time on my attitude toward Charles Wentworth.

I wrote to Hugo thanking him for the book (one of his favourites) and saying that part of Madame S's previsions had come true: but not her vision of the mink hat!

The day before we docked Annabelle felt very sick and asked me to read *Vathek* aloud to her.

We docked early in the morning. To arrive in New York harbour early in the morning is an experience which demands an exquisite description. I have never read one. Perhaps music would describe it better than words.

Mrs Strudwick was on the dock. She embraced Annabelle with emotion that I had never seen in her formerly. She had changed in the last five years. I had not seen her since Annabelle's wedding. Her hair was altogether white; she looked much older; and her expression — which used to be self-assured, and arrogant, in a calm way, if anyone disagreed with her or failed to please her — was serious, and also gave me the idea that her comprehension of life was more real, and therefore more humble. Briefly, she was sympathetic to me, and this before I realized the different existence she was now leading.

For I returned with them to Boston. And there in the apartment they now lived in on West Cedar Street, I met Mr Strudwick *père* again; although not until the day after my arrival, when I had been warned by Mrs Strudwick that I should find him very much altered. I had already perceived that Annabelle, who had visited him in his room after her arrival, had been shocked, in some way: though she only remarked that she was glad she had come to be with her mother even for a short time.

Mr Strudwick inhabited the only big room in the apartment, and I was conducted into it by a woman who seemed like a secretary but was a hospital nurse out of uniform. She asked me outside the door not to encourage him to talk about politics or business. She had a conscientiously tranquil voice. She said 'encorrige', rolling her rr's emphatically under the front of her tongue. Mr Strudwick jumped up from a chair by the bay window and came towards me with the special courtesy I remembered and liked — for he had pleased me formerly by being the Boston Merchant of a type more distinguished, more cultivated, and more aristocratic than existed at the same epoch in England — where a rich family could achieve without any precise dignity the facile distinction of titles. And, formerly, the so-wealthy Mr Strudwick had seemed to me, by a delightful paradox, the finest exponent of the 'unbought grace of life'.

But now his first impulse of courtesy hardly brought him across the room. I recall how he turned away and then, walking up and down, began to talk. And as I observed him — obsessed, neurotic, haggard, inconclusive in gestures, endlessly repeating his fears, and muttering over each of his remorses like a bitter rosary — it was evident enough that, for him, the grace of his life had been bought with its security.

Poor Mr Strudwick! He hasn't been the only one, above all of his world and generation — his lovely world, his privileged generation — for whom the loss of a fortune was also the losing of the very beauty of living; who, without having the least interest in 'being rich' in the vulgar sense, had a sensitivity of imagination to see how financial disaster must destroy, not only all the accumulated exquisite ornament, but the very pillars of fine living, how it had carried away hospitality and generosity, and changed leisure itself, that had been orderly and lovely as a garden, to a mere unending inability to sleep, and so to escape …

But, if Mr Strudwick had been defeated (ignobly or piteously according to one's way of judging human failure), she, Mrs Strudwick, had most evidently — I was to see this from day to day — gained a victory. For victory is courage, not success. And in this new life of theirs no change was as remarkable as the way in which her arrogance had become dignity, her assumption of privilege had changed to a sense of simple obligations and denials which, in their turn, had developed in her an appreciation of small gaieties and ironies.

Annabelle saw all this as clearly as I did. She said: 'Mother's become perfectly darling' — a description perhaps too sentimental and ignoring the strength that made it possible to be 'darling', and to be cultured — for the Strudwicks read and discussed as much as ever, under a strain. Within a few days I discovered that it was she who was with Mr Strudwick during his 'bad nights', the nurse coming only during the day; that it was she who helped the Swedish girl in the apartment, answered all business correspondence, took his place on several committees, fulfilling her own obligations in connection with various charitable organizations, and kept up all sorts of relationships by letters or visits — since she had, as always, the highest conception of relation between human beings, and would no more have left a letter to an old aunt in Virginia unanswered than she would have permitted her appearance (and how beautiful and how elegant she still was!) to have betrayed the fact that she no longer had a personal maid.

March 15th

During my stay Tad came to see us. He hadn't changed since my first visit to Boston. He still seemed a college boy, only with small lines at the corner of his eyes, and a darker sunburn so that his frequent smiles demonstrated that his teeth were still whiter. During our conversation he told me that he was about to motor to New Mexico with his sister, and suggested that I should come with them. As I was always ready to enter any door that opened before me, my first impulse was to agree; then I hesitated, because I had promised Pierre that I would bring Annabelle back to England. But Annabelle herself interrupted to say that surely I must go, and that in any case she had just heard that a cousin of hers was going to Europe soon, and she could arrange to go with her. During this conversation I asked myself if Tad corresponded to any of Madame Smith's descriptions of men: but as he did not I felt cordial towards him and without that vague hostility that is in any tendency to fall in love. I think that I must have said that I would decide during the next day if I would go with him and his sister, or not: and it was during those days that I received the letter from Hugo that was to have an unpredictable effect.

His letter was on the dressing table in my little room when I came in from a visit that I had made with Annabelle to the Museum. While we were looking at the furniture section, Annabelle had remarked how Hugo would be interested in a room that they have arranged there, with charming painted French wallpaper of the eighteenth century; and the fact that we had spoken of him seemed to make the arrival of his letter significant.

In his letters Hugo expresses himself always copiously, and with warmth that is only occasional in his manner when one is with him. The letter was written from Pryde; it contained news of Miss Tanagra, of the dogs and Pomeroy, and of the garden, all described in such a way that I felt as if Hugo had suddenly walked into the room. In the second part of the letter there were the two phrases which, during the next few hours, made me decide to move towards Europe rather than away from it (that is, to New Mexico). I express it in this way because the more I look back the more I realize that I never made a decision, but seem only to have let my existence take one direction or another entirely under the influence of an incidental circumstance or an unexpected emotion. In this particular moment (how many moments are crises in one's life?) I am sure that an added influence on me was the intensity of the steam heat in my room. I sat on the bed, as I read Hugo's letter, and the dry, too little oxygenated air in the room made me imagine the gardens at Pryde in the autumn, heaps of glistening brown leaves along the paths and the chrysanthemums dishevelled by the night rain.

But, of course, principally, there were those two phrases, in the arabesques of Hugo's handwriting. The first: 'Ever since you left I have had a sensation like a prolonged disappointment — or perhaps it is most like an elevator going up and down without stopping in my solar plexus ...'

The second: 'I can't help hoping that Madame Smith was right.'

I told Annabelle that I had decided to return to Europe, and not to go to New Mexico. I think she guessed that this decision had something to do with Hugo, and she did not try to persuade me. The same evening I heard her saying on the telephone in the next room that Blanche was going on the *Normandie* the next week, but that she herself was remaining with her parents a little longer, just the same. I asked her if it was still all right for her to sail with her cousin later; and she said yes, she had just been talking to her on the telephone.

Tad was very sorry that I decided not to go with him and his sister. (It is nothing to do with this story, but it is curious that he had an accident on that journey; he himself wasn't much hurt, but the sister was very badly hurt.)

When I left I went into Mr Strudwick's room to say good-bye to him. He was seated in his chair at the window, and at first he didn't seem to recognize me. Then I could see his attention drag itself painfully out of depths of miserable preoccupation, while his black eyes became gradually focused on my face. When I said that I was about to depart he was still silent; and then he said that he was sorry I had had 'such a poor time' with them; but that I could 'see for myself how things were with them', and he used the word 'ruined' several times.

And then suddenly he seemed to gain a sort of mastery over his inner obsession, and rose up, and, beckoning me to stand beside him at the window (below which cheap traffic rattled and fussed, opposite which there was a façade of an equally bleak apartment house), he said, in quite another voice: 'Just look at that *wonderful* sky, Mademoiselle Blanche!' (It was that American winter sunshine of which we should say, as of diamonds, 'of the first water.') And then he added, with all his former dignified cordiality: 'I hope and believe that means you're going to have a beautiful trip, Mademoiselle,' and asked me several questions about my journey; and hearing that I was about to sail in the *Normandie*, he made several compliments as an amateur of shipping, on the merits of the French Line; and I recollect that he was telling me how he and Madame Strudwick had enjoyed a journey on the *Ile de France*, when she came in to tell me it was time for me to depart.

As she shut his door behind her she said, in a tone that touched me very much, that he seemed 'almost his old self'. Then she added that Vernon had telephoned to her from New

York to say he had arranged for her and his father to go out West next month for a change. I understood that it was on a property belonging to Leonora, and that Vernon was paying for the journey. I was surprised to realize that he was in New York at this moment; because I had understood that he was in San Francisco for a time.

Both Mrs Strudwick and Annabelle came to the station (at Boston) with me.

When Mrs Strudwick was saying good-bye, she took my two hands in hers and said: 'Dear child ...' with tears in her eyes and something unexpressed in her tone; then she added: 'We shall think about you ...' She stopped again, and then said: 'Blanche, dear child, I can't help wishing some things — had been different.' I half knew what she meant. Even then, restraint and good sense made it impossible for her to say more; concentration of sentiment at parting had made it possible for her to say as much.

I arrived early at the dock, and when I had embarked I stood on the deck for a time, surveying the sparkling vivacity of the air, the quays and the shipping on the river, and permitting myself sensations which went through me like verses of poetry: some about the America that I was leaving, with its qualities of hope and freshness of heart; others about the Europe, familiar and mysterious, to which I was returning, And, as it happens in poetry, metaphor and truth became intertwined; and in thinking of America I thought also of Vernon, and in looking towards Europe I discerned, too, a personal silhouette, at the same time distinct and elusive, which was Hugo ... and then again, Vernon recurred, detaching himself, becoming clear and insistent and moving like a theme in music. (I think there is no clearer proof that one loves someone than his perpetual recurrence, sometimes in image, sometimes in echo, sometimes in a sensual memorization of touch or fragrance; in his insistent association with moments and situations when one least expects it, so that he enters on a conversation or a secondary reflection like a ghost coming through a door, making one's heart stop ...)

But when everybody began to arrive on board and crowd the decks I went downstairs to my cabin, which was panelled with dark wood so that the two portholes were like two big bright coins. There were several cardboard boxes containing flowers, one from Tad, another containing lilies from Annabelle. When I opened another box it contained a mink muff and hat, with a little note from Mrs Strudwick, asking me to accept these as a little present as they would suit my existence, and not the 'simple life' she was now leading. The muff and hat had evidently been relined by a furrier in New York who had sent them straight to the boat. I was extremely touched. I took the hat and tried it on in front of one of the many mirrors in my cabin. While I was doing this I saw in the mirror my door open and Vernon come in. He was followed by a steward. He was pale. He pointed to my luggage and said: 'All this, steward,' and the man said: *'Oui, monsieur,'* took up two valises and went out with them. I saw all this in the glass. Then I turned round, and he was still there, he was maddeningly close to me, his voice and his look said the same thing: 'Please come, darling.'

So I went with him, beside him, our hands not touching; we went along all those dark corridors and up stairways, and across a brilliant deck, through the crowd I suppose, but I didn't see anyone, for I was as in the power of a drug, and what I recall of that speechless transit, finally down the gangway on to the dock, and across the dock, down stairways into a waiting car, is a sensation of — how shall I describe its brilliant excitement, its peace, its quality of being lifted up and borne along as strongly and yet as simply as a creature impelled by hunger towards food? Also I remember an emotion of 'rightness', that was like a prelude; but a prelude which I had heard six years before.

I suppose that we drove through New York and crossed one of the bridges over the Harlem River. It must have been very cold, for it was an open car.

March 17th

Egerton is a village in New England. Its white, green-shuttered houses seem small between the immense trunks of elms. Its wooden white church has a steeple that is shaped like the tall hat of a Princess in a Fairy Tale.

The house where we arrived is more than a mile above the village on the lower slopes of the mountains; a crescent of pinewood behind it, and near it barns and pine sheds, for it had been a small farmhouse. We arrived in the evening when the moonlight was on the snow. The frozen air smelled of pines. The coloured man that Vernon had told me about was waiting for us indoors. There was a great fire of pine logs burning.

And now I do not know how to describe either that evening or the next two weeks. I keep finding only the flat phrase 'we were perfectly happy'. I do not know how to explain the kind of perfection. I find comments unrelated and without sequence, like a child describing a party.

We were extremely gay.

We were out of doors all day in the sun and snow. There were snowstorms, lasting for hours. We walked in one of these, and lost ourselves.

We slept in a room that had three windows, and a white wallpaper with small yellow stars on it.

When we woke in the mornings we would see through our windows the distant mountains and a corner of the black barn next to us, with snow on the eaves. The coloured man brought us our breakfast on a tray, saying every morning that it was certainly a beautiful day, and every morning smiled at us with the greatest affection, and seemed filled with delight that we had slept still another night together in that four-poster bed.

※

On one of our walks we stopped halfway up the mountain trail at a sawmill in among the pines. There was a lovely smell of new sawdust in the brilliant air. Logs were heaped up; and long golden planks, some without snow on them so they must have been sawn that morning. But now the clearing was deserted; so it must have been Saturday; and certainly afternoon, for I remember that as we sat down on a pile of long clean planks, our feet in the snow, the shadows of the pines lay right across the white-rutted track that passed in front of us.

It was while we were eating our sandwiches that Vernon said: 'Darling, I've got to make a curious condition'; and then he said that when we lived together we would have to have Sohni to live with us, unless his mother claimed him. Then he told me Sohni's story, and how Leonora, who was on a committee dealing with refugees from Germany and Austria, had heard of his case and offered to adopt him.

I said that it was good of her, and my idea of her changed as I spoke. Vernon said: 'Yes, in a way ...' and hesitated.

I asked him how, if Leonora had adopted the child, it could live with us. He said that Leonora had feelings of moral and civic responsibility. But that she didn't really like children; that she was kind to Sohni, but that since his arrival he had attached himself to Vernon, with an affection that was (said Vernon) 'almost frightening'. (When I saw Sohni I understood what he meant.)

We finished our lunch, side by side in that absolute peace of sun and pines and snow.

Part 3

A week later we returned to New York, to tell Leonora of our decision. (If one can call the collusion of two impulses a decision.)

Vernon had telephoned their apartment in advance, to find out if Leonora had returned from California; and learned that she had returned.

For me New York streets had a detailed unreality, and all the noise around us seemed far off. I was isolated within my happiness; and I think Vernon, beside me, felt also that everything except ourselves was a dream, for at some street corner he said: 'These people think they're leading real lives, Blanche.' But I replied that many of them must be in love, too; and his reply: 'Not as I am with you, Blanche,' touched me profoundly, by its lack of comprehension; and its innocent and arrogant denying of our passion to other people made him suddenly my son; so that, as the lights changed and he slipped in the gears (presenting to me that profile already so vivid in my heart that it was difficult for me to see it), I felt that there was still another way in which we needed each other. For he was evidently capable of being 'stupid' in matters where my cleverness was quite matter-of-course.

The apartment was on Park Avenue near the Waldorf. We walked through an immense entrance hall, like a luxurious crypt, to an elevator in carved wood that took us up directly opposite a door, to which Vernon had the key.

Inside, everything was evidently in the taste of Leonora. Vernon likes big pale spaces and few pieces of furniture; and this was all massive Spanish furniture, hangings and portières of brocades in purples, reds, and golds, imitation stone walls on which were hung ironwork candelabra, pieces of old armour, Persian rugs, and now and again a mirror of old dark glass. In the room with the vaulted ceiling in which we waited for Leonora an immense open fire burned, although the air was already too warm from the excessive central heating, which, as always, had its depressing effect on my state of mind. Vernon had told the butler to inform Leonora. While we waited he said, looking round: 'We shall soon be out of all this,' with a relief that was cheerful and confident; and demonstrated to me the curious way in which he must have lived his marriage without emotion as if it had been a railway journey.

But I had a feeling of apprehension. I could imagine, looking around, exactly the receptions given by Leonora in this room; and the people, energetic smart people with keyed-up voices and no shadows at all in their minds, who would come to them. Leonora was printed on everything: on the expert flower arrangements, on the little pile of new books, the best and the most recently published plays and novels and poetry, in French as well as in English; even, it seemed to me, on the view from the four long windows, of the slipping past of a shining stream of automobiles along the Avenue. I remember wondering how Vernon had escaped the imprint of all this vital elaborate taste. For in those eight years in which they had been married she must have used the many sorts of force which she possessed to make him hers, as completely as she had made this room hers. Her pride, and all that lack of self-criticism in her which she supposed to be self-respect, must have made her try to break down Vernon's intimate absence from her; to try and identify his ideas with her ideas; and to change his thoughtful respect and admiration for her into an uncritical worship. I thought, as we waited in the sombre luxury of that room, how often he must have escaped her, without his realizing at all what he was quite doing. Like many Americans of their background, they had become, in their relationship, strong and simple from lack of humour; and yet they showed themselves so identical in their need to idealize their problem; to interpret it morally, rather than (as two French people would have) in terms of 'good sense' *versus* 'love'.

Leonora entered the room quietly and with a certain pride in her carriage which I could not help admiring although it made me uneasy, too. She greeted us calmly but did not shake hands, and as soon as she was seated on the sofa, facing us, Vernon began by saying that we (he and I) had come to tell her of a decision we'd reached. He said: 'You see, Leonora, it isn't in the least a question of infatuation, or anything like that ... We've really cared about each other, a very long time.'

She asked, 'How long?' with admirable quiet. He looked straight in her face and said: 'For years.'

She said: 'I remember, there was some sort of a boy-and-girl affair before you came back from Italy.'

'It was more than that. I told you, at the time.' (I remembered now his account of how Leonora had been on the dock. And how his cables had never reached me.)

'Yes,' she admitted, but without admitting the least importance to a distant incident. 'Yes, I do remember.' Then she stated: 'But that was all over when we got married.'

'Yes. Naturally, in one sense.'

She drew herself up. 'There could have been no sense in which it wasn't over, Vernon.'

He looked at her and said that one was apt to think one had uprooted a feeling, and then one hadn't. I could see by his look that he didn't expect her to comprehend this. And she didn't. For her answer was that you couldn't love two women at once, and that he had married her. She said this conclusively.

It was then that he came at the motive from a new angle, saying that he felt that he and she hadn't really been 'in harmony' for some time, that he and I (Blanche) were probably in some way 'affinities'. That marriage, after all, was only 'sacred' when the relationship within it was something 'fine and alive'.

Whether he was being diplomatic or not I couldn't be certain. (I never am. He is always both transparent and opaque to me.) In any case he was speaking a language they both understood. And her answer, in the same language, was that she had 'never let their marriage down'. She said this with an exasperating nobility of manner, looking like Nefertiti while she said it; and yet with enough emotion to touch my feelings; and I asked myself if perhaps, apart from her possessiveness of him, she loved him.

But at this point he changed his tactics and said: 'Listen, Leonora, let's try and be real for a change. What counts is now. You don't love me.' At a movement from her ... 'No, dear, not in a way that you'd understand, if you ever did love anyone. And Blanche and I need each other, badly. For life, I mean. So we want to get married. We want you to give me a divorce.'

I don't think she answered his challenge immediately. What I do remember is that she behaved with the slightly dramatized courage and restraint of an aristocrat informed that his lands and chateau have been captured by an enemy. She showed fortitude followed by resignation. She said: 'Naturally, if that's how things are, dear, I shall give you a divorce.'

I had expected some kind of resistance: and I think Vernon had. For he began to thank her, evidently touched. She said that we were right to have come to her; that there wasn't any reason why we shouldn't all three remain good friends. And mentioned lawyers, and so forth, all this with gravity and consideration to us both. I saw that I had misjudged her; that she was capable of sensitivity. Vernon seemed almost troubled, beginning to speak to her tenderly, as if he must have hurt her badly to cause such a strange gentleness.

Then she said to him: 'Anyway, dear, I think Sohni would want to see you, before you go.' And Vernon said, yes; and anyway Sohni was the other thing he wanted to talk to her about; that, one thing, quite definitely, he proposed was to 'take on Sohni'.

She didn't answer this directly. But went across the room and out of the door; and came back saying she'd called him, and he was just coming. She added: 'He's been simply living for your coming home, Vernon.'

And then Sohni came in; through that heavy oak door with its red brocade portière. When he got in he paused, to look first at Leonora, then at me, then at Vernon.

I see him now, as I write, and I think I shall have this picture of him always — standing, a third the height of that pompous red portière on the opposite side of that overheated room; and then moving a step or two forward to pause again, beside a too big, high-backed, costly Spanish chair. I see him, his thin small hand on the carved arm of that chair, his lovely dark eyes on each of us in turn, with a different expression for each of us. I see him, fragile and timid and absolutely grave. And, in him, I see also all those children who then (it was 1937) and, in a lengthening procession, during the next three years, were to suffer, one innocent spirit after another, from the unexplained bullying of a cancerous Tyranny. To suffer (innocent even of a sense of injustice) fear and privation, loneliness, and the blank despairing loss of accustomed love. I see now in Sohni's dark eyes that appalling intimacy with fear; and in his hand, grasping the arm of the chair so hard, a habit of tensity; and in the way in which he carries his head, and in the compression of his sweet mouth, I see that he is used to unhappiness, and has demanded of his pride that it shall help him to seem indifferent.

I see him, not calmly, but with that generalized everyday despair that one has accumulated about the world in these last five years.

I see him, not only as his infinitely touching self, but as a forerunner …

And in those moments when Leonora was saying, 'Come along in, Sohni,' I was so seized by pity that I turned my face from the child, so that he shouldn't meet the violence of my pity.

Then Leonora turned to me and began telling me how he was going to go to school and how 'he'd soon start enjoying himself' with lots of boys his own age. I asked his age. 'Seven,' she said. And while she was talking I saw the child go to Vernon, his whole expression changing: and respond to something Vernon said and to the easy gesture of Vernon's held-out hand, with an eagerness that was like thirst. I saw him hesitate when he got to Vernon, his sweet shining heart-breaking gaze on Vernon's face. 'And how goes it, Sohni?' And then he added some joke in German, and the pale child face coloured with pleasure, and he murmured something in reply. And Leonora said to me, in a low tone: 'He'll miss Vernon.' And then, when he had the child standing by his knee, she turned to him and said, distinctly: 'Sohni'll miss you, Vernon.'

I think in that flash of our comprehension that the first thing Vernon and I realized, with unspeakable relief, was that Sohni did not understand: that he still understood too little English to comprehend 'missing anyone'.

Leonora added, in our silence that followed: 'You see, Vernon dear, having formally adopted him myself — which means I, personally, have promised to be responsible for him — it just wouldn't be possible to …' she hardly hesitated before she chose the phrase 'to consign him to the care of others'.

I was watching Sohni's hand slip with tentative confidence around Vernon's wrist, under the shirt cuff. Then Leonora looked at Sohni and said in careful, awkwardly pronounced German: 'You are happy that the Herr Vernon is back?' And I saw, distinct as two gestures, the child's instinctive recoil from any direct question, and, on his realizing the meaning of her question, the little tremor of feeling that was followed by a nod to her, and then that swift shy adoring look straight up into Vernon's face.

I shall remember always the child's profile of that moment; something still of the baby years in the sweet roundness of brow and cheek; and that look, so (I recall Vernon's word) 'frighteningly' sensitive; so beautiful and indescribably moving in its revelation of love.

It was that look that assured the triumph of Leonora.

March 22nd

I see that I haven't mentioned that I am no longer in the villa; that in January Camilla Blanche and I moved back here to Sussex. I have stayed on here with Annabelle, helping her teach the younger children, and we sew and talk in the evenings. The house is so lovely, the children so enchanting; there has been the snow outside day after day and enough logs to have big fires indoors. But it is a life lived in a shadow; and the absence of Pierre makes it all in a 'minor key'. That is how Annabelle describes it.

Vernon writes that he is going to try and get to France as an ambulance driver. He is, therefore, arranging his business affairs so that he can leave them: 'if possible forever', he says. By which he means — what?

March 23rd

After that occasion with Leonora at their apartment I sailed to Genoa and went to stay with my father, intending to spend the winter there.

When I told him what had happened he said that we, Vernon and I, should have left the child and that Leonora's need for self-admiration would have obliged her to give a divorce. He was severe and sad; he said that we had sacrificed ourselves on the altar of the great Nordic god 'Sentimentality'. From one point of view I felt that he was right. But I knew then, as I know now, that neither Vernon nor I could have acted in any other way.

Looking back I see that autumn was the beginning of the phase of suspense in which I am still existing (that is, March 1940). I had my one hope: that Vernon would be able to come to Paris in the spring.

It rained a great deal that autumn, so my father and I were much indoors in the company of the frescoes and the log fire. He had, as always, an excellent cook, and we ate well, occasionally entertaining neighbours — Italians chiefly, all either native Fascisti or accepting the Fascist policy. The Spanish War was in progress and all were pro-Franco. They must all have known that my father was not Fascist in his sympathies, but they accepted his own statement that he was 'philosophical, not political', and talked politics freely in his presence, much as women will discuss love in the hearing of a child of two years. The women, at those little parties, all had a sort of amorous friendship for my father, and as they were mostly handsome, even those of between fifty and sixty, he was warmed by their glances and touches, and by their warm exclaiming embraces whenever they arrived. The men respected my father from a superficial regard for scholarship, liked him for being a good host, and

I think were, at the same time, suspicious and tolerant of his liberal mind.

It was after one of those little dinners that my father said, after our visitors had gone: 'The greatest danger is that a nation like England with a sense of humour cannot prepare for war.'

'How ...?'

'A sense of humour implies a sense of relative values. This sense discourages the making of anything so dangerous and so ridiculous in shape as a gun.' He added that the Italians had 'gaiety but no humour ... and the Germans not even gaiety.' After this he followed a long train of thought, and I watched his face, like the mask of a charming and gentle satyr in the firelight. At one point I asked him why and he shook his head.

'It's a pity,' he said gently, 'really a pity.'

'What?'

Again he shook his head. 'That the mother of Hitler was not sterile.'

✖

This is part of a letter Vernon wrote me while I was still at my father's:

'... What you said, Blanche, is true, the more I think of it. We never could have been happy leaving the child. It never occurred to me that Leonora would react the way she did. Since that day she hasn't once spoken of you, or our situation. She is tremendously busy, as usual, socially and philanthropically. When I do see her she is very gentle towards me. She is a fine person really. No rancour. Luckily for myself I am driven with work. Next week we launch a new ship. I would have liked her called Blanche. I would have liked most things called Blanche. A house, for instance — a Maison Blanche on a bit of Côte d'Azur. And a daughter. As soon as I can find business that takes me to Europe I shall; and we'll be together, for a time.

You ask me about Sohni. I took him up to our place in Connecticut last weekend. (Leonora was away visiting her family in Philadelphia.) He had a perfectly grand time. We built a house in the woods and made a fire and cooked our lunch and our supper out of doors. He looks less delicate, I think. But, of course, his real trouble is needing his mother; and he must think about her a lot. As I told you, he knows his father is dead (without, thank goodness, realizing how). But about his mother it's difficult. Because there is that definite chance she might get out of Austria some time — she may be out of prison now for all we know. But one can't keep a child in suspense. Actually Leonora took my suggestion that we should say that his mother had to remain to look after a lot of other children in their garden at home. Sohni told me she did this. A whole lot of Jewish children that aren't allowed to play in the public parks used to go to her before she was taken off by the Gestapo. When Sohni asks me, When will she come? I have to say, Not for a long time. Yesterday Mother was in New York and came to see him. She took a fancy to him, and he was evidently charmed by her. Typical of Mother, she couldn't stand his little foreign-looking Norfolk suit with those long 'shorts'; and she's taken him off to buy a suit and made him look like an American! I think he was rather thrilled when she arrived to fetch him, speaking to him in her pretty German that she learned in her Dresden finishing school! When I come to Europe I shall persuade Leonora to let Sohni visit Mother at Boston ...'

March 24th

When I left my father I went to Switzerland to stay with some friends near Montreux, a painter and his wife who had many political friends. The talk was much of politics, and looking back I see that the conversation was interesting, although it did not interest me at the time. (For I always found politics a kind of unrecognized madness, changing the expression in the eyes of its victims.) Therefore, I did not pay much attention to what they said then (it was March 1938) and was annoyed by the fashion in which they exclaimed and made long sentences and prophecies about Hitler. It seemed to me they almost enjoyed the subject; and that they seemed to delight in recounting what was happening in concentration camps. (It has needed war to bring about the blockade of Germany, which five years ago would have stifled Nazism and prevented the war itself.)

From Montreux I went to Nice to visit Tante Julie and Otto. Balthasar came running out when I arrived to welcome me with vivacity and real affection. As he took my valises out of the taxi he said: 'Mademoiselle Blanche, you are too thin,' speaking with a mixture of severity and solicitude. He himself had taken on a little extra stomach and his hair was greyer, but he still sprang about on his deft feet, and his eyes were as huge and dark, his skin as brown and smooth, as ever, and before we had entered the villa he had informed me that the owner of the little *pâtisserie* — a widow, the widow of the *pâtissier* — had a 'fancy for him'. He added, throwing a glance at himself in one of the mirrors in the hall, that he could not imagine why. I asked him if she were pretty, and his little expressive tolerant gesture of denial came with the last word of my question. 'Ah, no, Mademoiselle. But — one cannot eat Beauty in salad!' (*La beauté ne se mange pas dans la salade!*)

According to Tante Julie, Balthasar had 'cut himself in four pieces' to seduce *'la dame de la pâtisserie'*— the widow, Madame Paillot; she who knew also knew without a doubt that Balthasar had a considerable little sum in the bank. Tante Julie said that Balthasar pretended it was a question of love but … Not that they did not get on well together; she and Otto had seen them one evening at a café in Nice and they had a very delighted air, both of them.

It was while I was there that Balthasar announced to us his engagement. He did so while he was handing the coffee at the end of dinner. Naturally, he said, he would not willingly quit Madame la Baronne (he maintained Tante Julie's title in conversation although she had been married to Otto for several years); he would be sad to do that, and he knew well that Madame la Baronne and Signor Behrens (here he brought on its tray the lighter for Otto's cigar) would not find another such as he … On the other hand, if it should happen that in spite of himself he was obliged to leave …

We congratulated him. Tante Julie rolled him out a lewd question from the corner of her lips that made them both chuckle. Otto felicitated him on having found a 'real pearl'. 'She has charms, thy Madame Paillot. She has the most agreeable arms!'

I think it was probably in that same conversation that Balthasar told us that he and Madame Paillot contemplated going to America to start a *pâtisserie*. He said that 'They' had said to him, 'Go to America!' Otto asked him if They had also advised Madame Paillot? But it appeared that she had only received encouragement from her younger brother, still on earth and well established in a hairdresser's business in Santa Barbara.

When Balthasar left us Tante Julie said that she understood now why he had been praising to her for several months the *valet de chambre* of Lady Brigg, a neighbour, and had remarked that this same *valet de chambre* was anxious to find a new place. And also that Balthasar had twice forgotten to clean the silver, and in apologizing remarked: 'Perhaps I am getting too old for this work.'

During this visit I became more than ever sensible of Otto's good heart, and we felt a real friendship for one another. I used to work with him in the garden, which was his great interest there. He had remade the garden, among other reforms banishing the odious majolica vases from the top terrace (an act which it seems caused Tante Julie's only real fury against him.) One of his own treasures was a little Bavarian eighteenth-century Cérès which he had placed at the end of a walk bordered on each side with shrubs of pink camellias. She was a Cérès of a deliciously young plumpness; dressed in her stone straw hat, wearing a stone fichu and carrying her basket of carved flowers and wheat on her smooth forearm, she might have been mistaken for her own daughter.

I remember that it was while we were standing beside her during one of our six to seven o'clock walks in the garden that he said to me that I was 'wasting my youth'.

'Your youth and your beauty, Blanche.' I had told him about Vernon and Sohni, and unlike my father he had understood the impasse, for though more worldly than my father he is less detached. But he said that I must let myself be loved by another man. A woman must be loved, he said. To be at her best morally, a woman must be kissed at least twice a day with real tenderness.

'But if she doesn't love the man?'

'She will do so, gradually.'

'You're an optimist.'

'No, just a good psychologist. I speak less of the senses than of the emotions when I say a woman must be emotionally satisfied.'

I told him he was sentimental and optimistic. Many women

were naturally restless, ambitious, or promiscuous from vanity. I remarked that Leonora was an example of a restless woman. He answered that she was an excellent example of a woman who wasn't loved!

When we walked back towards the villa, the sea, below our terrace, was getting dark in contrast to the sunset that was taking possession of the sky.

※

I think I went back to Paris because Vernon might come there. Without reason I hoped that since I had had no letter from him at Les Délices I might find one at my *appartement*.

I did not. Only several bills, and a glossy Easter card from Annabelle and Pierre with a picture of a yellow chicken coming out of an egg, and Pauline in a fairly bad humour because I arrived before she had finished cleaning the *appartement*. (She had had the whole winter to clean it, for I had only let it for six weeks in the autumn.) In an effort to calm her I gave her news of Madame and Monsieur, and of Balthasar's engagement. This last piece of news evoked from Pauline not even a word, but instead a sound which expressed, in its brief exclaiming, a remarkable mixture of contempt and admiration. A few days later she said while she was laying the table in my bedroom (the only room she permitted me to use because of the cleaning), 'Marriage, that will be something new for Balthasar.' And, at another time, she said: 'America! That will cost them something, a journey to America! And if the boat sinks! ...'

Then suddenly Vernon came. He cabled that he was going direct to the *appartement* on the Quai d' Orléans (that had belonged to his family for several years, so that when Mr and Mrs Strudwick came to Paris they should live with one of its most beautiful views before their windows).

※

He came.

But all those days together in Paris were deliberate escape. For we both knew we must go back to our lives as we had made them: so that while we were together the least moments, those fragments of a second, in which one lifted a glass, lit a cigarette, stepped into an elevator, selected a handkerchief, had enchantment, and pain ...

✕

It was the beginning of April. The weather cannot have been beautiful every day; but it seems to me as if it had been; and sunshine lies over each day, like an exquisite glaze. Everything we looked at together, museums, lilies-of-the-valley, old prints on the *quais*, the statue of M Clemenceau, cheese on stalls in the markets in the Champs-Elysées, has this exquisite and shining tenderness. And everything we tasted — the *canard à la presse* at the Périgourdine, the coffee with *chicorée* at the 'zinc' at the corner of the Quai d'Orléans where we went when we had slept too late for breakfast, the veal in the Forêt de Saint-Germain, the bad *vin ordinaire* at Fontainebleau — has an unforgettable 'bouquet'.

We walked by the Seine on one of those mornings which seemed to be painted by a Chinese artist. (Notre-Dame was a tree grown immense and tortuous to look like a cathedral; the water of the river had no crack in it; and the blossoms were of enamel on the boutiques of the Quai aux Fleurs — my mother's Quai! I told Vernon this.)

We went into the Louvre, arm in arm as all lovers go into the Louvre. We must have passed through the room where there is a battle scene by Delacroix, because I know Vernon said something about Delacroix; and then he turned to meet my look and his expression changed ...

We were so profoundly happy. And so unhappy.

We went on walking about among the pictures. (Just as

we had in the Brera, in Milan, six years before. Only now we were aware of the pictures, in as well as of each other.)

Standing before the Masaccio which Vernon loved so much there was an elderly woman whose vague black felt hat had only one definite characteristic, a pale blue *hortensia*, whose unexpected freshness might have been painted by Fragonard. From the brim (which was undulating as are brims many times damp and dried again) hung a little curtain of black net, spangled here and there; and those black *paillettes*, their size, their little diamond shape, the spacing between them, were familiar to me. Then, as we moved closer, they recalled? . . . Tante Julie! A hat she'd had, many summers ago; a hat that had a black veil with *paillettes* as if it had been spattered with chips of jet.

And then I saw that it was Mademoiselle Dubois! I exclaimed her name. 'But ... Mademoiselle Dubois?' She turned, and her yellowed bewildered-hare face stared at me through the sophisticated veil.

'Mademoiselle Blanche?' Her eyelids, and even her features (that had become more softened and lengthened), seemed to twitch; and such a shyness seized her that it was painful to be its cause. She became red, as if from fright; and when I was presenting Vernon to her, she darted at him between the now quivering sequins of her veil a series of expressions of an almost wild alarm. In my desire to help her to recover, I began to answer to her what must be the kind of question she would wish (but was still unable) to ask. I told her that Tante Julie had been living mostly in Nice, since her illness of six years ago, and that she had married again, a Monsieur Behrens who was very amiable and distinguished. I told her that my father was in excellent health and lived still in his villa in Italy. Here she gave a little gasp; not from nervousness, but in remembrance, I imagine, of Italy. I told her that I had travelled, and that I had now Tante Julie's *appartement*. She listened, with less apprehension and increasing interest, and gradually (it was rather like pushing a car to make its engine start) her own questions began to form themselves. So that, when I had begun to tell her that the long room where she used to do the mending for Madame la Baronne was now my dining-room, she interrupted. 'But, of course, I was stupid … I was so much astonished … just now … Of course, I heard it, Madame la Baronne is now married!'

I told her also of the changes I had made in the *appartement*; and then I said she must come and see me; and added that I had supposed that she was still in South Africa with the same people. (This was untrue. I had completely forgotten her existence.) She replied to this that she had been back in Paris for a long time, but had not wished to disturb me. She said the family in South Africa had not been 'very nice' (*pas tout a fait gentil*). Her manner seemed too 'shy' as she said this; and I saw that that minimum of pride which she had, poor thing, had been in some way outraged. (Poor, plain, elderly, and rather stupid, she must so often have lacked consideration, or even justice.) Vernon, at this same moment, glanced at his watch and asked if Mademoiselle Dubois would not do us the honour of lunching with us? And somehow he managed to make this request so gradually and with such consideration and persuasion that she was scarcely alarmed, and, after a hesitation which was caused directly by her natural slowness in adjusting her imagination to new projects, she admitted that, indeed, 'But yes indeed' she would like to … 'But willingly …'

Vernon chose a restaurant where one ate deliciously, where the atmosphere was tranquil and expensive, but not at all worldly. We had a table in a corner, and Mademoiselle Dubois sat between us. During luncheon Vernon asked her: 'Where do you live?' I had not asked her. Somehow she had always come from an address that Tante Julie must have known. With the indifference of youth, which is generally without interest in the details of undistinguished lives, I had never imagined Mademoiselle Dubois *chez-soi*.

But when she answered Vernon:— 'I have a little room, a quite little room. Rue Lincoln, Monsieur,' then I seemed to remember that she had, in fact, referred once (in some conversation with father, no doubt) to 'my little room — my altogether little room.' Vernon said to her, with that sort of sweet affectionate mockery which has charmed more difficult women than Cécile Dubois, that she was extremely chic if she lived there! (As he said this I remembered the *appartement* of Georges Charnaux was in the Rue Lincoln.)

Mademoiselle Dubois was explaining to Vernon that what she had, *hélas*, was no more than a little attic high up, 'very high up, Monsieur, and the *ascenseur* stops two floors below.'

The end of this conversation was that Vernon asked to be allowed to call upon her: and, excited beneath the customary hesitancy of her manner, she said she would, indeed, be enchanted. But it would not be at all … not at all (here the *hortensia* shook) what Monsieur was accustomed to … Then she invited me to come also; but evidently troubled by conflict between an idea that my coming would make Vernon's visit less strange, and another idea that my coming, after all these years of acquaintance, on a new social level, would be strange also. She added, after she had asked me to come: 'But would it be agreeable to Mademoiselle Blanche to come?' I reassured her as much as I could about this; ashamed that it should be Vernon who proposed this visit.

So we went, during the next few days. She invited us, in a little formal note sent to the Strudwick *appartement*, saying that she would expect us, 'with the greatest pleasure,' towards six o'clock.

We walked up the Champs-Elysées and on an evening that had a sweet disturbing warmth. It was as if a golden dust had been shaken into the air.

Her address, as she had told us, was in a 'chic' building. And the concierge's lodge reflected its prosperity, curtained with thick, clean lace, and crowded with heavy furniture so that there seemed only space for the concierge and his wife to sit close to their table. However, when Vernon opened the door and put his head in, the man got up, but sat down again when we demanded Mademoiselle Dubois, whose rent evidently brought in a poor percentage, and he only muttered the information. But his wife lifted her glance from her sewing and regarded us with interest. 'Mademoiselle Dubois awaits visitors,' she stated. Evidently she had had this remarkable news confided to her by Mademoiselle Dubois herself. She repeated her husband's information, graciously, impressed perhaps by our worldly appearance.

We took the *ascenseur*. And then we climbed. And it was in truth in the attic that we were received by Mademoiselle Dubois, more breathless with timidity than we were with mounting her stairs. But to her many apologies, mingled with little acclamations, Vernon replied by expressions of the most sincere pleasure at being with her, and as he admired her view, her little Empire sofa, her freesias, the little fan hung on the low wall in a glass case, her nervousness evidently gave way to pleasure.

Since then I have often visited the *petite chambre* and so it is difficult to know which things I recollect from that day. Certainly the wallpaper, whose imitation of turquoise-blue striped white brocade extends only half-way up the room because of the slope of the eaves; and that little sofa (inherited from a grandmother) with its gold claw feet, upholstered in a violet plush, which must have been chosen by Mademoiselle

Dubois herself; for this same 'violet' reappears here and there — in the two glass vases on the chimneypiece, in the sateen tablecloth which shows violet through the overcloth of écru lace and linen (which I recollected she bought in Venice), and in a bow which has always been on the neck of a white china cat that sits upright with an undeniably common air, on one of the many little fragile tables. (Each of these tables has upon it a little cover, of Italian linen work, or, perhaps an imitation of Tante Julie's taste, of Japanese machine-made embroidery.)

But the china cat recalls the question of Eugénie, who appeared that day while her mistress was pouring out tea for me, and port for Vernon. (It was a new bottle, in evidence with glasses on a tray of turquoise blue edged with wickerwork which had been bought '*dans le Army-and-Navy Store tout près de Victoria Station*.') Eugénie went directly to Vernon, and seating herself upon the arm of his chair regarded his face with attention. She was a white cat, and it appears that the white china cat was bought by Marcel (the nephew!) in compliment to her. But in fact it is only in whiteness that it resembles Eugénie.

For the china cat is *canaille* in its surprising mouth, in its flat head and exaggerated ears and flirting blue eyes; whereas Eugénie is distinction itself, aloofness itself, and has eyes yellow-green like Pernod.

Her relation with her 'mistress' was demonstrated at once by the assiduity of Mademoiselle Dubois, who brought a small bowl of milk and put it on the carpet beside the armchair, murmuring in a tone I didn't know in her, and recommending the milk like a headwaiter occupying himself with his most distinguished client. But Eugénie continued to regard Vernon's features; perhaps with admiration, perhaps with contempt. I remember that Vernon laughed at her (Vernon has the laugh of a man of quite another figure — a stout man's sonorous laughter); and this sound produced a very delicate emphasis of hostility in Eugénie's whole person; and, with a dignity of departure, as if she were slowly gathering up invisible skirts, she stood up, gave him a final glance over the shoulder, and descended from the arm of the chair to the ground, where, after much cold and refined hesitation, she bent over the bowl of milk, her eyes expressing no pleasure at all, but her tongue steadily although delicately employed.

'She is pretty, isn't she?' Mademoiselle Dubois asked us. It was easy to agree: the svelte whiteness of the cat, and its air of luxury, were in contrast to her owner's black dress with buttons fastening the bodice from neck to waist; and whose net and lace collar I was sure I remembered from fifteen years before. (1 seemed to recall that collar on the blue linen that she wore each year in the gardens of my father's villa.)

During the conversation I asked her if she had had a cat 'in those days'? But she informed us that it was only since three years, when 'a little inheritance' had come to her from her mother, that she had been able to give up any work — except 'making knitted things from time to time' for certain ladies who remained 'always very good to her'; and finding herself so much *chez-soi*, she had bought a kitten for company. She forgot her shyness while she told us about the 'sweetness' and naughtiness of Eugénie as a kitten. She said also that she had desired a white cat ever since she had read, as a girl, a story by Théophile Gautier, about a white cat that had a basket lined with blue satin. And then, rising and going to an alcove of the room which was hidden by a striped curtain, she brought out a basket containing a folded blue satin eiderdown. During the moment that she held the curtain aside I saw her own iron bedstead, a *prie dieu* on the wall beside it, and beside that the photograph of her nephew Marcel as a baby (which she used to have on a table of her room in Italy).

While she was talking to Vernon he happened to say

something about his returning soon to America, and she turned to me to ask if I was going also. And I realized that she thought Vernon was my husband. I said that I had to remain in Paris for a time, and made a change of subject.

When we were going down in the *ascenseur* I said to him: 'How stupid of me not to have explained that you were only a friend.' He didn't answer. I saw that suddenly he was having one of his *crises* of depression, when I could do nothing for him.

When we came out into the street I noticed that Georges Charnaux's was exactly opposite and I wondered whether he and Mademoiselle Dubois, as neighbours, ever saw each other in the street. And I reflected if Charnaux knew her, he would discover in her, no doubt, one of those 'minor' characters of his, sketched with a clever malice which is praised, by his critic-friends, as discerning wit.

✕

Vernon didn't go back to New York as soon as he had expected. Some business kept him in Paris and Le Havre. But it was worse than if he had gone; for Leonora cabled that she was coming over for six weeks, to join him. I was with him at his *appartement* when the cable arrived. I think it was during a conversation we had after that that Vernon said Leonora could have been different if she had been able to have a child; and I realized that this was a real reason why he felt affection for her — that is to say, from a masculine pity. In some way, because of this remark of Vernon's, we had a quarrel; and also I suppose because we were both so unhappy. Vernon became sullen first, because I said I was going immediately, since Leonora would be here soon; then when I began packing my things he stood leaning against the door of the bedroom, his hands in his pockets, looking down at me with an air of amused cruelty in his black eyes. A cruelty that hurt him also, for he looked ill. I knelt by my open suitcase folding my clothes clumsily because I couldn't see clearly, and my fingers were trembling. I accused him of enjoying the double situation and of being sentimental and egoist, and in the end the effect of what I said was that he was leaning over me with his hands at my throat. And then suddenly he was in tears, his head was on my shoulder. I held him in my arms, but still with the horrible despair of our quarrel in my heart; and this despair went on for hours after. (And even now, as I write, I can feel the sick physical evocation of that despair.)

※

When Leonora arrived I left Paris and went to some friends at Etretat. It was on my return that I heard from Cécile Dubois that Madame Vernon had been to visit her and had been very kind and ordered three sports sweaters. I saw that Mademoiselle Dubois was perplexed, and while she was telling me of Madame Vernon's graciousness her soft startled glances were asking me questions, though too timidly to expect any answers.

I wondered what I should tell her. Then, as one may with a child, I found that the necessary simplicity of my explanation expressed the truth. I said that Vernon and I loved each other but that he could not leave his wife because they had an adopted child who loved him more than her.

Cécile Dubois seemed to reflect on what I said. I saw her perplexed look on the knitting (one of those sports sweaters, in ice-blue) that was on her lap. Whether any moral judgments (she is Catholic) or half comprehensions of physical love were part of her reflection I do not know. Certainly she hesitated: but only I think because she would have liked to find in her modest vocabulary some way of expressing to me that, in any case, whatever she was capable or incapable of comprehending, she was our friend. But suitable phrases must have failed her:

and all that she could find to say was, shaking her head: '*C'est bien triste . . .*' But she did not say it sadly. She said it with dignity and deep affection.

※

On September 3rd, when the war was declared, I was in the Touraine at the château of some friends. I was doing a portrait of my hostess, for during the last two years I had worked seriously at painting, and was enjoying it. My hostess (Denise Guillaume) was sitting for me when her husband came in with the news. We had expected it, and an English boy who was staying had left three days before. All the same the shock was intense and horrible. I put down my palette and we all went out into the garden. We stood on the terrace saying little phrases like 'So it's come', and 'It was impossible to avoid it'. A road passes the gates. Through the tall ironwork of those gates we could see the people of the village passing, on their way from the church.

I do not know the Guillaumes well. They had been brought to see a few of my portraits the year before in Paris, by Hugo. They had liked them, and had suggested I should paint Madame Guillaume's portrait. In fact I had been a little bored staying with them. A life of rich industrialists in their summer Château; too gravely snob to be gay. Monsieur Guillaume owned an immense iron factory somewhere. She dressed at Lanvin and was a handsome blonde with taste only in dress.

At lunch she was absolutely silent, and then, suddenly, burst into tears. Her husband was embarrassed and impatient, but showed a certain tenderness as he led her out of the room. I see her blonde high coiffure, her fine shoulders shaking in her pink linen dress. Late that evening I went to her room to say my good-byes, as I was going back to Paris the next day. I found her almost unrecognizable from crying. She did not get up from the armchair in which she had been crouching, but when I came to her she seized my hand and asked me to forgive her and cried out that she was afraid for someone she loved. Hugo told me after that her love affair with a German naval attaché in Paris was well known.

When I got back to Paris I found that letter from Annabelle telling me that Pierre had been mobilized and asking me, if I had no other projects, to come and stay again with her.

April 10th

Yesterday I had this letter from Vernon, from New York:

I am on my way to France (direct) to join Aunt Mary Strudwick's Hospital Unit, ambulance driving. This is the best I can get. As a job it may mean awfully little to do — worse luck. Or it may not. At any rate, when there is any fighting I'll have a chance to help. Leonora's already in France. Did you know? — Nursing. I think at Biarritz, but the outfit she was going to hoped to go up behind the Maginot Line. Sohni's staying here with my mother. She adores him. Queer when you think how strong her habit of anti-Semitism was.

Write to me care of my bank, in Paris.

Doesn't this war make you wonder if we, I mean the free citizens of our Northern Democracies, have been, after all, such Just Stewards of our great good opportunities? Now and again I get a kind of grim angle on what's happening, and see it as a logical retribution for all the wrong we've all just allowed to go on ... for the inertia of imagination that's made us all able to tolerate all the obvious faults in our social and political arrangements. In fact, retribution for a lack of moral splendour all round!

Part 4

June 6th

In Annabelle's house, Sussex.

I see that a whole section of my retrospect ended with that letter from Vernon, written early in April.

Between then and now so much has happened. Already the months of last winter, first in that mediocre villa on the edge of the cliff, then here with Annabelle, are unreal. Equally incredible are the two weeks, in Paris and in Nice, which followed that telegram from Cécile Dubois. That extraordinary telegram.

Now I am back here with Annabelle in Sussex, writing in the bow window of my pretty room.

Across the lawn the children in their summer cottons are having tea at a table under the copper-beech tree. The Czech girl, in her short-sleeved dress of scarlet and white cotton stripes, sits with them. Camilla Blanche is in the little chair of her own that Pierre painted yellow for her last summer, when she was still in her cradle. Camilla Blanche's hair shines on her round head, her face is like those sun-painted peaches of Provence. She is beating the blue tablecloth with a spoon. The tapping sound comes across the lawn. Her brother speaks to her with the authority of his five years. 'No, no, Camilla!'

Camilla Blanche is no longer the miniature enigmatic visitor to life with the face of mother-of-pearl and the flying, strange little smiles whom I lived with in the villa last autumn. She says entire words now in a witty velvety tone. And when she stands for a whole minute on her feet she looks round, in expectation of wonder and admiration.

※

I remember how when the Czech girl (that works here now) brought me that telegram I thought it might be from Vernon. Then I read it. Sent from Paris: COME AT ONCE IF POSSIBLE. CECILE DUBOIS.

It was unimaginable that she would send such a telegram unless for the most urgent reasons. And even if, poor darling, she was in the last despair of poverty, or gravely ill, without hope, even then she would not have enough egoism to derange a friend.

It was in the end of April that that telegram came. (The Finnish war already over by two months. The war in Norway almost over … The war in Holland, in Belgium, in France, not yet begun.)

I will not narrate details of my difficulties in getting to Paris. Sufficient to say that it was through the influence of friends of Hugo that I was able to go at once. I dined with Hugo the night before I left London. He is in the Censorship. I found him changed since the war began. An inner sadness seemed to be sickening him, making lines on his face, and darkening the skin around his brilliant-blue lazy eyes. During dinner he said that, however banal the phrase had become, he was haunted by 'The lights are going out all over Europe'.

After dinner we stood in the shadow street, the dark shapes of taxis sliding past, a blue phantom omnibus passing across the end of the street. Above us the sky was brilliant with stars.

We had managed to be talkative in the restaurant. But now we were both too sad to speak. We embraced, clinging to each other in our desolation of heart. Then he turned, swinging away from me, and, after two paces, he was part of the dark.

June 7th

I had telegraphed to inform Mademoiselle Dubois when I should arrive, and at the *appartement* I found a message from her inviting me to come to her for tea towards six o'clock. Evidently then it was not illness that had made her summon me! I had time to unpack, and to look out of my window on to the side street with that little anguished recognition of all its familiarities. Opposite was the lingerie-shop window full of rose colours where Tante Julie had often commended half-dozens of nightdresses fragile with lace, sewn by just such girls as sat in the window opposite, above the shop — girls with bent heads, the cheeks much rouged, black dresses, intent fingers.

Now and then on the pavement a soldier passed, like an echo of a sound one hadn't heard.

Why indeed had I been called by Mademoiselle Dubois? As I walked up the Champs-Elysées I asked myself whether, in connection with a possible bombardment, she desired me to execute some precise if humble bequest. To take charge of Eugénie perhaps?

The *ascenseur* in her building in the Rue Lincoln had not ceased its habit of complaining as it raised itself four floors. And the shabby staircase by which I climbed to the highest landing was even more depressed since its one window had been stuck with black paper, and only a greyish light rose from below mingled with the old smells of the concierge's dinners.

I had scarcely taken my finger off the bell of Mademoiselle Dubois's door when it was opened, and she exclaimed: 'Ah, Mademoiselle Blanche ... my dear Mademoiselle Blanche!' and I was once more in the room with the blue ribbon-striped brocade wallpaper, and the many little tables covered with Italian linen and false Japanese embroideries; and Eugénie, no less luxuriously white, no less sardonic in her full maturity, sitting on the purple plush sofa, ready to receive me with indifference.

I had only to glance at Mademoiselle Dubois's face, turned

now to the light, to see that she was excited or agitated: her hare-eyes gleamed above her long flushed cheeks, and, proof that she was dominated by some strong feeling, she was not shy. She repeated phrases of welcome, asked me to sit down, asked me how things were in England since the war had begun, asked me how that beautiful Madame Annabelle was and all her children — but did not wait for my replies between these questions. From the fact that her dress was neat, that she had pinned a little pale blue velvet bow in her newly waved grey hair, I concluded that her agitation was not caused by sorrow.

She offered me port or tea, and I accepted the former, seeing the bottle. (Was it the same bottle she had opened for Vernon a year ago?) With the bottle in one hand and the glass in the other, she went for a moment to the window, which was open at the bottom, and looked down into the street, an expression on her face which made me wonder if she was one of those war victims who detect in the familiar life of accustomed neighbours increasing indications that they are spies.

But she came away from the window without any comment and while she poured out my port I asked her if she had heard from Vernon, as he was now in France, somewhere in the North-east, I thought, with his ambulance. I added that his wife was also in France, nursing in a hospital, and that the little boy they had adopted was in Boston with Madame Strudwick. I told her all this because, as I have shown, both Vernon and I had been able to confide in Cécile Dubois, not because she would understand, but because she would not; that is to say, she had always been too simple in thought, too timid, to do anything but accept, in her unquestioning affection and gratitude and love, whatever we told her; ready, like a good children's nurse, to murmur in sympathy for our difficulties, and to mutter in anger against whoever should hurt us. So that now I was surprised that she did not show her usual intense interest in what I told her, except to repeat: 'Madame Vernon …' after my mention of Leonora. Then she asked me if I had had a good journey, and asked me the time. It must have been between half-past six and half-past seven, and I suppose I told her so.

Then she went back again to the window. And then suddenly made an urgent gesture to me to come and stand beside her. An intensity emanating from her mind would have caught at me if that movement of her arm hadn't.

She was looking down, not on to the street, but at a window on the first floor of the building opposite. 'There they are!!!' she whispered. '*There they are!!!*'

And then I saw them; or rather, I saw her: by the open window, putting on a pair of white gloves, her profile turned to talk to the man who stood at her shoulder.

The whispering in my ear: 'She has been there every day, since a week …' (A whisper, though indeed there was only Eugénie to hear, behind us on the sofa.) 'The first day I saw her go in. I saw her suddenly in the street down there. One day, the second day, they came to the window, and …' (a hesitation) 'and she was wearing a sort of pink wrapper' (*une espèce de peignoir rose*) 'and he …'

The whispering stopped. 'One could see that they were very intimate,' added the whisper, and with a side glance I perceived the colour flushed up to the intent shining stare. 'It was then that I telegraphed to you, that same evening.'

I forget if, or how, I explained my next movement. No doubt I acted exactly as my hostess had expected, for she was opening the door for me to go, and I remember her saying several times that in 'no other case' would she have mixed herself up with such matters (evidently a protest to her own conscience). And I remember that even as I found myself in the street Leonora came out of the door opposite but did not see me, and began to walk towards the Champs-Elysées.

June 9th

Leonora was already at the corner of the street when I caught her up and called her name. She turned; started; then said my name, and, after a second, gave me a smile showing her white teeth. I told her I wanted to speak to her. My agitation must have been evident. Probably it calmed her after the shock she hardly betrayed at seeing me. She said: 'Come on, then, and see me at my hotel.' I said that the nearest café would do. We crossed the Champs-Elysées and sat down at a front table of a café opposite. I asked her at once if she was still determined not to let Vernon take Sohni. She looked startled at this question, and at the same time a little vague, as if she had almost forgotten the whole question. But then, as she seemed to recollect what Sohni 'stood for', her face took on that expression of tranquil serious arrogance, and she simply repeated what she had said in New York: 'I personally have promised to be responsible for him.'

I didn't answer. My heart was beating less rapidly. I made myself pause. Then I said that since she was Georges Charnaux's mistress, Vernon now had the right to divorce her.

Any real respect for Leonora begins from the second in which she understood what I had said. After a deliberate hesitation she asked: 'How did you know?'

I explained. Her comment was, sarcastically, 'Blackmail?'

I replied that she had deliberately used her 'right' over Sohni to keep up an appearance of sanctity in her own marriage.

She coloured at this. But she only asked: 'Would he divorce me?' as if this were part of a calculation she was doing in her own mind.

People were passing us with the sunset on their faces and long shadows tied to their feet.

Leonora put down several statements as if they were cards on which she might bet. One was that she would not allow

Vernon to divorce her. Another was that she had a 'supreme responsibility' towards Sohni. Another was that neither Vernon nor I would understand her relations with Charnaux. She put down these cards with a perfect assurance. And yet it seemed to me it was an assurance of habit, an assurance based on the past.

At one moment she looked at the crowd passing to and fro in front of our table. And a quite different sequence of thoughts must have made her say in a quite other voice that tomorrow she would be going back to her hospital. She turned her face away to look up toward the Arc de Triomphe.

At last she turned round again, leaned quietly towards me, clasped her hands together on the table, and looked down at them while she said to me in her hard quick voice that 'her conscience was perfectly clear.'

This remark seemed to me to have no real connection with the situation, and I repeated that if she did not give up Sohni — 'whom you do not love,' I said, 'but whom you have chosen to identify with your own exaggerated self-respect' — Vernon could oblige her to do so by, simply, a threat of a divorce which her same 'self-respect' feared. I said finally: 'You desire to remain admirable. You do not think you will seem so if you appear in the newspapers as the mistress of Charnaux. You yourself have made this crisis. You could have given Vernon and myself happiness, and Sohni security, five years ago. But there again your self-respect was more important.' (While I was saying all this I felt it was fortunate that Vernon was not present. Because his chivalry, as insensitive sometimes to real values as her self-respect, would have made it impossible for him to threaten Leonora!)

While I was speaking the lovely light of the evening — that light of the 'divine hour' — made a transparent copper patina over her masklike features, her big pearls, the white collar of her dark dress. Light, to me, has the same disturbing power as Music. And it was perhaps the light that influenced Leonora, the deepening golden air penetrating through her hard personality to some quite other personality that lived in her also; that had been evoked perhaps (this is what I came to suppose) by the first 'unmixed emotion' she had ever had in her life, a real passion for Georges Charnaux. For, suddenly, while remaining perfectly, precisely, in the same pose, she was crying. The tears brimmed out of her Egyptian-shaped eyes. She moved her gloved hand and took a handkerchief out of her bag: and slowly dabbed it against each of her cheeks. She was unaware of the crowds passing us. She did not notice my surprise. Then she said: 'I'm sorry, Blanche.' Sorry, for what? I wondered! Not for her own behaviour, that would not be in her character. Then she said nervously that she supposed that just now when I caught her up in the street I had produced a 'reflex and habitual reaction' in her. She said that everything had changed for her lately. She said that only since she got to France this time, since the war, she'd realized that there was — I expected the word — an 'affinity' between her and Georges Charnaux. Her phraseology was evidently unable to express something altogether real that she wanted to say, not only to me, but to herself. And this clumsiness touched me, more than her tears, whose origin might have been self-pity. She said: 'You see, Blanche, I ...' She baulked it. And I stated for her: 'You're in love with Charnaux.'

She bent her head. 'Yes.'

'You're in love with each other,' I insisted for her. She answered 'Yes,' her expression changing in response to some tremor of sensual remembering, so that I saw, suddenly, the woman in her who had found in (that odious!) Charnaux what she hadn't found in Vernon, or any other man. Automatically she had translated her sensations into a word like 'affinity'. And equally, she hadn't the least apprehension that this late passion of hers that was her first love must be to Charnaux, that expert amorist, an opportunity to marry a 'rich American'. She now said that, in fact, Georges wanted to marry her.

I said: 'Why are you unhappy then?' for I wanted to know why she thought she had cried.

'It's all so — difficult. I feel it'd be selfish, wrong perhaps.'

I emphasized the irony: 'To do what you want? And let us, Vernon and me, do what we want?' And then I asked her, curiously, whether, if I hadn't found her out (almost *'en flagrant délit,'* I said, and she winced), she would have continued only to have a secret *affaire?* To which she replied — her tears had ceased, but she was still in a visible state of uncertainty between her two personalities — that 'it was true that one felt old ties were sacred'.

And then I realized her true reason for temporizing (I realized it more precisely, I am sure, than she did herself). What *might* happen, for her, was Vernon being killed. Ambulance is not a safe job, as events have shown, whereas the Ministry of Information, where Charnaux was, could not be said to have a high rate of casualties. Widowhood was more dignified, even more beautiful, than divorce. But, I added, I am sure she did not really *think* such possibilities, and was only influenced unconsciously by them.

However, I made sure before I left her that she would divorce Vernon; and give up Sohni. I drove her in a taxi to her hotel: and then went back to my own *appartement*; just in time to go to the cellar below it, for there was an *alerte* while I was paying the taxi and the sound, very distantly, of our anti-aircraft guns.

※

When the All Clear was sounded and I could go upstairs to my *appartement*, I wrote to Vernon, telling him about Leonora and Charnaux and what had happened. My plan was to wait in Paris until I had his reply, which might take several days. As I was writing the concierge's wife came in with a letter for me from Tante Julie, in answer to a telegram that I had sent, telling her that I would be in Paris. In her letter she told me that Otto's heart was worse, and asked me if I could come, even for a few days.

June 10th

I went by a night train to Nice, and arrived at Les Délices on such a festal morning as the Mediterranean arranges in May. This brilliance followed me into the hall, whose parquet was strewn with diamonds from the bevelling of the mirrors; and Tante Julie came out of the door that leads to the kitchens in a white peignoir that was caught in the cascade of sunlight that poured from the window half-way up the stairs. She caught my hands in hers, which were cold.

Then she led me into the *salon* where the shutters were closed so that our low voices should not be heard upstairs; and, replying to my questions, said that the doctor had been again yesterday evening and had said that although the heart itself was little worse than it had been for several months, the whole resistance had grown less. She added, the tears straining the darkened crescents below her eyes: 'I don't think he desires to live … The good doctor is of my opinion.' She added: 'It is this *filth* of a war!'

Her hair was pulled back, its flat brass contours defining the fine massiveness of her skull. Her skin was pallid and dry from lack of sleep, and the lines deep and heavy from her nostrils to the corners of her mouth; and one could see how massive her jawbone was, holding up the flesh, and how the eyes owed their real beauty to that wide arching of their sockets, and the solidity of the forehead above them.

She repeated: 'This — war' — using the adjective that Otto would never permit. And then, with a brutality and bitterness that had long ago, generations ago, discounted any glory or any sense in war, she added: 'But we shall win ...' And, in that moment, I saw the essential peasant in Tante Julie, ready to defend: not a flag — one can well leave flags and symbols to the Germans; not a government — one knows very well the government that robs you; not even the soil itself — which repays grudgingly, which uses your strength and cheats your hope; nor Liberty — as one wrote it in class, and learned about it from the excited history discourses of a young master whose cuffs were frayed, whose shoes were cracked, and who spoke of France with passion. No; profoundly mistrustful of ideas or ideals, resentful of politics, contemptuous and fearful of war, what Tante Julie was ready to defend sulkily, stubbornly and to death, was quite simply *the habit of being French*. As a peasant she would be, to the death, French in her good sense, in her ingrained avarice (caused by toil for small gain), in her warmth of heart (never exaggerated to excessive generosity), in her matter-of-fact sensuality, and in that sturdy acceptance of life which had no need to sentimentalize its cruelties. (And, equally, a *demi-mondaine* she would be to the death, expert and gay in love, moderate in excess, provident in luxury, tolerant in friendship, and as courageous in losses as flamboyant in gains.)

I asked if Otto would be able to see me, and she replied that indeed he had asked to see me. She added that she had told him I was coming here for a little holiday.

As she took me to my same room that I always had, I asked her about Balthasar. She told me she had had two letters from him; that he was in Santa Barbara, he and his wife, and that their little business was prospering. I said I wondered if his Spirits had told him the war was coming, and Tante Julie replied that he had no doubt foreseen it for himself, as anyone could.

When she came to fetch me to conduct me to Otto's room,

she was 'made-up' and the coiffeur had been. She had on a white cloth costume and much jewellery and a pair of purple espadrilles. She asked me, with a little anxiety, if she was 'well' and I understood that she desired to please Otto.

We found him propped against two pillows and the nurse went into the next room, leaving us with him. He didn't look ill as I had expected, only very clear-skinned and a little transparent, as if he were in a shadow; and in the pleasant room whose light came through the red and white awning on the balcony I had a first impression of tranquillity and clean linen and the perfume of jasmine from out of doors. It was only when I had sat down beside his bed ('Sit near to him, he makes less effort to speak') that I realized that he was as if weighed down to the last tone of his voice, and to the least movement of his eyes, by an immense fatigue. When I kissed him the effort or emotion of receiving me brought tears to his eyes; when he had said: *'Ma petite Blanche, tu es toujours a belle,'* and was holding my hand, I could feel, after he had spoken, the absolute lassitude of the cool fingers in mine. Tante Julie went into the adjoining room with the nurse; and I began to talk to him so that he should not speak.

I told him of my long winter, remote from reality, at first so oddly alone with Annabelle's baby and nurse. His eyes smiled faintly at my description. I told him of Annabelle and of Hugo ... and finally answered his 'And Vernon?' All the time I had known he would ask, and had known what I would reply.

I said: 'Leonora has consented to a divorce. And she will give up the child.'

He took a breath slowly and quietly. Then he whispered in that tranquil room: 'So you will ... get married.'

I told him that Vernon was with Mary Strudwick's Ambulance Unit. At first I thought he didn't hear, for he had ceased to look at me and was staring, his eyelids drooped over his brown eyes, toward the windows. But after a silence he said: 'Now there is only … the war to separate you.' His hand moved and clasped mine, and relaxed again. Then I saw a faint colour rising under the transparency of his skin, and his so charming smile showed for a moment under his elegant white moustache, and he made the following sentence: 'I have a sort of certainty for you …' and added with simplicity, 'that you will be happy.'

The nurse looked in to say I must not remain but visit him again in the afternoon.

When I did so he seemed to me paler, and the expression of his eyes less serene, as if his thoughts had been doing him harm. He asked me how I had found Paris — and how the people seemed in the streets, there, and here in Nice also. (For he knew I had been out with Tante Julie during the afternoon.) I told him how hopeful everyone was. But he questioned: 'There is no bad news?' (This was the second or third of May.) I told him, no, nothing new. He accepted this, and said, as if in excuse, that lying there he became too imaginative. He said also: 'While I lie here the lovely places of Europe come to me like ghosts.' I remember he spoke of 'such a massacre of innocent gaiety'.

June 12th

I stayed three days. I was with Otto for a little time every day. Tante Julie and I made little shopping expeditions together in Nice. I bought several foolish and pretty things, a round *bonbonnière* of pink satin, garnished with Valenciennes lace, a bed jacket of white ostrich feathers, a delicious belt made of straw and false pearls — perhaps as souvenirs. And Tante Julie bought linen, sheets, woollen stuffs by the metre, kitchen saucepans in enamel, and everywhere jars of her special skin food. She refused to pay the augmented prices (imposed already for all such things), and succeeded in paying only pre-war prices by a mixture of obstinacy and pathos; for the tradespeople had all known her for many years and when she admitted, tears in her eyes, that Monsieur was no better, they would shake their heads, and the sincerity of their sympathy would make them vulnerable to a sudden '*Eh bien*, I take these three pairs of sheets for 1000 francs.'

She would recount to Otto her bargains — or her wise resistance to profiteering (Tante Julie for some reason liked the English word and always pronounced it 'profee'tering' — and I remembered that once years before she had described de Montal in a hostile recollection as a 'dirty profeeter'). And it was evident that Otto enjoyed these accounts, given in immense detail with all that she, Julie, had said, verbatim. Even in his increasing obscurity of sadness and weakness, I could see how he still enjoyed: 'And I, I said to him, "One hundred and fifty francs a metre!!? What do you take me for? An American Tourist?" — The dirty toad! "And do you prefer that I go to the Maison Girouard at Cannes, where I can get just such a *lainage*, even better, for ninety-five?" Naturally he did not know, the dirty fellow, that I had been last week to the Maison Girouard and bought up what remained — you remember, Otto, that yellow face cloth that I got there for two hundred and ten francs the metre. So then he said, "One hundred and thirty-five?" "Ah — no," I said, "you make me an honest price or I go elsewhere," and he went to consult his wife — the poor woman, I had talked with her often, she is changed to break your heart — since five weeks she has no news of her son; he is *aviateur*, you know that, Chéri? The poor things, I had the heart full when I left them. Eh bien, I paid one hundred and fifteen! Which isn't bad, you think? For after all I would have paid twice that at the Maison Girouard, but one must admit that Girouard is not cheap, and the tablecloths I got from him I would have got for less, but much less in Paris. I told him that. "Ah," he said to me, "in Paris it is different." "How different?" I have said. "The only difference it is that in Paris one is honest!" You have seen the tablecloths, Chéri. But they are really pretty! Blanche, *ma petite*, go downstairs and in the salon on the sofa at the end you will see the package of them.'

Tante Julie would not have two nurses: and I do not know how much it was economy, how much devotion which caused her to take over the nursing of Otto at night. I think he usually dozed through the night, and hardly spoke to her. And she said to me that again and again when he looked so quiet and pale, above all in the hours of dawn, she was seized by a terror. I tiptoed in one night after she had just dismissed the nurse, and found her sitting in an armchair with a lighted candle on a table beside her and a book unopened on her knee. She never read, indeed I don't remember ever seeing her read anything except a newspaper or a fashion paper. She was wearing that white peignoir that she wore on the morning I arrived. For some seconds she did not see me come in. Her eyelids were lowered so that her eyes shone in long unseeing slits, and in the candlelight her face and the gold-white bulk of her body were already immobilized by fatigue. In the shadow, on the other side of the room, Otto's bed and sheets seemed to be sketched faintly in white chalk, and I could hear him breathing. Then my silent presence made her start awake.

'What is it ... *what is it?*' she whispered. '*Ah* — it's Blanche.' There was such a look of fear in her green eyes. She said nervously: 'I had a bad dream.' She glanced at the gilt clock on the chimneypiece. 'And yet I can't have been asleep, it is only two minutes since I sat down.' Then she glanced at the candle for more reliable confirmation, and said: 'Look, it was a fresh candle and it has only just begun to burn.' She shivered. 'He's asleep, isn't he? He's *asleep?*' I reassured her in a whisper. She turned her face to look at me; and some trick of the candlelight that, a moment before, had defined all the lines and sagging of age now, by another trick, made her beautiful as she was when I used to go with my father to visit her, and she paraded her copper-winged head from mirror to mirror through the little *salons*. She shivered again and muttered: 'I don't like to dream. These times give one bad dreams.' I perceived that the book on her knees was a prayerbook. I stayed with her for a few minutes but then she urged me to go back to bed.

June 13th

The next morning I had a telegram from Vernon saying he had forty-eight hours' leave to go to Paris and would meet me there.

I went in to say good-bye to Otto. He had already heard the news, but he did not speak of it. Another lovely morning was on the balcony with the striped awning and the room smelled of jasmine, as on the first morning of my visit. I said that I would write to him. He held my hand, and could not decide to relinquish it. Both of us felt that we would not see each other again.

When I left him at last I went down into the garden to be alone; and I walked alone and found myself beside the little Bavarian Cérès. In the superb morning sunshine, her marble hat deliciously tilted, her basket full of carved corn and flowers, she seemed a figure on a tomb; the pretty tomb of such a pretty world.

June 14th

When I got back to Paris there was a telephone message on Vernon's behalf saying that he was unable to get leave yet.

And a telegram from Vernon himself asking me to wait and he would soon write.

Naturally I decided to wait. Pauline was still there, although making her preparations to return to Lille when I went back to England. I told her that I was living with the lovely Madame Pierre Morel who used to come to the *appartement*. She remembered her well, and that she had had a beautiful diamond brooch evidently of great value. I told her that Madame Morel was no longer rich, and she muttered with disapproval of these times which make big fortunes disappear. It was very bad moreover for *'nous autres'*, she said. But when I told her that Monsieur and Madame Morel had been, until the war, extremely happy all the same, she nodded sentimentally and conceded that money could not do everything. When I gave her my news of the illness of Otto she shook her head and said that no doubt 'this war' (she had a tone of long-suffering exasperation when she mentioned the war, as if it were a destructive kitten, not belonging to her, which nevertheless she had to endure in her kitchen) — 'this war' was 'too much' for the kind Monsieur Behrens. 'He does not like to see suffering,' she said. 'Even that time when I burnt my hand with that accursed electric stove which Madame had once installed, Monsieur Behrens, really, one would have said, he suffered also.' And I remember Tante Julie's account of Otto bringing orchids and champagne to the bedside of Pauline (in that sort of cupboard that was Pauline's bedroom, behind the kitchen!).

I told Pauline also that I was waiting for Monsieur Strudwick. Her comment was: 'It is what I have always said to Balthasar, an American like Monsieur Strudwick is a husband many times more distinguished than *those who pretend to be princes* …' Her gnarled colourless hand closed in the smallest, most expressive gesture of meanness: and

I saw that by this time Hugo had become more or less identified in her mind with her own simile — that he was a taxi driver pretending to be a prince, and her next remark (echoed directly from Tante Julie in the old days): 'Men are no longer the same,' made of him also a taxi driver without proper virility. 'Balthasar has told me one or two things,' she said; and with 'Ah ... that Balthasar!!!' she gave me to comprehend that she decided to leave many left-handed revelations unspoken.

I asked her if she had heard any news of Balthasar. She admitted no more than that the concierge had heard from the wife of the wine merchant (whose relations moreover with Balthasar one had remarked on at one time!) that he was making a success. I told her that Tante Julie had had news from him from Santa Barbara, and that it was evident that everything went well with him. 'Ah ... one could be sure that *ce Balthasar* would never be on straw!'

June 18th

I waited — I was going to write 'three days'; so habitual it is to express in terms of time a period which one had felt in altogether other terms.

Earlier in this journal I have said that I had three Parises in my life: the inherited Paris of my mother; the dulled Paris of my adolescence; and the Paris which, for Vernon and me, was a mirror in which the invisible enchantment of our love became visible, our delight taking on the form of the river, our wonder assuming the properties of Notre-Dame, our sweet or foolish moods reflected in a striped awning, a bunch of mediocre violets, a shabby green bus careering headlong toward Montparnasse.

But now I experienced, not three days, between May the sixth and May the ninth, but a fourth Paris. A Paris at whose gates there was already a dark angel; a Paris where, already, the sunshine, opening the tulips in the little walled gardens of Passy and Neuilly and Auteuil, in elegant hidden parterres behind the Rue de Grenelle, held in its warmth a sort of hesitance, and the wind, stirring the lilacs in every *parc*, at Bagatelle, at Versailles, at Fontainebleau, brought with it a presentiment that even that white and purple fragrance couldn't stifle. The streets were busy as ever, the cafés full, the restaurants crowded, the narrow streets busy and vociferous, the elegant *quartiers* radiant with summer, the green alleys of the Bois darkened with strolling people, and the lake gay with boats and romantic with swans. It would be untrue to say that this war-Paris of women and soldiers and children and old people wasn't full of life; that the Grands Boulevards, the Quais, the Halles, the Left and Right Banks, the Place Vendôme equally with the Place de Clichy, the Rue Royale, with the Avenue de l'Observatoire, didn't align themselves, as seductively as a row of French can-can dancers, as massively as the columns of the Madeleine, in a superb and profound insouciance. Nor is it an exaggeration to say that the women had never been so pretty, their deliciously painted faces decorating the streets like flowers; while the old women (I used to go and talk with them while Pauline did her shopping) in the Halles, in the smaller markets, the Quai aux Fleurs, were never so vivaciously full of good sense and truculence, so warm-hearted and so avaricious, so mystic and so realist, so shrewd, so coarse, so witty ...

It would be untrue to say that the Paris of that beginning of May wasn't gay.

But it was the gaiety of a heart that, just now and again, missed a beat.

To say that I heard no word of apprehension is no evidence, because during this time I did not see any of my friends. A state of war disperses one lot of people and gathers in another.

Of the people I knew who were still in Paris, there was none I wanted to see. To hear certain music, to see certain scenes, one can only endure to be with certain intimate friends, or alone. I was in such a mood in my receptivity to my 'fourth' Paris ... I was elated, sensitive, desiring only to move in a solitude, so that waves of comprehension that I caught from the life of the whole city might not be interrupted.

For there was only one person who would have felt with me, understood with me: Vernon. Only to Vernon could I have said: 'I have still another Paris. Its citizens are women's faces painted like flowers, and old women in shawls selling fish (who read only between the lines of their newspapers); its visitors are our own soldiers. And they — the soldiers and the flower faces — are in the cafés; and the fragrance white and purple is everywhere ... And, perhaps, it is only I who carry this apprehension in my heart. Perhaps I, only, imagine what the old women in their shawls read between the headlines.'

Perhaps, during my long '*flâner* around', while I lingered in the so-Second-Empire tranquillity of Passy (where there emerge from the doors in the garden walls crinolined and top-hatted spirits designed by Renoir) — in this lingering it was perhaps a sentimentalism to feel: 'Here is yet another Frenchness' (as Annabelle says). A Frenchness of lace blinds, of heavy Louis XV sofas, of yellow plush divans, of the good rich cooking, the knife-and-fork rests, of 'family life' in short, made secure by saving, agreeable by good living, solid by grandparents ... And, side by side with this, there is also what I knew years ago through my father — the nobler and gayer simplicity of professional family life, where the table is very simple, the carpets worn, the children beloved, the books well-bound, and the very intellect of France inhabits and is nurtured.

June 19th

During these three days I received a letter from my father, forwarded by Annabelle. (Naturally, he could not mention politics, but what he could not say was clearly indicated.)

My little Blanche:

Here the pigeons are well, the asphodels flower, and the blossom of the orange trees embalms the atmosphere of my breakfast on our terrace, and a charming wind from Venice makes the shadows of the young vine leaves dance like grandchildren on my venerable knees. A barge is passing on the canal; slowly because it is indifferent to time; happily, or so I conclude from a contented expression on its black visage, because it has no greater ambition than to arrive, sometime, in Padua.

For myself, I am physically at peace. But my heart troubles me. And it is not a case for a doctor. I know the cause: it is because I look one moment at my flowers and the next at the newspapers.

It seems that all over Europe there is a Spring of special beauty. From all my correspondents and old friends — in France, in England, in Holland — I have news of their flowers, and their weather; and I can hardly open a letter from which there does not escape the breath of wood violets, a vision of tulips, and I receive, through the good grace of many censors, news of battalions of small roses moving in the vanguard of the Summer.

I also have news from the newspapers.

I have always tried not to live in the past. Rather to carry with me in the present the people and days and places I have loved in that past. Thus, as you know, your mother has passed many hours with me in this garden, receiving with her little half-smile many ponderous foolish confidences of my heart. I have often been enchanted by her little profile gilded by this so-beloved light; and at night she has been at my window beside me ... (For one must not leave someone one loves in the past as on a railway platform, so that they get smaller and less and less distinct.)

But since these last months, Blanche, she has not been with me. And by my resolve. Even this last month of incomparable beauty I have not risked her being here; in case, leaning over my shoulder, she should see the newspaper.

I must stay alone in 1940 now ... I must 'evacuate' her into the past, and visit her there; as, when a young man, I used to visit her in the drawing-room of her *maman*. I have told you how she would sit on a Louis XV chair, with a pale blue riband round the waist of her muslin dress and her hair difformed straight upward to the most appalling little 'pompadour' by the coiffeur who came twice a week from Nice ... Together, in the past, we will read in the newspaper a favourable notice of Mademoiselle Bernhardt's appearance last night at the Comédie-Francaise, and an impressive account of the Coronation in London, of Edouard VII ...

But the next morning Pauline entered with my breakfast, and said to me that the concierge had heard on his TSF that the Germans had entered Holland.

At midday I had a telegram from Vernon, informing me that he could not come. And — all on this blue telegram, for the first time in our whole correspondence, but in French: 'I love you' (*Je t'aime*). It was written with a scratching nib in the sloping handwriting of some neutral official of the Post Office in the Rue d'Anjou … And yet, like the little black valise of a conjurer, it contained revelations and wonders packed close, and which Vernon, taking his stand on the platform of my imagination, deployed for me only …

I decided to remain in Paris. Not only where I should have still a chance of seeing Vernon, but because suddenly, as Pauline put down the tray beside my bed and reported the information of the concierge, the war became real; that is to say, I knew it emotionally.

And that day it seemed to me Paris was like a friend whose temperature is rising, but who, to the visitor's eye, does not seem to be at all ill. On the contrary, in a curious way, more distinct in beauty. Everywhere there was a sort of dramatized *bienêtre* (well-being).

But that same evening I had a telegram from Pierre. Here are its exact words: DARLING BLANCHE, I ADJURE YOU, I PRAY YOU, TO RETURN TO ANNABELLE. I EMBRACE YOU. I KISS YOUR HANDS. PIERRE.

I was first surprised by the telegram. (I supposed he knew from Annabelle that I was in France.) Then annoyed. Pierre, always as egoist as he was charming and touching and *gamin* — always assuming that his green eyes, his innocent amorous expression, his variety of smiles, his witty winning gestures — Pierre always supposed that I was at his disposition, to look after Annabelle. It suited him to forget that I had my own life, and that now that war was breaking out like a fire that has been underground, Vernon would also be in danger.

My first impulse was to ignore the telegram. Hadn't Annabelle herself, thanking me for my 'help' all winter, urged me in her last letter to stay on in France, so that I could be nearer Vernon?

And yet, an hour later I had decided to go back to England. And had told Pauline she could leave for Lille the next morning. (Incidentally—how curiously lacking in apprehension of what was coming I must have been, to have encouraged her to go on that journey to Lille!)

In the plane, returning, I was angry with myself for giving in to Pierre's telegram. Its urgency was foolish, I thought. I had no idea why I had obeyed it.

✖

I had no idea until three weeks later. As for Annabelle, she was surprised to see me. I didn't mention Pierre's telegram to her, because it would have distressed her to think that, for her, I had left Paris, and perhaps a chance of seeing Vernon sooner. But she was very evidently glad to have me back. And when I told her how it had all happened about Leonora and Charnaux, and Dubois, she was full of sudden happiness for me and Vernon; and then, in spite of herself, stirred to amusement by the idea of poor Cécile Dubois playing the role of detective!

✖

It was one of the evenings during that terrible last week of May that Annabelle and I sat in the garden late, and the evening felt as if it didn't belong to us; seeming, at the same time, so beautiful in our hearts, and so far from our lives; as love must be to old people. There was such a perfume from the syringa. Annabelle said: 'It seems queer it doesn't rain.' She meant that rain would have seemed more real.

In the glimmering light her face showed clear, like the blossoms on the syringa. She spoke a great deal of Pierre's plans for the garden which would 'have to wait now'. She said: 'Maybe when he gets leave he'll do some work.' She said also that she was haunted, these days, by:

Nous n'irons plus aux bois, les lauriers sont coupés.

She said: 'That refrain keeps recurring.'

Her voice repeated in that darkened air, so sweet with the incense of the syringa: *'Nous n'irons plus aux bois.'*

She said after, with a kind of simplicity of horror: 'To think what they've done.' She meant by 'they' the Dictators, the Politicians (not only German).

She said also: 'When you realize that most people in this world only want a little decent happiness ... the Germans too,' she added. And then with that emphatic yet absolutely real idealism that she inherits from her mother: 'Don't let's forget all the goodness in Germany, Blanche. Don't let's pretend that Germany isn't full of women, like you and me, just aching all the time with anxiety, and,' she added, like an unwilling whispered confession, 'and so afraid — for their children.'

Instinctively we both looked up at the sky. It was gay with stars.

(Two nights before a bomb had fallen on a farmhouse two miles away. The inhabitants were killed; one was a baby ten months old. The day after we had passed the place. Police and ARP men by the black jagged walls. A perambulator in the yard. A charred smell that caught us as we drove past, Annabelle accelerating.)

As we were going in she said to me, slipping her arm through mine: 'I'll be so happy for you, Blanche, when it's all over, and you and Vernon can have a home.'

When we were in the light of the hall I thought suddenly: 'How tired she looks!' And, as it happens when you live much with someone, I saw in that second what it had been impossible for me to notice from day to day, and from year to year: that her young nectarine beauty was altogether gone; and that paler thinner face she had now had loveliness from the lights and shadows of her expression, a charm from the modelling of the bones, the smallness of the head itself, and a sweetness — no longer from texture and bloom (as children have sweetness), but from that quality of hers that I have always loved most, her serenity of spirit.

We went up the staircase arm in arm, and then, just as she was going into her room, she said 'Blanche ...' to me, and yet as if she weren't speaking to me, but somehow *through* me, to her own witnessing spirit ... 'Blanche, whatever happens, I hope I shall never stop being grateful for the good years ...'

June 20th

I have heard from Tante Julie that Otto died three days before the Germans entered Paris. (Tante Julie's letter is dated June 13th — the day before.) She says very little in her letter. Just that 'it is this war that made him ill' and that it was the news of these last days (that is, of the German advance) 'that has killed him'.

What she states, with fierce characteristic misery, is also a simple truth. It was in fact the war that shocked his spirit and body into illness. And it is not difficult for one who knew Otto as I did to realize that the Germans advancing into France were advancing into his very soul. I can only be thankful from the depth of my heart that he died before he could hear or read or know that phrase — which seems to contain the very meaning of desecration — 'The Germans are in Paris.'

June 26th

It was about this time — two weeks ago — that I received the letter from Vernon's mother:

My very dear Blanche:

I want to say to you that your dear letter and one from Vernon, written at the same time, have made me very glad. You must know that in time past I would have found just this news difficult to accept: and now I, and Vernon's father too, feel that, if happiness is ever a word one can use again in this world, you and Vernon will be happy.

I find it difficult to understand the way Leonora has acted in all this. Apart from the moral side, it is her selfishness which I condemn. But Vernon writes that I am 'please, not to condemn, but to understand'. So I try to. He adds, by the way, so *truly* I know: 'If only we could replace all sorts of condemning by all sorts of understanding in the new world that'll have to be made after this war.'

But, to go back, dear Blanche. This is just a note to say to you that I am with you in my thoughts, as I am with my other daughter. And my comfort in these days is to feel that you and Annabelle are together. The mails are slow, and who knows what may not have happened by the time this letter (written May 20th) reaches you. I think of you, and Annabelle, and Pierre, and Vernon; and I think of the darling children (the new photographs of Camilla Blanche reached me last week, how darling she is!) and I pray for you in my thoughts, in the queer way we 'Puritan Agnostics' (wasn't that Vernon's phrase?) come to prayer in these times. Finally, dear, I want to add a special message of affection and welcome from Vernon's father. I daresay Annabelle told you of the miraculous change in him these last months? Somehow this world-tragedy seems to have wiped out his neurotic condition. And now he is not just 'his old self'; he is a *new self*. He is busy day and night: committees, speaking, writing, to help England. He has metamorphosed his 'nurse', by the way, into a secretary: and I should say she must sometimes long for the time when he was a nerve case, and not an absolutely unrelenting 'boss'.

A postscript, evidently added the next day before the letter was posted:

So strangely things turn out, dear. I was just going to end my letter by news of our darling Sohni, who has been with us here, as you know, since Vernon sailed, when John called me from the office he has now and said he'd a most wonderful piece of news for me. To cut a long story short, it's this. Sohni's mother is here! *How* she's here is a story you'll hear some day; and it's a fairly heartbreaking one; but the saving great wonder is that she is here — that after all she's been through she's with her boy. John has been working on this for some time, trying to find out about her, via London: and didn't tell me as he was too much afraid of disappointment. She came here to the apartment yesterday evening. John brought her. She is a very lovely woman, not more than twenty-eight but looking thirty-five or forty from what she's been through, dark eyes like Sohni's, and small and slender. I hadn't said anything to Sohni during the afternoon. But when she came I went first into the room we have made his schoolroom where he was having his supper, sitting up at the table and reading, in his crimson dressing-gown that Vernon bought him. I told him I had some wonderful news for him. He sat up very straight and said: 'Vernon is back?' But I said no, as good as that: better maybe … And then I knew he just 'got' what I meant. He went so pale I was frightened. And then his mother came in behind me. (I hadn't meant her to, but of course, she couldn't wait in the other room.) She ran to him and fell on her knees beside him. The way he took her terrible quiet emotion was the most impressive, manly thing you ever saw. He just put one arm around her shoulders, and laid his cheek down on her head, and I saw his little right hand patting her, steadily, as if she'd been the child. And then I left them.

The arrangement at present is that they are to stay here, as our guests. That is what John and I both wish.

Part 5

Annabelle had said: 'Whatever happens.'

But Pierre has returned to her.

He returned during the second week of July.

(She has, at least, her certainty.)

He returned the day before Camilla Blanche's first birthday. Annabelle had heard from the hospital where he was that he would come about then. He had not permitted her to come and see him while he was there because he would cure more quickly alone. But she received every day a message on a postcard, that is to say ever since he was brought to England, from Dunkirk.

I helped Annabelle make the birthday cake for Camilla Blanche. It was white, decorated with pink roses and little yellow ducks, and in the centre a pink candle, remarkable as the column of the Place Vendôme. We were in the big white kitchen together in the afternoon. She said while she was colouring the sugar: 'Pierre likes good-looking cakes. He took our wedding cake on our honeymoon and put it on the *table de nuit* in the hotel. He said the Taj Mahal was nothing to it ...' She had a full heart in those days before he was to come. But she said little, because of me.

Because of my uncertainty.

My uncertainty, which had begun as a small doubt: then during a long period it was an uncertainty; then for twenty-four hours it changed to a hope, because of the letter from the other ambulance driver who had seen Vernon in Lille. Only then it became the fear, which has substituted itself for my heart, existing precisely in that region, and beating steadily in imitation of a heart.

But I will continue about Annabelle and Pierre. (Otherwise, if I stop doing so many little things, if I stop dusting, cooking, talking with the children, showing the gay-skirted Czech how to conduct a vacuum cleaner; if I stop, then I am again at the cinema in my own brain. Those moving terrors.)

Pierre was to come in the evening, toward six o'clock, in a car lent by someone, I think, to bring him from the hospital.

Annabelle ordered that the children should wear their best clothes, and all that morning there was the fragrance of ironing in the corridors, and Annabelle herself wore a 'yeast pack' on her face long after it had dried, so that she had the appearance of a half-modelled Galatea; and in the afternoon Annabelle went into her bedroom to remake herself a beauty out of her disused and littered *maquillage* (to reinstate, for Pierre's eyes, her beauty that had left her and become part of his heart). At five o'clock when I saw her again she was very chic and I hardly knew her, she had so nearly her younger face. She said to me to come down with her to wait in the drawing-room where all the morning she had been arranging innumerable roses, from the garden. Camilla Blanche was brought into the drawing-room also, in a white dress and her hair shining and her eyes like dark lozenges in the heart-shaped fondant of her face. The other children were outside under the cedar tree, the other side of the lawn, restless and expectant, in a Prussian-blue shadow.

Annabelle was wearing a grey linen dress and some old scarlet beach shoes that Pierre had bought her. While we were listening for a car we heard guns in the distance, and though we heard them often when the wind came from the south-east (from Kent direction), during those minutes we felt as one should feel every time at the sound. And Annabelle said: 'Look, there's a telegraph boy. He's not coming.' And I thought: 'It is for me. Now I shall know.'

But it was for the Czech girl from her young man asking her if she could change her free afternoon to meet him in Brighton the following week. She came in to ask this, and while she was speaking, with a salmon-pink face, Annabelle ran out past her into the hall, and the Czech continued to speak to me, asking me if I knew if there were buses on a Thursday to Brighton? I told her across the perfume of roses in the room that she must ask the milkman, and by now I heard, or knew, that Pierre had arrived and was outside in the hall, and in the corner Camilla Blanche began to cry for a brick that had slipped under a sofa, and outside I saw the older children coming across the grass, but hesitating, their white clothes flashing.

I waited, it seemed long, after the Czech had picked up Camilla Blanche and carried her out. And then Annabelle came in with Pierre, his arm in hers, and I saw that his eyes were bandaged. His green eyes.

August 14th

When I saw the telegraph boy I said to Pierre: 'Now the young man of the Czech girl wishes to know if she will marry him on Saturday, instead of Monday.'

We lay in garden chairs in the sun; each in our darkness.

'No,' he said. 'It is not for the Czech girl. It is for you.'

When Annabelle brought me the telegram I forced myself to take it.

It was from Tante Julie. ARRIVED CLARIDGE AFTER A DIRTY VOYAGE.

Annabelle said: 'I'll telegraph her to come here.' I thanked her. When she had gone Pierre spoke: 'Is that all she says?'

'Yes.' I looked at his profile.

He said quickly: 'No, no, Blanche … don't allow yourself such feelings.' He held a matchbox to light his cigarette. He said: 'I hear emotions like one hears the leaves of a chandelier in a mistral ... *Joli, ça?*'

He took his cigarette out with his left hand after the first puff, and caught my hand with his right, and held it quickly to his lips. Then he said: 'When did you last hear from Vernon?'

'Not since I came back from Paris.'

✳

We were all expecting Tante Julie and the telephone rang. Annabelle went and then came back to say it was for me and that she had no doubt missed her train.

The telephone is in the passage outside the kitchens. There was an odour of the repast that Annabelle was preparing for Tante Julie, a perfume of onions and simmering butter.

The thin voice in the telephone said: 'Plymouth wants you.' I waited. Then it was, suddenly, the voice of Vernon. He said: 'Are you all right, darling?' — and ten times: 'Are you all right?' I found the breath and words to ask him: 'And you — and you, darling?' And then the thin voice asked him: 'Have you finished, Plymouth?'

August 20th

I think that the return of Tante Julie will complete what I have been writing all these months.

She came the day before Vernon. That is to say the day that he telephoned. (He had arrived from France that morning.)

She arrived in a hired Daimler in time for that so-well-prepared-and-seasoned luncheon. She descended from the car, her black clothes and veil of a widow so profoundly black that the lawn behind her became an emerald green (as does the grass of churchyards when mourners traverse it). She was hardly made-up — a touch, not more, of a garnet red on her lips, and a big crucifix of garnets suspended round her neck. Her gloves were of black suède and she carried her old travelling cushion with its crest and little gilt crown stamped across the corner.

She embraced me. She held me in her arms. She repeated: 'My child, my dear child,' her emotion rich and unhappy and perfumed with chypre. She embraced Annabelle. She looked at Pierre. And, after that second in which she saw, she went to him, and took his hand and said her brief: '*Bonjour, M'sieur*' to him with a simple implication of tribute that made an expression flicker across Pierre's lips, and I heard him say his conventional welcome like an expression of gratitude.

We went into the house. And in her room I told her that Vernon was coming. But she did not know he had been missing. She herself had got on a boat at Marseilles five weeks before. They had been five weeks on the journey. She told me about it. She said: 'I was all the time so content that Otto was dead, and that his soul is in peace.' She crossed herself and added that she had been able to bring away almost nothing and of clothes only two dresses and what she was now wearing. She took off her hat. Her hair had evidently been newly dyed to a nasturtium darkness in London. She looked out of the window at the summer garden and the woods beyond and asked me how many acres Pierre and Annabelle had, and then fell into a sort of aphasia of unhappiness, sitting at the frilled dressing-table before the glass, her black-veiled hat held on her knee between her big white jewelled hands, She spoke of Otto, and of Les Délices; and of Pauline (of whom she had no news since she went to Lille when I left Paris). Among all sorts of phrases of description — of the refugees coming south, of terrors, of her voyage back; and among exclamations, that were one moment curses, the next prayers, she said often: 'Shall I ever see my fine *salon* at Les Délices again?' and then, what should she do now without all that had meant 'life' for her? 'But I am not the only one,' followed by a simple, almost classic, repetition of: 'What sorrow everywhere! What sorrow!' I saw a black shawl over her nasturtium hair, and her hands gnarled and interlocked below her chin, and her eyes, innocent of Rimmel, raised to the sky where the Saints, august and capricious, hid themselves, and seemed not to observe bad harvests and evil men.

She asked me if I had any news of Mademoiselle Dubois. I told her no. I added that I supposed her still in her *petite chambre* in the Rue Lincoln. She and the cat, Eugénie, who would be indifferent to the sound of German boots passing on the pavements below at night.

She asked me if I had news of such and such friends; and I had no news, nor she herself. They were in France. They were inside a nightmare, which we dreamed, and they experienced.

She said: 'And thy Vernon, he comes to-morrow?' and looking at me she no longer had the black shawl and the gnarled hands, but was 'the woman with the laces' who had been Semiramis, for my father, a woman who in the deciphering of men had arrived at a comprehension of love; a woman whose eyelids retained the shadows of delicious moments; whose hair was an epigram at the same time cynical and philosophical on her own flamboyant dawn; whose heart was extremely experienced, having lived in such sociability with other hearts (sharing the mystery of its own beating, which kept alive a Julie, with similarly mysterious beatings which kept from death the Jeans, Charleses, Roberts, and, no doubt, the Louises and Raymonds). It was this heart which made it possible for her to understand, and to make me feel, almost without words, that she understood what I had suffered; and what I felt now. What she said, in fact, was only: 'To-morrow you will be happy' (*Demain tu seras heureuse*). The 'thou' gives better her comprehension.

※

Towards seven o'clock she demanded of Pierre if she might borrow a spade. He told her there were several spades and described to me where to find them. She thanked him. We had all been, since tea, sitting under the cedar tree, for the afternoon had been hot. Then she said to me: 'Come, my child,' and she got up, indicating that I should follow her. She walked towards the house; still in deep black, but in the dress of georgette which had been so creased on the journey, and which I had ironed for her, before she would descend for tea.

I followed her up to her room.

She went to a sort of old hamper, such as she had always travelled with, her luggage being always a mixture of baskets of various sizes with the chefs-d'oeuvres of Vuitton. This one she unstrapped; and undid, also, a great length of cord, which she rolled up carefully and put in a drawer. Then she took out of the hamper a pair of mauve *crêpe de Chine* sheets on which I observed in black the monogram 'J B,' but still a little coronet. Under the sheets was a despatch case, which she unlocked with a key on a chain other than the garnet cross. She took another key out of the despatch case, and going to the chaise longue took her travelling bag, zipped it open, and drew from its interior a small and very much worn iron box. She put this on the dressing-table, and having gone to the door of the bedroom, looked out into the landing, and then fastened the door, she returned to the box and unlocked it. She bent over it, nodded quite to herself, touched and evidently turned over its contents, and then shut the lid and locked it again, replacing the key, this time on the chain, together with the key of the despatch case.

Then she took the box under her arm, put on her silver-fox cape, and demanded that I should find her the spade.

The stables, at Annabelle's and Pierre's, contain all that is in daily use, or in absolute disuse. The chassis of the white Packard, the perambulator of Camilla Blanche, the skis, the pony, the machine for making soda water at home; also the garden tools.

Tante Julie waited in the yard, her silver foxes resplendent in the late sunshine. I brought her out a spade. 'It is too light.' I found one that I had seen the gardener use on his rare but strenuous visits. She inclined her head.

She had already, according to English usage, been escorted around the garden. (By Pierre, who showed her each blossom and stopped her to point out the quality of each view.)

Whatever she had retained of that tour, she had evidently understood the map of the entire estate, for she led me along the back of the house, down the wide grass walk, bordered with lavender, that bisects the top kitchen garden, and through a door into the red-walled garden. Here she paused for a moment standing with the door of this fragrant roofless house, inhabited by England. Then she led me across to the further door, and out into a strip of land, half orchard half rubbish heap, where there were some broken flower-pots, a sand heap, and several cold-frames. Beyond this strip was a field of deep grass and beyond that a little wood, which Annabelle called the Copse. Tante Julie crossed the field, her black skirts brushing the rich grass, and the first beginning of sunset painted a light as beautiful as tolerance over the copse and the grass and Tante Julie's hair.

The grass ceased where a steep bank, evidently a suburb for rabbits, rose to the high level of the wood. Tante Julie mounted the bank as if it were three steps covered with red carpet.

'Now the spade.' She laid down the iron box.

I followed her. She took the spade, and then bent her head to examine the ground at our feet, prodding it here and there. Fragile ferns and leaves of wild strawberries made a tracing over the substance of last autumn's leaves which were now half soil, half leaves, and coloured like the dregs of wine.

Tante Julie lifted the big spade, set it on the ground, raised her right knee and placed her big wide foot, in its black suède lace shoe, upon the spade. I stood back, as if I expected at least an explosion, or else from a pure impulse to watch.

To watch Tante Julie dig. I couldn't have helped her, if I had tried, or she had told me to. With strength and skill equally astonishing, and with no more grimace than a sort of brooding obstinacy, without any evident fatigue and without removing the fox cape from her shoulders, Tante Julie, in the light of that English sunset, dug a hole three feet deep on the threshold of that English wood.

When she had done she laid down her spade. Then looked about her, not with any air of achievement, or respite, but to be sure that no one observed her. Then quickly she seized the iron box, and knelt down, stiffly, and lowered the box into the hole. Then she got up again, took up the spade, and began to shovel back the earth. When this was done she went into the wood and came back with several small plants which she had uprooted, and, bending so low down with difficulty, put them into the soil, and firmed it around each plant with her broad thumbs. She stood up again.

'... They can't take root now. All the same ...' she pulled a handkerchief out of her cuff. Chypre traversed the wood-perfumed evening, disturbing some English bird so that it began singing in a nut tree close by. 'All the same,' she continued, 'I don't think They will find them.'

I took up the spade and followed her as she turned to go down the bank. As we crossed the field she said over her shoulder, for I was walking behind her: 'Although I have the idea that They won't come.'

We went through the deep grass back towards the garden wall, now coral against a sky of pale green. Peace itself was distilled in the air.

I could still hear that anonymous English bird singing

its sweet vague astonishment at chypre. I thought of Tante Julie's jewels that had journeyed from the depths of India, of South Africa, of Peru, to shine in the imagination and show-cases of Cartier, of Tiffany, and having become symbols, at one moment of riches, the next of desire, the next (for Tante Julie) of success, and even of an absolute security, now rested in a hole on the edge of an English copse.

Tante Julie turned to me as we re-entered the garden.

'Pouf! How hot I am! Take my fox, my child.'

THE END

Notes on the text

BY KATE MACDONALD

Part 1

October 6th 1939

The Good Earth: 1931 award-winning novel by Pearl S Buck that dramatized the life of peasant farmers in China, which became a best-seller, and a film in 1937.

October 10th

Ronsard: sixteenth-century classical French poet and scholar, whose popularity revived in the early nineteenth century.

poule de luxe: literally a hen of luxury, a trophy mistress.

boulevardier: a gentleman who lives his life in the boulevards, where a café is his club and his friends are urban, modern, untrammelled by domestic restrictions.

pharisaical: from the Biblical Pharisees who required the letter of the Law to be followed, without considering a higher truth; a tendency towards self-righteousness.

grossier: rude, crass.

La Fontaine: Jean de La Fontaine, collector and reinterpreter of myth and fables, whose *Fables* are a standard work in French literature.

Bagatelle: a small chateau set in the Bois de Boulogne, in Paris.

***Exposition* of 1936**: the Exposition Internationale des Arts et Techniques dans la Vie Moderne (International Exhibition of Art and Technology in Modern Life) took place in Paris in and around the Trocadéro Gardens in 1937.

flâneur: a man (*flâneuse* for a woman) who walks the streets to observe and enjoy without necessarily taking part in urban life.

Greuzâtre: probably a play on grisâtre, a pejorative term for greyish, incorporating a reference to the oeuvre of Jean-Baptiste Greuze, famous for his portraits of subjects in character.

November 3rd

dickey: a spare seat for a single passenger that folded into the back of an open-top car, and had no shelter from the weather.

November 25th

Valenciennes: a delicate hand-made lace, renowned for its quality and price.

appointments: her personal articles for bed and washing.

pensionnaire: a boarding-schoolgirl, not a young lady of means.

the Printemps: one of the leading department stores in Paris.

December 2nd

Molinard's mimosa 'friction': possibly a reference to French parfumier Molinard's famous solid perfume compact released in 1921, perfumed with mimosa.

pantoufles: slippers.

seedcake: a light sponge cake flavoured with caraway, which is the flavour of *anis*.

Mais enfin ...: In the end, it went well, quite correctly.

Ruy Blas: a tragic drama from the 1830s by Victor Hugo, in which Ruy Blas, a valet, is disguised by his master in a Spanish court intrigue but Blas rises to meet his supposed noble identity and wins the love of the queen.

Madame, il fait grand vent et j'ai tué cent loups: a quotation from a love letter read aloud in *Ruy Blas*, which Vernon and Blanche have just seen: Madame, there is a great wind and I have killed one hundred wolves.

knocked: a common way for spiritualists to claim that the spirits of the dead are communicating, by a rapping or knocking which can be decoded into letters and words.

l'homme qu'il faut pour Mademoiselle Blanche: French, the right man for Mademoiselle Blanche.

December 6th

Yale-Harvard Game: usually played in mid-November, this college football game is the most significant sporting event in the continual rivalry between Harvard and Yale.

ravis: delighted.

December 10th

rubbers: rubberised overshoes, protection against rain and snow.

December 11th

Nijinskys and Massines: two of the leading male stars of the Russian ballet, the most distinguished modern dancers of their day.

waxed: grew stronger and louder.

pères de familles: fathers of families, who should be staid and responsible.

December 14th

tailleur: tailored, close-fitting.

Altiora Semper: Latin, always higher.

cut in: the practice of exchanging places with another man during a dance to take his partner, socially sanctioned but not always welcome by the unfortunate man if his partner was a popular one.

White Rock: an American brand of soft drinks and mixers.

December 17th

actually *demi-mondaine*: not actually a courtesan or prostitute, but certainly thinking in practical rather than ethical terms of relationships between men and women.

bistred: coloured with bister, a brown sooty pigment used in drawing.

cattleyas: a species of orchid.

bigoudis: curlers.

the Boeuf: Le Boeuf sur le toit, a Parisian avant garde nightclub.

December 21st

comme il faut: as they should be.

la Diplomatie: the Diplomatic Service, which required an impeccable background and strenuous social training from a good family.

The Green Star Line: an invented shipping line, indicating great wealth.

January 2nd, 1940

partir c'est mourir: to part is to die.

souffrante: suffering.

l'air bien souffrante: the look of being very unwell.

Part 2

January 4th

strophe and antistrophe: from Greek classical drama, where the two parts of the chorus respond to each other's lines with another capping it using the same rhythm and rhymes.

January 26th

Bruges: Bruges is in Belgium, but perhaps Leonora had not realised that it was not France.

February 3rd

laic: relating to the laity, a secular thing.

More English: William III was Dutch, although his wife Mary II was English, the elder daughter of James II.

blued: an early example of the blue rinse appearing in fiction.

détraquée: deranged, unsettled.

ratafias: small almond biscuits, often served with Madeira or sherry.

February 21st

pourboire: a tip.

dot: a dowry.

February 27th

sirène: a mermaid.

TSF: *Télégraphie sans fil*, the French equivalent of 'wireless', an early radio.

garçonnière: a man's flat or set of rooms.

March 2nd

Député: the equivalent of a Member of Parliament in the French National Assembly.

grisaille: from art, paintings or drawings executed in shades of grey and other neutral colours.

deranged: a pun on the English meaning, acting in an eccentric or mad way, and the French, from *déranger*, to disturb oneself or to be put out.

soixantaine: her sixtieth birthday.

paillettes: sequins.

Thyssen: possibly Friedrich Thyssen, head of the German steelmaking company founded by his father; initially a supporter of the Nazi party but later distanced himself from it.

March 14th

Vathek: the Gothic novel by the English novelist and eccentric William Beckford, originally composed in French in 1782.

Part 3

March 24th

chez-soi: at home, in the third person.

canaille: vulgar.

C'est bien triste: it's very sad.

Part 4

June 9th

en flagrant délit: in the act.

June 10th

if she was 'well': that is, did she look attractive, desirable, beautiful.

Ma petite Blanche, tu es toujours a belle: My little Blanche, you are always a beauty.

This was the second or third of May: Germany invaded France on May 10th.

June 12th

bonbonnière: a box for presenting sweets.

lainage: woollen material.

June 18th

flâner: walking and observing without engaging or being drawn into the scene, see *flâneur* above.

June 19th

Nous n'irons plus aux bois, les lauriers sont coupés: 'We'll go
the woods no more, the laurels are all cut.' Originally a line
from a well-known children's song, repurposed many times by
different French writers, and probably referred to here from the
eponymous poem by Théodore de Banville from 1843.